Skinny Lenny's Front Step & Other Stories

Tony DeSabato

ISBN: 1543152279
ISBN 13: 9781543152272
Library of Congress Control Number: 2017906576
CreateSpace Independent Publishing Platform
North Charleston, South Carolina

Dedicated to my parents, Tony and Eleanor, who taught me to live with integrity, laugh with abandon, think critically, observe the world, and love my family and friends.

Also by Tony DeSabato: *Brewster Flats*

FRIDAY NIGHT DINNER

DINNER AT THE DIDOMINICO HOUSE on State Street had become ritualistic on weekday evenings. Promptly at five thirty, Nicholas's father came home from work after having shed his greasy overalls in the machine shop, where he washed his hands with Mione soap, a gritty cleanser that removed most of the daily grease and grime—and some of his skin. He washed behind the counter of Integrity Automotive Parts, the mom-and-pop operation where he machined parts and rebuilt engines. At home, he washed one more time in the old pedestal kitchen sink that looked as if it belonged in the bathroom. This time, he used Ivory soap to get rid of any residue and to try to chase away that awful smell that came along with Mione soap.

The family assembled for dinner in the kitchen. The dining room was only for decoration and overflow seating on all holidays except Christmas. At Christmas, the dining room table became a train platform for the Lionel train set (027 gauge) with an engine that puffed smoke, a coal tender that whistled, and an auto-carrier car that hauled four model Ford cars—red, white, blue, and yellow. It had been a gift from Santa.

They took all their meals in the kitchen. It was a smallish room, but it had all the necessary ingredients: a once-white gas range that needed to be lit by matches, a too-small refrigerator that only recently had replaced the icebox they had had for many years, the well-used sink, and the family washing machine with rollers on top. Nicholas's mother used these to press the water out of the laundry before hanging it on a clothesline in the backyard, where a fig tree and a grapevine from the old country seemed to be flourishing.

Nicholas's grandfather sat at the head of the gray-and-white Formica-topped rectangular table; his father, opposite his grandfather, was at the foot. Between them—on his father's left and on his grandfather's right—were his mother and his brother. Nicholas was to his grandfather's left and across from his brother. His sister was between him and his father. The kitchen never felt crowded.

Nicholas never had to wonder which day of the week it was. His mother, Rosa, took care of that with the menu. Monday was escarole or pastina in broth followed by chicken cooked just the way he liked it. Every Tuesday and Thursday, she made some other form of pasta, which they called spaghetti or macaroni, regardless of the type. This was always served with beef and veal meatballs, all in tomato gravy. His mother simmered this for hours. Non-Italians called it red sauce. Wednesday nights brought pasta *fagioli* with sausage or pork chops. The daily salad was dressed in wine vinegar and olive oil and served after the main courses. Dessert was a choice of a banana, an apple, or an orange, with the occasional treat of figs from the backyard, sliced pineapple when his brother was being spoiled or strawberries when Nicholas was being treated.

Nick, called Nicholas by the family to distinguish him from his dad, had no trouble getting from Monday through Thursday. Friday, however, was another matter. Friday was beans and fish—Regina beans made with a brown sauce that tasted so nasty Nicholas swore his mother used mud from the backyard over by the fig tree. It took all the courage, discipline, and willpower his nine-year-old self could muster for Nicholas to down enough of the hideous first course to avoid hurting his mother's feelings and to escape his father's reproaches. These usually included some form of, "You should appreciate what you have," or, "Someday you'll realize how lucky you are to have food at all," or, "I work hard every day to feed this family. Finish your beans."

As bad as the beans were, Nicholas found the fish categorically more difficult. His mother would buy this unidentifiable seafood species from the open-air Italian Market on 9th Street, which was one block away. She deep fried it to make sure it wouldn't poison them, and then she served it not filleted as the main course after the mud beans. Nicholas prayed for a tuna casserole each week. His prayers went unanswered.

Nicholas well remembered one Friday night. He almost never made it through the fish, but that night seemed worse than ever. It was a warm spring night, and they had a guest over for dinner. Tony Bel, the stock car driver, came over because Nicholas's dad was working on his stock car, and Tony Bel was helping. The beans nauseated him to the point of panic. He broke into a sweat that soaked his undershirt, welding it to his chest. He soldiered on. He had the feeling he had used up his father's tolerance the week before when he got caught pretending to eat his beans while actually quietly offloading them to his sister's bowl. This night, he somehow managed to down them. The absence of harsh words gave him time to figure out a new strategy for the fish. He carefully rolled ideas around in his brain. Nibbling wouldn't work. It would prolong the torture, and he knew he still wouldn't be able to keep the fish down. A deliberate approach wouldn't work. It would take too much concentration. He didn't dare put the fish on his sister's plate. He continued to think about it. Then it came to him: he would down his piece in two quick bites, forcing it past his mouth as quickly as possible. This way, he might be able to sidestep the taste completely. He'd have to deal with the texture, though. He carefully prepared for the moment and isolated the fish on his plate. He'd use the dago red that had been made in the basement as a chaser. He strategically placed the two-ounce glass by his right hand so he could grab it with his other hand. Wine had been part of every dinner, going back to his earliest memory. He positioned his fork carefully in his left hand and hoped for the best. He checked to make sure nobody was watching him, and then he stabbed at the plate. One quick bite. Half gone. Almost.

He tasted the fish in his mouth and felt it stick as it was going down his throat. He looked from left to right and back again. Still, no one was watching him. He coughed. He coughed again and then again. Then he leaned back in his chair and started wildly waving his arms before grabbing his throat. He gagged and gasped.

"I can't breathe," he finally squeaked almost inaudibly.

"Give him some water," shouted his mother, and she pushed away from the table to pour a glass at the sink.

He tried to drink it, but the water leaked from both sides of his mouth. He still had no air.

He struggled, punching the air with balled fists, but that only made it worse. He started to feel light-headed. His father pushed away from the table and came straight at him. His arms were extended, and his hands were open. Nicholas ducked and banged heads with his father, who had also ducked. Before he knew it, Nicholas was dangling upside down and staring at the harsh gray linoleum floor that matched the tabletop. He didn't have time to figure out what was happening to him and why. His father, holding him by the ankles, shouted to Tony Bel, "Hit his back. Hit his back. Hard!"

He felt pounding and then more pounding. His father dropped Nicholas's head almost to the floor and then pulled him up. Together, his dad and Tony Bel continued these maneuvers until the fish bones shot across the room and landed on his mother's shoes. Air filled his lungs, and he blurted, "I'm okay. Turn me over!"

Upright now, Nicholas felt his world spin more slowly. He could now see his brother's tears and his sister's terror. As his world started to return to normal, his mother embraced him, and his father checked to make sure he was okay.

"Mom, I really have trouble with the fish," he whimpered, and a single tear trickled down his left cheek, just missing the corner of his mouth.

"I know, Nicholas, I know. We'll find something else."

GRANDPOP'S CELLAR

1018 State St.
Philadelphia, PA 19147
March 11, 1960

Miss West
6th Grade
Jackson Elementary School

Dear Miss West,
I know I was supposed to write a description of the outside of my house for class, but I have a special street and a special house with a special room in the cellar, and I wanted to tell you about them. I hope what I wrote is okay.

Respectfully,
Nicholas A. DiDominico Jr.

Grandpop's Cellar
By
Nicholas A. DiDominico Jr.

Our street is like every other one in our South Philadelphia neighborhood. Cars park on both sides. Many times each day, a gigantic bus shakes its way up State Street and rattles our windows and, I guess, everybody else's too. A fire hydrant, which everybody calls a "plug," makes a good start and finish line for the races I have every day with the other boys and girls on our block. Some of the kids are in our class, but some are a little older, and some are a little younger. Our street is like the others, but it's different too. It's special. It's one of a kind with lots of life and family and love, and all of us have dreams and hopes. It's our street. Our home.

All the houses on our street, except the end ones, share two walls with the two houses next door. We call them "row homes." I used to think people were saying "roll" homes because we have a bakery, Bocelli's, where we get our Italian bread and rolls. When we have a few extra coins, we can get square pizza—actually, tomato pie—made in a brick oven. After that, I thought they meant "row" like in a rowboat. I didn't understand that at all because we don't have a stream or a lake, and we're more than ten blocks from the Delaware River. Later, I found out it meant our houses are all in a nice, neat row. Our row home is three stories high, like most of the others, but ours is special because we have bow windows on the second and third floors. These bow windows confused me too. I never saw any ribbons on our house, and we never had a bow and arrow, although my father keeps a shotgun in a safe place. Then my grandpop told me in his broken English that when the front of the house sticks out in a semicircle, that's you call that a bow window. I think other people call it a bay window, but my grandpop told me that was wrong. We have the only bow window house on our street. That makes our house very special.

I live in the house with my older sister, Rita, my younger brother, Richard, my mother, Rosa, and my father, Nick Sr., but everybody calls him Nad. I used to live with my grandfather, Sylvino, and his wife, Annina, before they died. My actual grandmother passed away when I was two, so I didn't really know her. Annina was fun. She played with me. She spoke almost no English, but she knew how to talk to me—with cookies. When I was a little kid, she would put me across her knees, tickle me, and roll me over and over until she made a chocolate cookie appear out of nowhere. I got to eat the cookie. She was always teasing me.

My grandfather worked for many years as a manual laborer on a construction crew. He came from Chieto, Abruzzi in Italy to America as a young man to find a better life for himself and his young wife, Elizabeth. She had diabetes, and had her leg cut off, and then she died. Grandpop started out digging ditches, and then he became a foreman and then a superintendent. He kept a bunch of construction tools. My dad works as a machinist. He can not only fix your car, but he can completely rebuild the engine and remake almost all the parts as well. His tools are with my grandpop's.

With of all these tools, our house doesn't have a basement like other houses. We have a cellar. I love the cellar. When I was little, I could go down there and play forever. I would try putting parts of old clocks or of our old toaster together. I could take apart some of the machinery, and sometimes I put these things back together so they would still work. I wasn't as good as Grandpop or Dad. I pretended I was building a stock car, like my dad did. I wasn't allowed to watch television, so when I finished my homework, I would go down to the cellar. Sometimes, I still do.

To get to the cellar, I would have to walk down wooden stairs that have about twenty coats of battleship gray paint on them. My grandpop bought the paint when they were trying to get rid of extra stuff at the Naval Base at the very southern tip of South Philly. He got a really good deal on it. There's a rail to hold onto that my grandpop made out of two-inch cast iron pipe that was being thrown away from one of his jobs. My grandpop never wasted anything.

The cellar has two parts. There's a wooden door with a fancy spring lock that keeps the back part hidden from the front. The door is green, and the door is important because the front half of the cellar is very different from the back half. The first half has wine in it. My grandpop built a platform that goes from the front wall to the green door, and on that platform, he put seven large, old wooden barrels. This was where he kept his homemade wine made in different years and with different kinds of grapes. Each fall, my grandpop would go to the Italian Market, 9th Street to us in the neighborhood, and buy grapes for mashing. He had this mashing machine with a handle you had to turn. He figured out an easy way to make it work. He put an old washing machine motor with some gears and a fan belt on it. He would dump the grapes into it, turn it on, and watch the grapes get mashed so he could get the juice for his wine. My grandfather was very clever.

The rest of the front cellar has my mother's clotheslines. When the weather is bad and my mother needs to dry the clothes, the cellar comes to the rescue. I used to make my mother mad when I was a kid by running back and forth through the clothes that were hanging there. Sometimes she would have to wash them again.

The front cellar was fun—especially around wine making season—but the back cellar was the best part. You could get down the cellar from inside the house, but you could get in from outside too. Both the front and the back of the house have openings with heavy metal doors. We used these openings to bring in tools, equipment, grapes, and other big stuff.

The back cellar was Grandpop's workshop. It had all those tools I told you about. There was a lathe, a drill press, hand drills, jackhammers, pickaxes, two-man tree saws, and sledgehammers. He had all kinds of hand tools hanging on the wall. Ratchets, wrenches, sockets, and screwdrivers still hang from the ceiling and the walls, and some are stored in drawers. There's grease everywhere because Grandpop used the cellar for so many years, but everything is still neatly organized. All the tools are kept clean. Everything has a purpose, and each tool is important.

Between the workbench and the flight of stairs, there's a storage closet that extends under the stairs in one direction and toward the back of the house at the other. The closet is always locked. I have some memories about that closet from when I was a kid.

One morning, I knew I had to get inside that closet. I asked my dad about it, and he gave me a grown-up answer. "That's where we keep the expensive, complicated tools. You shouldn't go in there without Grandpop or me. Those are very expensive tools, and some of them are dangerous."

I knew I had to get into that closet. I started searching for keys and couldn't find anything for weeks. Then one day I saw my grandpop open a small drawer in one of his wooden toolboxes. He took out a key and opened the door to the closet, but I couldn't see in.

Early the next morning, before anyone woke up, I climbed onto my grandpop's workbench and found the secret key. I could hear the blood pounding in my ears. I was going to get in.

I couldn't reach the lock, so I pulled a big can of bearing grease over to stand on. That was when the biggest surprise came. I walked around the room, but at first I couldn't see very well because it was so dark. I decided to use my hands to poke around. I began touching things. Tools filled the room. I touched them one by one. I then felt some equipment, supplies, shelves, and even the walls as I worked my way around the room. I pushed against one of the walls, and it started to swing open like a door. I fell into it and closed my eyes as tight as I could. I couldn't even see the darkness. Then a bright light came on, and I had to close my eyes even tighter. I tried to calm down, and I slowly loosened the grip on my eyelids then started to stumble over something. I fell and landed facedown on the floor and thought I would just stay still for a minute. I began to wiggle and turn until I managed to sit up cross-legged. Kids can do these things pretty easily. I put my hands over my eyes to block some of the light so my eyes could adjust. I had to figure out where I was and what I was seeing.

In this special part of the closet, I saw so many toys and games. I thought I must be in a gigantic toy store or the North Pole. On one side, there were tricycles, bicycles, and even unicycles. They were large, medium, and small and in many colors: black, red, yellow, and more. There was even a path where you could ride. I could take any one I wanted and then go back again and again for rides. There were two-wheel scooters and toy cars and trucks that I could sit in and pedal all over the place. There was a track set up for roller skating and a circle set up for marbles. There were toy fire engines and cranes and tractors and Lionel trains. Everything I could imagine was there.

It took me a long time to figure out all that was there, but I finally got it all sorted out. Then I got another surprise. Off on the other side of the room, I saw row after row of chests. They looked like pirate chests—big, heavy, fancy, with lots of color. I went over to one row and opened lid after lid. Wow! Gold coins and gold nuggets and jewelry of all kinds were in there. The next row of chests had gems in them—diamonds, rubies, and emeralds. I stopped to catch my breath. This had to sink in. Who knew about this? I wondered. Did Grandpop know? Mom? Dad? We're rich! Why don't we use this?

Day after day, I went back to the storage closet to play. Finally, I decided to tell Rita. She wasn't interested at all. It's a dirty cellar, and she didn't want to crawl through some dark room that smelled like grease and oil. Anyway, she said she liked the toys and games she had. Next, I turned to Richard, but he was so little he couldn't really understand what I was talking about. The cellar always scared him anyway. So, I kept going there alone.

After a while, I began to find it harder and harder to make my way into the secret part of the closet. As I got older, I went there less often.

One day, when Dad and I were alone, I again asked him what was so special about the closet that we had to keep it locked. He gave me the same answer as before—special tools that are expensive and dangerous. "Anything else, Dad?" I asked.

"Well, you know," he said, "I have some faint memory that, as a young boy, I found a secret hiding place behind the wall in that closet. I've never been able to find it since. But I remember there were some old, broken toys in there and some old, big storage trunks that were falling apart. I think maybe Grandpop sealed that section off when he made his workbench. That's about all I remember," he said.

But I remember more. I remember it all. I remember everything about Grandpop's cellar.

THE END

Miss West, I know I didn't do the assignment as you gave it, but I thought you should know something about my grandpop's cellar.

The Pit Fall

It happened in early August, before my birthday. Rita was there too, but I've never been able to talk to her about it. Maybe I can now because it's been so long. If she doesn't remember how it happened, I can help her because I have one of those brains that has memories that go way back and hooks things together into such a clear picture that it could easily have happened only a few minutes ago. My memory is so good that it can add details long after the fact to show the whole story. I've played this memory over and over so many times that I think it's actually happening again, and there's nothing I can do about it—nothing I can do to stop it or change it.

I know it was the summer of my sixth birthday because Mom was pregnant with Richard, who was born in November on the same day as my sister's birthday. It was Thanksgiving that year. I also know it happened in the summer because that was when we went to the stock car races.

Dad was a mechanic and a machinist; he built cars and engines and could even make new parts for them. Just after I was born, he and three or four of his neighborhood friends decided to buy an old '39 Ford somebody had tried to make into a race car. They wanted to really fix it up, build a new engine, and race it on one of the half a dozen or so tracks in and around Philadelphia.

The first track they raced was a tiny quarter-mile asphalt oval at Municipal Stadium deep in the heart of South Philly and not far from our house. I saw my first stock car race there when I was about two. It was freezing on a late spring Friday night, and mom held me in her arms with a blanket wrapped around me. We were ten rows behind the race official, who used flags of all colors to control the race. I came to know that the green flag started the race; the yellow one meant to slow down because there's an accident or some other problem on the track; the red one stopped the race, either because of rain or while they cleared the track; and the checkered flag, the most powerful of all, was for the winner of the race. Dad had to explain to me that the white flag meant one more of something—either one more pace lap or one more lap to the end of the race. The black flag meant the driver couldn't race anymore. They had signals with other flags too, sometimes crossing them. I was never able to hook up those signals with anything in my brain, so they're not part of my memories.

Dad and his buddies didn't like the Municipal Stadium track. It was small, and the competition was weak. It was really an old football stadium where they played the Army-Navy game each fall and where the Philadelphia Eagles sometimes held practices. Dad's car had no trouble winning every race there. For the most part, the crew preferred the larger ovals, like Langhorne and Nazareth. Both were in Pennsylvania. Before long, they became part of the regular races in New Jersey and once in a while at Flemington, Pitman, and Atco, but mostly they raced at Pleasantville and Vineland. Most of my memories are from Pleasantville and from when I was a little older—maybe nine or ten. That was when Richard began to have problems but before we lost him two summers later. After Richard died, I stopped going to the track with my father. I've hooked up Richard's problem with stock car racing, and after his death, I didn't want any part of stock cars or of Dad, for that matter.

The Pleasantville asphalt oval was tucked in off a tiny road cleared through the scruffy pinelands in South Jersey and was a few miles before Atlantic City. It was totally different from the heavy red clay at Vineland, which was where it happened. Even though I bailed out on racing after what happened to Richard, my memories of Pleasantville are all good. I even loved the name. I figured nothing bad could happen in Pleasantville, but after a while, I confused it with Plasticville, which was a town made up of a set of buildings on my Lionel freight train set-up Santa brought one year. We still have that set, but we don't put it out anymore. I think maybe I'm too old for it or maybe too young. I loved the long, black, powerful locomotive with a whistle-blowing coal tender and the red caboose with a smokestack. The engine pumped out lifelike steam from pellets dropped into the smoke stack before powering up. I especially liked the rolling stock that carried new cars to Plasticville, with its garage, city hall, library, dinner, railroad station, two houses, and a signalman whose lantern warned of the oncoming train. Richard liked the train too.

At Pleasantville, Dad could almost always sneak me into the pits during races, even though the rules said I was too young. The pits were more exciting than anything. During the heats, the crews that had cars out there racing glued their eyes to the track while all the other crews fiddled with their cars, tires, and fuel. The sounds of engines without mufflers gurgled through straight exhaust pipes and muscled out all normal talk. Only shouting worked, and it worked better with wild arm waving and hand signaling. I had to wait until the parade lap to get Dad's attention for a hot dog and a Coke, so cold in one of those little bottles that I would swallow half-formed ice through its neck to cool me from the fume-filled heat and humidity of summer in the east. I was happiest in the pits at Pleasantville with Dad and the crew.

On the rides to the track, Dad and I rode with Tony Bel, the driver, in Dad's aqua-and-white '50 Ford with the supercharged engine and two four-barrel carburetors. It was so souped up that Tony Bel once got it to one hundred miles per hour in second gear on a closed road because he and Dad just wanted to "see what this baby'll do." I wish I'd been there for that one. Dad's partner, Jerry, drove the tow truck with Toppi riding shotgun. They were Italian like us and the rest of the crew, including Tony Bel, short for Belfiore. Tony Bel was my hero because he drove smart but like a madman. Dad made sure Tony had enough car to pass on the straightaway, but that wasn't the real challenge. It took more than a fast car to pass on the turns, especially on the outside or up high on the track, where any mistake by you or the guy you were passing could put either of one of them right through the fence, in the hospital, or worse. Tony Bel's eyes and hands and the pit of his stomach took care of passing on the outside or on any of the four turns. He would pass anybody, anytime, anywhere. He passed them when and where he caught them.

When he wasn't racing, Tony Bel was a happy-go-lucky, lighthearted, easygoing kind of guy with twinkling, soft eyes; a hop in his step; and an open, toothy smile he flashed to almost anybody but especially to attractive women, attached or otherwise. On the track, though, he was a demon. He was feared and respected and quick to take a yard or, rather, a nose, a wheel, or a car length, whether or not it was being offered. Off the track, he was mostly liked, unless he had made a pass at your lady.

Jerry Terlizzi handled the fuel and oil. Before Richard, Dad used to make me laugh by calling him "Jerry Tin Lizzi." He made this mixture of nitro and glycerin for the fuel and this oil additive he told me was castor oil. They made a smell—almost a taste—I've never come across anywhere but at the stock car races. They called it acrid and pungent. I called it "Aftershave?" in honor of the teal '39 Ford sedan with a red question mark as the number, the name "The Critter" stenciled on the hood, and "Toppi's Torpedo" splashed on the roof above the windshield. Toppi was the welder who was also a mechanic and worked on the car He didn't seem to have a last name. I guess with a name like Toppi, he didn't really need one. He put the car back together if Tony Bel wound up through the guardrail or hanging upside down with only the safety harness keeping him from flying through the windshield or into the top as he rolled side over side or even end over end as we prayed that nobody would zoom by and spear him.

On the rides home, we would always stop in the wee hours of Sunday morning at the same diner on the Black Horse Pike. We'd get coffee, hot chocolate for me, and fresh baked apple, peach, pumpkin, or blueberry pie, often a la mode. At Gents' Diner, we would meet up with the other racers from Philly, South Jersey, and the nearby areas. There was always a friendly rivalry, but the Delaware River offered a natural boundary. Dad always said that if we ever had a problem with the farmers from Jersey, we shouldn't count on any help from our Gents' buddies; the Jersey crews would stick together.

I remember one night in particular when Jerry Tin Lizzi took a lot of heat not only from the rival crews but especially from the Question Mark crew because of his awful performance in a special owners' race. It was the craziest thing. One night, the race organizers set up this race so the owners rather than the drivers would race the cars in a five-lap heat before the main event. It was supposed to be a fun, low-competition exhibition. Our crew appointed Jerry to drive. He started out great, passing the whole field in the first three laps. Then, all of a sudden, on the backstretch, he was all alone, and the car plunged down toward the infield, got sideways, and started to roll. He mangled it up so bad that not even Toppi's torch could put it back together before the main event. Jerry said the left front tire blew, but Dad told me he thought Jerry peaked in the rearview mirror to see how much of a lead he had, lost concentration, and overreacted by jerking the steering wheel to the left then to the right, knocking the car around all over the track. Jerry didn't get hurt, so it was okay to give him some rough words the rest of the night, mostly at the diner. We didn't come home with any trophies that night.

I don't have nearly so many memories of Vineland, and, of course, the strongest one drives me crazy. We raced at Vineland on Sunday afternoons if the car held together Saturday night.

Earlier that year, during Easter break, I was having the cocoa and toast we had every weekday morning. I was sitting in the same gray vinyl-covered kitchen chair at the matching Formica kitchen table, as I always did. Mom sat next to me after Dad left for work and after Rita went off to do whatever eight-year-old girls who think they are sixteen do on spring mornings in the city when they are off from school.

"Nicholas," she said. I was always "Nicholas" or "little Nick" to make my name different from Dad's. "How would you like a little brother?"

"Sure," I said between bits of toast with butter dripping off. The butter smeared most of my face. "But it sure would be great if he and I were the same age so I'd always have him to play with."

"Well, we can't work that out, but I'm having a baby, and it might be a boy. If so, you'd have a little brother."

"It might be a girl, too. For Rita."

"Whether it's a boy or a girl, I'm sure you and Rita will love it with all your might. For your sake, Nicholas, I hope it's a boy."

I wondered if she said to Rita, "For your sake, Rita, I hope it's a girl." One Sunday later that August, the whole family drove to Vineland. It was the night before Tony Bel eked out a victory over our biggest rival, Sil, short for Sylvie, Mitchell, short for Machollini. We called him Sillie Macho because he was a tall, square-faced, loud guy with a mangy complexion, blacksmith arms, a barrel chest, and a big, wide nose. He liked to throw his weight and his words around. He used to win all the races before the Question Mark started to show up at Vineland.

The night before at Pleasantville, Sillie managed to pass Tony Bel with three laps left when Tony Bel had trouble getting around the traffic caused by some slower cars. When Tony Bel cleared them, he took off after Sillie like a man possessed, getting so close to Sil's bumper that it looked like Tony Bel was pushing Sil's back coupe, painted with a white circle containing a bold black number eight with a king's crown on the top, all the way around the track. What was really happening was that every time Tony Bel went to pass, Sillie moved the Royal Eight Ball to block him. On the last lap, though, Tony Bel made a quick dive to the inside, and when Sillie tried to block, Tony Bel took the outside line and brazenly passed up higher. Desperately trying to counter, Sillie sent the Royal Eight Ball spinning in a most unkingly way. Three or four more cars passed him, and he finished out of the money. During the victory presentation, after Sillie disappeared in the pits, I did notice Sillie's girlfriend come up to Tony Bel. She was a platinum blonde with a perfect face, and she was wearing a skimpy blue halter top and white, almost see-through pants. She handed him a piece of paper and touched him on the shoulder like more than a friend. I remember because Dad saw it too and went up to Tony Bel afterward. Dad was wearing that you're-about-to-get-a-lecture look all over his face. Tony Bel smiled at Dad and just walked away.

At Vineland that day, the main event didn't start out so well for "the critter." Tony Bel got jammed up early, and Sillie forged a big lead. Our friend from South Philly, Lou Monte, followed. We cheered for Lou whenever we could. With two laps to go, Tony Bel found himself with open track ahead, and he almost closed the gap. Lou caught Sillie first. Sillie started his usual blocking routine. In turn two, though, he waited too long, and when he went to block, Louie's ten car was already beside him. They touched, and both spun out, clearing the way for Tony Bel, who sailed in for the checkered flag.

In the pits, we were all there to greet Tony Bel—Dad, Mom, Rita, Jerry, and Toppi. I was there, too. Dad went over to the next pit to see if Lou was okay, and he returned with his arm around Lou. Then things got crazy.. Sillie rushed our pit, grabbed Lou from behind, spun him around, and punched him. He screamed, "You took me out."

Lou doubled over, and then Sillie went after Tony Bel. He was screaming and cursing. "Stay away from me and my girl. If you come back here, I'll put you through the fence and plant you in the cornfield."

We all watched, paralyzed, except for Tony Bel, who just looked at Sillie, shrugged, said nothing, and then flashed that smile of his. Sillie lost it and threw himself at Tony Bel. Tony Bel's coffee went flying in the air, and Sillie shoved Tony Bel down the side of the Question Mark. Sillie was throwing haymakers that looked like they were landing. Tony Bel went down hard, and Sillie went after him. Only Dad reacted. He pulled Sillie away. Sillie went after Dad, who bobbed and weaved and came back with a combination of punches that staggered Sillie. He went sprawling just as Mom arrived. Sillie stumbled into Mom, knocking her down hard. Very hard. Rita and I started crying, and Dad screamed that Mom was pregnant. He rushed Sillie with fists flying. When it was over, Sillie was bleeding from his left eye, and his nose was off to the side of his face. Dad's right little finger was pointing back toward his elbow. I watched him shove it back into place with a wince as he came back to Mom, who was trembling and crying but otherwise okay.

The next day, we were all relieved when the doctor reassured us that Mom and the baby were okay. In November, Richard was born, and he seemed healthy. Rita and I loved our little brother, and he loved us right back. He was a great baby. He didn't cry. He went to sleep without a fuss. He was always pleasant and cheerful. We both took care of him when he was small, and I especially loved playing with him when he got a little older. It was only after he turned four that the trouble began.

We shared a room from when he turned two. We talked one another to sleep each night, and the first to wake always nudged the other. Then he started to complain each night, and Richard was never a complainer. He told me he had a headache in his forehead like he had eaten something cold (like ice cream or Italian water ice, which we called lemonade, even if it was cherry flavored) too fast. I fell asleep first, and Richard woke me to tell me how bad it was. He had these headaches again and again. It wasn't every night but often enough that I would wind up holding him in my arms a couple of nights a week trying to rock him back to sleep. The doctors couldn't find anything wrong with him. He could see and hear fine, and when we played, he could move around great. He ate well too, but the headaches were brutal.

About a year later, Mom and Dad told us the doctors figured out that Richard's problem was a brain tumor. The next year was impossible. Everything went bad. Dad couldn't help Richard. Mom couldn't. Rita couldn't. I couldn't. The doctors couldn't. The only chance was to operate, but Richard never made it out of the hospital.

Our lives changed completely. Our family ceased to be.

I was now alone in my bedroom. The ceiling became my closest friend.

I asked questions about brain tumors. One of my friends told me his uncle had died from one that came from a hard fall. One of my teachers told me sometimes a person is born with one, and it grows when he grows. I figured it out—I hooked up the tumor with Mom's fall at the race, and I started to hate stock car races and Sillie Macho. Why did Dad have to get involved? I wondered. It was all Dad's fault. I stopped going to the garage and the races. When I was called "little Nick," I told them I was just plain Nick—no more little Nick. Mom and Dad tried hard to keep the family together. They talked about God's will and how blessed we had been to have Richard at all. They said Richard would have wanted us to carry on as a family without him. They tried, but we didn't recover, and then Dad surrendered.

Harsh voices downstairs when Dad would finally come home replaced the sound of my brother's peaceful, even breathing in the bed next to me. Dad's clothes smelled of smoke and booze, his steps were unsteady, and his voice was broken and hollow. Sometimes he came home tattered and bruised from a fight or from falling or from walking into a step, a wall, or a parked car.

"Nick, you can't keep doing this." The bedroom carpets muffled her voice to a roar. "You still have a wife and two wonderful children. What about us?"

"What about you?" Dad shot back. "You're better off without me. I have nothing left to offer. I'm spent. I'm done."

"That's not true," Mom came back at him. "I need you. Rita needs you. Little Nick needs you."

"Rita has you. And little Nick? He won't even talk to me or stay in the same room with me. And you? You don't need me. You're the strong one."

I tried to shut out the shouting, and I spoke less and less to my parents. But each night, before falling asleep, I always said, "Good night, Richard," and first thing each day, I said, "Good morning, Richard."

Finally, the fighting stopped. No truce was declared. Dad just didn't make it home. The bus driver said he never saw him walk out in front of him.

He was in a coma now, but the doctors said he'll get better. By the time he wakes up, maybe his legs will be healed, and he'll have the strength back in his arm.

Now that it's just the three of us for a while, maybe I can tell Rita what really happened. I called to her from my bed. "Rita, do you remember when Mom told you I was going to be born?"

"No, but I remember when she told me about Richard. She came into my room one night and asked me if I wanted a baby sister. I told her I liked you just fine, but it would be nice to have another baby in the house. She told me she was pregnant, and she said she hoped for my sake it was a girl. She said she would talk to you the next day."

I told her what Mom told me, and we both laughed for the first time in a long time.

"Nick," Rita offered, "Richard's gone, and we can't change that. You have to start being like your old self again. Dad hasn't recovered, but you have to."

"Rita, it was Dad's fault Richard died," I blurted.

"What? Dad loved Richard like there was no tomorrow. Sometimes, I thought he loved him more than he loved you and me."

"I figured things out." I explained about the fight and Mom's fall and how Dad should have minded his own business.

"Nick, it doesn't work that way. Dad's fight and Mom's fall had nothing to do with it. You can't carry this grudge forever. It doesn't work that way."

I explained how I hooked together what I had been told with what happened. We talked on and on till we were totally exhausted.

"Rita, Dad knew it was his fault. That's why he started drinking and going out and fighting with Mom."

"No, little Nick," she corrected. "Dad loved Richard. It has nothing to do with guilt. It has everything to do with love."

For every question, she had an answer. So, I finally dragged myself back to my bed. I looked up at the ceiling and went over everything she had told me. I thought about Mom and Dad, about all the trips to the races, and especially about being in the pits. I thought about how much I had loved being little Nick before all this happened. Of course, I thought about Richard. My friend the ceiling helped me refigure everything, and I realized I had been wrong about Richard, about Sillie Mitchell, and about the races. I had been wrong about Dad. I shivered with the realization. I was tired. How do I begin to make this right? I wondered. I have to find a way. Morning neared. I was ready to sleep but not before going through my ritual. "Good night, Richard...Good night, Dad."

THE GAUNTLET

DOMINICK PURLINI AND ROCCO CICCATORE left their homeland within a few years of one another to start new families and new lives in the dream-lined streets of America. Dominick and his wife, Assunta, took the boat from Italy in the mid-1940s, leaving their home in Abruzzi for the Italian enclave in South Philadelphia. This was just a few years before their son, to be named after his father, was born. They settled in with Dominick's sister, Josephine, and her husband, Vincent, in a small, two-story row home on Ann Street, an east-west oversize side alley just north of State Street between Eleventh and Twelfth. Josephine and Vincent had somehow found a way to buy the house shortly after they came over a few years earlier.

The brown brick-front row home boasted two nice-size windows on both levels and three gray-white marble steps leading up to a solid walnut door with no windows. On the first floor, the dining room, living room, and kitchen held up the second floor, which was carved into three and a half bedrooms and a bathroom with a claw-foot tub, a sink, and a toilet but no shower. Not only did the four adults live there, but so did Dominick's three nieces. They were almost adults themselves and were soon to be married off. The nieces crammed into the second-largest of the three small bedrooms. Out back, the previous owners had bricked over most of the little yard, leaving only enough room for Vincent and Josephine to plant a fig tree and a grapevine, both from the old country, next to a small, rickety wooden outhouse. The adults called this shanty a "bugghouz," which was broken English for backhouse. It supplemented the inside plumbing almost nine months a year. The bugghouz became unusable in harsh winters, from December through February. That was when the street became wholly impassable, and heavy layers of snow prevented the thick first coat of ice from melting, and the chilled, cramped conditions made brittle the bonds of the immigrants thrown together, isolated from the community at large by language and culture. Even normal conversations took place in a roar, and when tempers flared, as they often did, especially when Vincent and Dominick came home tired from their long days at the slaughterhouse just off the docks, voices rattled windows, and only blood and marriage vows restrained the adults from hurling pots or pans or throwing punches.

Summertime brought less tension, except on the hottest of days. Everyone played outside. In daylight, the younger kids, on a street void of much traffic, invented games with boxes, broomsticks, balls, belts, cans, and bottle caps. In twilight, the adults, sitting on their steps still gritty from the daily cleansering, talked, drinking Cokes or Italian water ice. Lemon and cherry were the only choices from the store of the corner of Twelfth and State. The street games were physical, and the kids often came home crying. They were banged and bruised, maybe even a bit bloodied, but never seriously broken.

It was a rough-and-tumble world into which Dominick the Butcher's son arrived. He made it rougher. He played harder and more ferociously than even the bigger kids on the street. Dominick the Butcher spoke in his native dialect to encourage his son's aggressiveness. Before long, an aura began to attach to Dominick the Butcher's only child. Butchie Pur had a given name, but only the members of the Purlini family ever used it. On the street, he was always Butchie Pur—not Butch, not Butchie, not Pur, and never Dominick. In the early years, he was just another little street-game-playing kid out on the asphalt from sunrise to sunset. But as his body matured into all compact muscle and sinew, he acquired a mean streak; no one knew how or why. Maybe it was because his English was weak or because his father seemed so harsh and severe--out of touch with the New World. Maybe it just came naturally. He began to dominate the alley and then the neighborhood. As the strongest, fastest, toughest kid around, he developed a following of seven or eight other boys who played off his strength and acquired and nurtured his mean streak. Soon kids from other blocks found ways to stay away from Ann Street.

Butchie Pur started his run-ins with the police when he was almost eleven years old by breaking windows and tossing bottles. Now, at almost sixteen years old, he had already been picked up by the cops more than half a dozen times for fighting and breaking into cars. They never actually caught him stealing one, although he had hot-wired a Ford from another neighborhood and took a short joyride through the city. He made stops for quick scores in an Irish candy store on Second Street and a Jewish deli on Seventh. He used a copper pipe disguised as a gun under a towel. Jimmy and Louie were with him, but the cops never caught them. His reputation spread throughout the enclave, and everyone knew Butchie Pur was a punk. A bad punk. People knew to stay away from him and his corner. No longer confined to narrow little Ann Street, his turf spread to the corner water ice and candy store at Twelfth and State--12S. This was diagonal from the elementary school where he managed to graduate despite learning almost nothing except how to terrorize half the faculty and all the students. His counterpart, Rocco Ciccatore, terrorized the others.

Rocco lived over by Thirteenth and Wharton. His father, Rocco Sr., knew the Purlini family from Abruzzi. Rocco Sr. owned a poultry store in the Italian Market four blocks away from their house. Hucksters sold most of the fruit, produce, and fish on Ninth Street from dilapidated wooden carts. Only the few clothing, cheese, meat, and poultry merchants worked from stores. The chicken store owners regularly carried their coops of live chickens, turkeys, and ducks out to the sidewalk so customers could pick out the birds they wanted and could watch, if they chose, as Rocco's father or sometimes even Rocco, beheaded, defeathered, and cut them up into dinner-size pieces. Just as Dominick Purlini Jr. was always Butchie Pur, Rocco Ciccatore Jr. was always Plucker—just plain Plucker. Plucker's reputation had begun to spread a few years earlier when, on the slightest dare and without a shiver of hesitation, he used his father's Ninth Street technique, borrowed a pocketknife, and used it on an unsuspecting neighborhood street cat now referred to as "Headless."

Butchie Pur and Plucker had worked out a separate peace in their grade school days. Plucker thought he was as strong and fast and tough as Butchie Pur, and maybe he was. Early on, maybe because of the family connection back in Italy, the two boys never hassled one another. Butchie Pur gave Plucker respect, and Plucker never pushed Butchie Pur. Butchie Pur was first, but he was first of two equals.

Except when they weren't playing hooky from tenth grade at South Philly High, Butchie Pur and Plucker both guarded their corners. Butchie Pur sentried Twelfth and State; Plucker patrolled Thirteenth and Wharton, which was one block south and one block west. Butchie Pur and his boys controlled the southbound trolley route on Twelfth Street. This went from State to Wharton and beyond one block to Dicks Street, the eastern access to Pizzi Square. From Thirteenth and Wharton, Plucker had open season on the kids drawn into Pizzi Square from the south and west. They came to play hardball, rough touch football on the cinder-topped square, or to shoot some hoops on one of the three full-size basketball courts the city had concreted over and decked out with perforated tin backboards and steel rims with chains instead of cord nets. The world had cast Butchie Pur and Plucker from the same mold. They were tough, strong, mean, and reckless, and when their corners joined forces to form the Southwarks, they became overpowering—especially to unsuspecting kids traveling through their turf.

For some reason, Nick DiDominico had only a vague knowledge of the street lure about the Southwarks. His world was enough different from theirs. Like most of the other kids in the neighborhood, Nick was second generation. This meant his grandparents had immigrated. Nick's father, Nicholas Sr., Nad to everyone, had acquired some skills working on neighborhood cars as a kid. He had an aptitude for the mechanical, and he landed a good job as a mechanic in the neighborhood. First, he worked in a mom-and-pop machine shop, and later he worked in the local public property garage, where he worked on police cars and fire engines.

In this neighborhood, people either let their offspring fend for themselves almost completely, or they permeated their lives with emphasis on education, on bettering themselves, and on learning to speak proper English while keeping Italian as a second language to help preserve their heritage. Anyone could immediately tell the difference between the parents' styles by watching the kids. Nick's freedoms grew as his conduct reflected his parents' values.

Nick lived over on State Street between Tenth and Eleventh, half a block from Shot Tower Playground, which was between Ninth and Tenth and between State and Wharton. Shot Tower took its name from the still-standing tower erupting out of and over the neighborhood on one side of the playground. According to myth or legend or history, during the Revolutionary War, molten iron was dropped from its summit into vats of water below to form shot. Shot Tower was actually a nicer playground than Pizzi. It had a grass-and-dirt baseball diamond, a football field, a clubhouse, and two boccie alleys. It was used mostly for organized sports coordinated by the city. None of the kids from Nick's neighborhood played any sports, and all of Nick's classmates from the Catholic school lived nearer to Pizzi Square, which was on the other side of the parish. So, early in sixth grade, when Nicholas Amadeo DiDominico decided he was more interested in sports than being a corner kid just hanging out on the alley off Tenth and State and getting into trouble, he knew he would have to go to Pizzi Square to find a game. In sixth grade they shuffled the classes in his school and Nick had just made two new friends from the smart side of the parish. At recess, Johnny Colini and Paulie

Tedesco told Nick that they had fun playing football or basketball every day after school at Pizzi Square, and they said he should come over to play with them. Johnny and Paulie didn't think to tell Nick about Butchie Pur and Plucker because, as neighborhood kids who had been playing at Pizzi since they could first walk, Johnny and Paulie were exempt from Southwark hazing.

The late-September Monday crackled with a typical autumnal breeze. Outside the city, the leaves were changing colors. The State Street sidewalks remained the same—not that Nick would have noticed any changes on his morning walk to school. The first part of the day passed quickly enough, and soon it was recess. As was rapidly becoming the norm, he, Johnny, Paulie, and others played wall ball during the break. The game had been Nick's introduction to sports. They played using the wall of Pizzi fire station, the parallel school wall that matched it in height, and the thirty-foot space between them. The only equipment was a rubber air-filled ball covered with pimples or stars. They liked pimple balls better; they were thicker and bouncier, and they lasted longer. Early on, Nick established himself as a sure-handed, mobile leaper on defense and an artfully aggressive thrower on offense. He figured out quickly he could ricochet a pimple ball off both the fire station and school walls, making it almost uncatchable. Nick loved wall ball.

That day, after recess, Nick uncharacteristically lost his concentration in school.

"Nicholas DiDominico," called Sister Marita Carmel from the front of the chalk-dusted sixth-grade classroom, which was on the third floor and looked out at the fire station. "Nicholas DiDominico," she called again to vacant ears. "Nick-o-las Di-Do-min-ick-o," she now screamed, startling him out of his trance, which drew smirks and giggles from the rest of the class. "Where are you, Nicholas DiDominico?"

He groaned. "Sorry, Sister."

"Nicholas, the capital of North Dakota, please. What is it?"

Somehow, he managed to pull "Bismarck" from a space in his brain not completely piled high with thoughts of his first after-school trip to the Pizzi Square.

"Thank you, Mr. DiDominico. Now, try to stay somewhere with us in the state of Pennsylvania for the rest of the day, please. Can you do that?"

"Yes. Sorry, Sister."

Off the hook for a while, Nick's thoughts returned to Pizzi Square. Excited about playing with his new friends, he felt adventuresome. Normally, he left the neighborhood only for school or church. It had been several years since his mother had taken him for long walks in his stroller through Pizzi Square en route to Broad and Passyunk, where she would pay the phone and utility bills. Nick ran into his house after school to change his clothes as quickly as he could. His mother always made him hang up his dress pants, white shirt, tie, and blazer so they would be ready for the next morning. He pulled on his dungarees, a T-shirt, and his black high-top Chuck Taylor All Star Converse sneakers as quickly as he could, and he bolted down the steps to the front door.

"Nicholas, where are you going so fast? No homework today?"

"Mom! Remember? We talked about it last week. I'm going to Pizzi Square to play some ball with a couple of the kids in my new class. They play there every day, and they asked me to come over. Remember?"

"What about your homework?"

"I'll do it right after dinner."

"No television till you finish your homework."

"I know."

"Be home by the time Dad comes home. Five thirty."

"I know. I'll be home."

"Have fun."

"Okay."

"Be careful."

"I will."

Nick sprang straight up State Street with his head down. He looked up only to cross Eleventh. He was closing in on the Monroe Hamilton Elementary School at Twelfth. He was en route to Pizzi Square. His head was still down when he felt the first jolt to his chest. It stopped him cold in his tracks. He looked up to see three big kids locked arm in arm. They were blocking his path. Four bigger kids backed them up, and they were laughing at him.

"Where do you think you're goin', punk?" one of the three shot at him.

"Hey, get outta my way," Nick fired back. "I'm just goin' to play some ball over at Pizzi Square."

One of the front three, a skinny kid with a big nose, slouched, and he held his right fist in his left hand at waist height. He leaned in toward Nick but spoke to the biggest of the kids, who was standing behind him. "Hey, Butchie Pur, he's just goin' to play some ball over at Pizzi Square. Is that okay with you?"

Nick was now being completely surrounded. He had heard of Butchie Pur and his reputation once or maybe twice, but it had completely slipped his mind that to get to Pizzi he'd have to go through 12 S, which was the way that the kids in the neighborhood referred to the Southwarks. He tried to back out of the circle without touching anybody. He knew if he touched any of them, he'd get jumped immediately. His way was blocked, so he stood his ground. He fought the urge to ball his fists—that too would have gotten him jumped. He tried not to panic and tried not to try to escape. He tried to figure something out. So far, he was coming up empty.

"I don't know, Louie. I don't think it's okay for punks from other corners to just come by a Southwark corner. Let me check the rules here."

Butchie Pur pretended to page through an imaginary book he pulled from his back pocket. Everybody laughed except Nick. Nick was normal size for a twelve-year-old. He hadn't yet experienced that willowy growth spurt due sometime soon. As a result, he was in proportion and well coordinated. The other boys looked to be fourteen, fifteen, or even sixteen, and they were closing in on their adult heights. He tried not to make eye contact without looking down.

"Nah, it's not okay. Ask him if he has any money."

"You gotta pay a toll to get through here, punk," Louie hurled at him. "You know? Like on a bridge. For safe passage."

Again, everybody but Nick laughed.

"I don't have money. I just want to play some ball."

"Butchie Pur, he says he don't have no money. Just wants to play some ball."

"Costs money to get through here to play ball. Send him back home," Butchie Pur ordered.

"Go home, punk. Butchie Pur says for you to go home and stay there or come back with some money for the toll."

Nick thought of himself as the toughest smart kid in his class and the smartest tough kid too. He stood in the middle of the circle and wished he were Bobby Massi, the toughest tough kid. That way, he could fight his way out. He really wanted to be Sammy Rizzi, though, the smartest smart kid. That way, he could think his way out. He knew he couldn't give them money, and he couldn't just push his way through. On the spot, he decided that if he went home now, he'd never get to Pizzi Square. He came up with an idea. "Hey, you with the mouth." He looked right at Louie.

He was one of the younger kids, and he had obviously just gone through his first real growth spurt. He was all wobbly legs and dangling arms. The mouth probably meant he was the easiest of the gang.

"You're acting pretty tough with Butchie Pur and all his boys behind you. But what about you on your own, Louie? How tough are you on your own? Did they make you pay a toll to hang with them? That's probably the only way they'd let you in."

"Let's get him, boys," Louie shouted. "Let's smash this punk."

Butchie Pur stepped into the circle. "I don't know, Louie. It seems like this punk here is callin' you out. Hey, you." He motioned to Nick. "You callin' Louie out?"

"I'm callin' him out to a fair one—if he's got the guts to go it alone."

"Hey, Louie, he's callin' you out to a fair one. You up for it? If not, maybe you should pay his toll."

"Ah, come on, Butchie Pur. We never do fair ones. That's not the way it works."

"It don't work that way 'cause nobody ever called one. Punk here is callin' one. Okay, boys, back off. Mikey, on the count of three, you push Louie in, and I'll push the punk in. Ready? One, two, th—"

On the count of two and a half, just as Butchie Pur touched him, Nick lurched at Louie with a right jab to his left ear. Then he threw an uppercut to the stomach. Nick's dad had done some club boxing. When Nick was seven, his dad started to show him how boxers stood with balance and bounce. He worked with Nick, who was left handed, regularly. "Stay on the balls of your feet. Bounce. Keep your right hand high. Near your right cheek. Keep your left one lower. In front of your left ear. Most people are right handed and will jab with their left hand. Always circle away from their left. If they try to throw haymaker roundhouses, you'll have plenty of time to slip them. When you throw a punch, mean it. Put some snap in it at the shoulder and the elbow, and throw your whole body weight behind it. Always try to throw a combination of punches. At least two—one high and one mid. If you can't avoid a fight, always, always, always beat the other guy to the first punch—but only if you can't avoid it. Especially if he's bigger than you."

His father's words raced through him.

The combination punch had the dual effect of ringing Louie's right ear and knocking the breath out of him. He stumbled sideways, mostly dazed. One of his boys propped him up and pushed him toward Nick, who tried to bounce but found himself planted. His arms were suddenly pinned to his sides by a ferocious bear hug. Another boy got off one punch, catching the left side of Nick's nose and his left eye. Nick felt the eye drain down his face and the red-hot sting of pins and needles spread through his nose and into his cheeks and throat. He fully expected to see his own blood splash out in front of him, but a loud voice froze the action.

"Stop!" Butchie Pur's shout shattered the chaos. "Butchie Pur told the punk here it was a fair one. Stop. Let the punk go. He got Louie fair. Louie, you want some more?" Louie was in no state to answer. "I didn't think so. Hey, punk, you go to Pizzi to play some ball. We'll see about next time next time."

Nick looked at Butchie Pur and nodded. Without changing his expression, he made eye contact with each of the other boys except Louie. He turned up Twelfth, curbing his instinct to bolt. He walked straight and didn't reach up to his swollen eye and nose. Today, Twelfth and Wharton was empty. Plucker's boys were on Thirteenth. Nick ran into the park to find Johnny and Paulie tossing around a football with a bunch of other kids.

"Nicky," called Johnny when he saw him, "over here. We need one more for six on six. Glad you could come." As Nick came into view, he added, "What happened to you? We haven't even started to play yet, and you're all banged up."

Nick told him the story in full.

"Wow, Butchie Pur's gang. 12S. The Southwarks. I should have thought about that," Johnny piped in. "Nick, you have to be on the lookout for Butchie Pur's sidekick too. His name is Plucker, and he's almost as mean as Butchie Pur. He once turned a cat headless. He hangs out on my side of the Square."

"You mean I can't get around Butchie Pur's gang?" Nick said.

Paulie added his two cents. "You might be able to get by Butchie Pur, but then you'll run right into Plucker."

"Maybe I should just forget about coming around here. And what about going home? Do I have to go through the same thing to get home?"

"I don't know," Johnny said. "How about coming home to my house and letting your folks pick you up later?"

"That won't work. My mom doesn't drive and I have to be home by five thirty when my dad comes home from work."

"I think we should play now. Maybe they won't be out when it's time for you to go home."

They chose up sides, and Nick fit right in with the group. On defense, they lined him up to rush the passer first.

"Count one Mississippi, two Mississippi, three Mississippi. Then rush. Unless the quarterback starts to run." Johnny instructed.

Nick made a couple of good tags behind the line of scrimmage, so when one of the pass defenders twisted an ankle, Nick moved back to the secondary. He knocked down a few passes and barely missed picking one off. On offense, he caught everything thrown near him, but on one play, they lateraled to him in the backfield for a flea-flicker, and he quickly showed that somebody else should do the passing. All in all, he had a fun time. He even forgot that his nose and eye were swollen.

Before long, shouts from parents echoed from the edge of the Square.

"Johnny!"

"Paulie!"

"Frankie!"

"Ronnie!"

The game broke up, and suddenly Nick realized he could no longer avoid the trip home. He left the Square at Twelfth and Wharton, and he decided to go home a different way—down Wharton to Tenth and then over to State. He decided walking rather than running, would draw less attention. He kept his eyes alert to as many different directions as he could without looking like one of those swivel dolls in the back of a brand-new Chevy. He managed to get home just as his dad walked through the front door.

"Hi, Dad."

"Where you been, Nick?"

"I went over to Pizzi Square to play football with guys from school."

"All the way over to Pizzi? Have fun?" Nick's father stopped short when he saw his son's face. "What happened to you?"

This question brought Nick's mother into the living room.

"It's nothin', Dad. I was rushing the passer, and I slipped on the cinders. Somebody's forearm came up and I fell into it. It was an accident. We kept playing."

"You sure, Nick? It looks like you have a black eye and a bloody nose. You sure you didn't fight?"

"I'm sure, Dad. It was just my first time playing with these guys. I was a little bit nervous and clumsy. I got better as the game went on. I had fun. They're good guys. They asked me to come back again tomorrow after school."

Nick wasn't sure about tomorrow, though. He knew he'd have to get through Butchie Pur's gang again and maybe even Plucker's. He'd try to figure something out after his homework.

Sleep came hard to him that night. His face now throbbed from the sucker punch, but it bothered his head even more. If one sucker punch could come from nowhere, he could be barraged before he knew it. He wanted to go to Pizzi again, but terror seeped in steadily. He fought off the urge to cry. He was almost thirteen. Maybe he should just forget about Pizzi Square and Johnny and Paulie. Maybe he should stay on his own street. He knew he'd been lucky with Louie. He'd gotten the jump on him, but what if the whole gang jumped him? What if Butchie Pur himself came after him? He knew he'd be a goner then. After hours of self-torture, he exhausted himself to sleep.

In school the next day, the word spread quickly that Butchie Pur's gang jumped Nick; he had been roughed up, but he held his own enough to get to Pizzi Square to play ball. His black eye and swollen nose marked him with honor. At recess, Johnny and Paulie asked him if he was coming over to the Pizzi Square after school for another game. They said they'd probably need him to make the sides even. Nick said he would try, but he was worried about the gang.

Johnny piped up. "Nick, I grew up in the Square with Plucker. He's older, but he knows Paulie and me from before we even started school. I'll try to talk to him to see if they can cut you some slack. He never bothers the neighborhood kids. I'll tell him you're a good guy just trying to get into a game. I'll say you're my good friend, okay?"

"Thanks, Johnny. You think he'll cut me some slack?"

"I don't know, but I'll talk to him right after school and call you at home."

"Good."

Nick raced home and changed. When the phone rang, he grabbed it.

"Nick?"

"Yeah, Johnny? You talk to him?"

"Yeah. He said he won't give you any trouble unless you cross Butchie Pur. If it's okay with Butchie Pur, it's okay with him. What do you think? You comin' over to the Square?"

"I don't know. I don't know if I can get by 12S."

"How did you get home last night?"

"I came down Wharton and never saw them."

"Maybe you can come that way. Okay?"

"I'll try."

Nick had choices: stay home, try to avoid 12S, or go right by their corner and take his chances.

"Mom, I want to go to the Pizzi Square again. Okay?"

"Okay. But be careful. No more black eyes. Be home by five thirty."

This time, Nick walked out his front door and tried to figure out the best route. He decided to take the same route as yesterday, but this time, he kept his eyes open. As he approached Twelfth-Street, he started to look around, but the corner was empty. He turned down Twelfth and headed toward Wharton. There they were at the mouth of the Square—about thirteen or fourteen of them. Butchie Pur stood in front with another big kid next to him. Plucker, he figured. Nick thought about turning to run home, but he guessed they'd run him down, catch him from behind, and beat the crap out of him. He thought he might have a better chance if he faced them straight on.

"Hey, Plucker, is this the punk you got the call about?"

"I guess so, Butchie Pur. He's the only punk I see."

"Hey, punk. You got around us last night, but you can't get around us now. Louie here says he wants a piece of you, punk. You want a piece of Louie?"

"Butchie Pur, I don't want to fight. I just want to play some ball. I'm not causing trouble."

"Where you from, punk?"

"Tenth and State."

"Anybody from Tenth and State comes by a Southwark corner is causing trouble. That's the way I see it. What do you think, Plucker?"

"I think so too, Butchie Pur. Punk's got to learn the rules."

"Plucker, I'm not a corner kid. I go to school with Johnny and Paulie. I don't want to fight. I just want to play ball."

They surrounded him and closed in slowly.

"Well, Tenth Street kids either got to fight or pay a toll. You bring money today?" Butchie Pur was having fun with this.

"I don't have any money."

"Well, then you got to fight. You want another fair one?"

"I don't want to fight."

"Your choice, punk. Pay a toll, or we all get you, or you get a fair one, just like yesterday."

With that, Butchie Pur grabbed Jimmy on his right and pushed him toward Nick. Nick was not quite ready and took Jimmy's left on the chest. Jimmy was three or four years older than Nick and had the size to go with his age. He also knew how to handle himself better than Louie did. Nick got up on his toes and began to circle, but Jimmy snuck a few punches in to his midsection. Nick's combinations fell harmlessly on Jimmy's arms and shoulders, but his boxing style kept Jimmy at bay for the most part. Then, as he was circling, Nick either tripped or was tripped and lost his balance. Jimmy rushed in, bear-hugged him, rolled him onto the cinders, and pinned him.

"You give up?" Jimmy shouted in his face.

"This was supposed to be a fair one," Nick shouted back. "Somebody tripped me. Let me back up, and let's have a fair one."

Jimmy dug his knee into Nick's gut as he got up. By now, all the kids from the Square had come over to watch the fight. Butchie Pur and Plucker turned to talk on the side.

Butchie Pur took control. "Hey, punk, you still want a fair one?"

"I don't want to fight. But if I have to fight, yeah, I want it to be a fair one. There's only one of me. How many of you are there? Ten? Eleven? Twelve? How fair is that?"

"Well, punk, if you want to come from Tenth and State to Southwark turf, you might have to fight my boys one at a time."

"I don't want to fight; I just want to play ball."

"Hey, Plucker. This kid got friends? Maybe we can even the sides up."

"Johnny, here, and Paulie."

"Hey, Johnny and Paulie, this punk your friend?" Butchie Pur demanded.

Johnny and Paulie looked at each other and froze for an instant. Nick thought all three of them might be jumped. He looked for a way out but found none.

"Yeah," Johnny spoke first.

"Yeah," Paulie joined in.

"You guys ask him to come over to play ball?"

"Yeah," Johnny said.

"You know how stupid that is without checking with Plucker or me first?"

"We didn't think, Butchie Pur." It was Paulie this time.

"They didn't think, Plucker." Butchie Pur mocked them to his accomplice. "Plucker, what do you think? Should we beat the shit out of the three of them or cut them some slack?"

"I've known Johnny and Paulie since they peed themselves. Probably doin' it again right now. They're okay, Butchie Pur. Punk here's got spunk. If they vouch for the punk, I'd cut them slack."

"You heard it, punk. You got slack. You two, don't go askin' kids from other corners over here without checking with Plucker or me, you hear?"

"We hear," they said in unison.

"Hey, punk, what's your name?"Nick hesitated a little too long. Butchie Pur's voice grabbed him.

"Punk, I'm talkin' to you now. You don't show respect when I'm talkin' to you, you get a fair one with me. You hear? We're gonna let you by, punk. And since we let you through here, we gotta know your name."

Butchie Pur broke from his snarl ever so slightly. The change in his face was obvious to Nick. It was as close to a smile as the situation would allow.

"Nick DiDominico, but I go by Nad, like my old man."

"Well, Nick DiDominico. Looks like you got some 'nads. Either that or you're a moron. You a moron?"

Butchie Pur was almost jovial, and Plucker seemed to be enjoying himself too.

"I try not to be," Nick answered.

"Okay then. You go by Nad from now on, you hear? And don't cause no trouble, 'cause if you do, there won't be no fair one."

Butchie Pur and his boys strolled back to Twelfth Street. Plucker's gang went to Thirteen.

The game started quickly. Nick DiDominico, now Nad, ran a fifteen-yard buttonhook for a first down.

CASABELLA

To know fully, to grasp the total meaning of every nuance and subtlety, we need to look back so the filters of time and experience—maturity, if you will—can remove the distortion, the confusion, the apparent chaos, and whimsy from what we are living. Our feelings of sadness and joy, pain and pleasure, disillusionment and satisfaction seem real enough at the time, but only after we make changes into other passages of life can we distinguish clearly which of those feelings have united with the inner linings of our personalities, the fibers of our souls, the cores of our beings. The feelings, events, and people in our lives lack a completeness in the here and now. Only after time can we truly understand how things were. When you are different, when they are different, or gone, that fifth dimension—perspective— rounds out the focus, retroactively, in a way that cannot be achieved *in media res.* We can perceive only portions of vitality, beauty, and genius in the present. Their depth and fullness, nature and scope, brighten and sharpen with distance. Light from different angles must illuminate them so we can understand every element of all the ingredients. Only then can we embrace their total impact and importance. Both the presence and absence of those feelings, events, and people are imperative. It may be sad, but only verisimilitude is readily discernible in the present. Real truth is more elusive. For truth, we need reflection. We need experience. We need more life. We always need more life.

I

My parents christened me Nicholas Amadeo DiDominico in the fall of 1948 in the Church of the Annunciation B.V.M. in South Philly. My name was originally my father's, but no one, not even Mom, called him anything but Nad or Naddie. I knew these were his initials, but when I was about sixteen, my uncle told me that Dad had really acquired the nickname when he was in his early twenties.

That winter, a local thug called Biggie had invaded the neighborhood. He wore a black overcoat and a gray fedora and tried to intimidate one or another of the corner guys whenever he found a chance to isolate one. The tough guys claimed Biggie's mouth had more fury than his fists, yet there was a bad feeling on the block. Biggie stood tall with a longshoreman's build, a drunkard's temper, and a bully's disposition. He got lucky early on and singled out a couple of the lesser guys from the corner. He danced in and out of the neighborhood at odd times, so the legit guys had a hard time catching up with him. One day, he swaggered into the neighborhood, and by chance, he encountered my dad and demanded a payoff from him. "Protection insurance," he called it. My uncle said my father told him to go look for a job. Biggie shouted that his job was collecting insurance from small-timers and that he was on the clock. He punctuated his words with a cocked fist and a push. Nad bobbed, weaved, and countered with a combination of left, left, right, left, right, right, left that broke Biggie's nose, bruised some ribs, and sent him first sprawling to the street and, eventually, out of the neighborhood forever. My uncle said everyone started calling my dad Nicky Gonads. Then someone realized his initials were N A D and "Gonads" became "Nad." It became his permanent moniker. I was Nicholas or Nicky, Nick in our house, to my extended family and in the neighborhood. In high school, without ever actually earning Dad's nickname, I began introducing myself as Nad. To this day, I'm Nicholas, Nicky, Nick, or occasionally Clanks to those I know from before high school and Nad or Naddie to the rest of the world.

As Nicholas, I spent my youth playing street games in the neighborhood as part of a quartet of ragamuffins. Chubby was the oldest by almost a year; Larry was only a week older than me; Chooch was a month my junior. We started out playing with cardboard boxes. The popularity of big cardboard boxes knew no bounds. The thrill of a new refrigerator or washing machine on the block engaged us for days. One box would become a castle for Arthur, Lancelot, and the rest of the Knights of the Round Table. With another one, we built the Alamo for Jim Bowie. We went through caves for Zorro, foxholes for GIs, and spaceships for Buck Rodgers.

Eventually, the boxes became tattered remnants, and we looked for other ways to amuse ourselves. We played street games—hide the whip, kick the can, chase the white horse, block ball, dead box, a game we called gobagershky, and buck-buck. We felt the last three games were special. They were our games in South Philly. It didn't occur to us they might have been played in other places. In fact, we didn't realize at the time there were other places. South Philly was the whole world. Gobagershky might have been played only in our neighborhood, though.

Dead box was a true street game. You needed a street to play it. Our street ran the width of South Philly from east to west and was, therefore, no good for dead box and the other street games. Fortuitously, two little streets located just around the corner presented a better and safer haven for play. On summer mornings after the horse-drawn Abbotts wagon dropped off milk for cocoa, I would start to work my way out the front door. I alternatively yelled, "Mom, I'm goin' up the little street" or "Mom, I'm goin' around the corner." It was always my goal to be out there before the old Italian huckster steering his horse and buggy up the street started shouting about Javelle Water, promoting his glass bottles of the strongest bleach in the world for twenty-five cents a bottle. Only on the worst days did I fail to hit the street before the umbrella man knocked on our door and asked to repair our umbrellas or to sharpen our knives and scissors on a ramshackle little cart. It had a foot-activated, belt-driven sharpening stone, bolts of black cloth, spokes, and handles cannibalized from unsalvageable umbrellas from other South Philly neighborhoods where he had pushed his workshop on previous days piled in the front.

One morning when I was about nine, Chubby greeted me as I left my house. "Hey," he said. "Let's go. Let's play dead box."

This was before I picked up the neighborhood nickname "Clanks," but that's another story for later. Chubby, built like a broom handle, all pipe cleaner arms over downspout legs, acted like the leader of our small group on the streets but not in school. Neither Chubby, Larry, Skinny Lenny, nor Chooch showed any inclination toward book learning; they left that to me. What little torso Chubby had looked emaciated, and his face was narrowed as if it had been pressed in a vise. Chubby had high energy and high volume with no filter. He was always the first to learn the street games, mostly from watching his older brother, Petey.

"Sure. Dead box?" I asked. "What's a dead box?" I couldn't believe we had a coffin to play with. "Is the dead guy still in the box?"

"You're so stupid," Chubby offered supportively. "No, there's no dead guy. It's not a box box. It's a game. Do you have a tinny?"

"I have a pinky and a thumb, but I don't think I have a tinny. Which one is that?"

"Come on, Nick. Don't you know anything?" Chubby reached into his pocket and pulled out five bottle caps and a piece of chalk. "Here," Chubby said with the irritation of a teacher going over a times table for the tenth time. "Pick a tinny."

Bottle caps back then had cork in them. Chubby had already removed the cork, put a penny in each one, and melted wax to seal in the penny. Thus, he had converted the bottle caps into tinnies. Your tinny was an important part of your identity. If you found a good one, maybe a special 7 Up or Frank's Vanilla Cream Soda tinny that won you some games in dead box, you would try to hold onto it for a while. You'd keep it hidden so your mother wouldn't mistake it for junk and trash it. Chubby was cool; he had brushed all the paint off the top of his tinny and painted it black.

Chubby ran around the corner where Larry, Skinny Lenny, and Chooch had already chalked out a portion of the street into roughly a five-by-three-foot rectangle with a one in the bottom left corner, a two in the top right corner, a three on the bottom line, and so one. All in all, twelve numbers were placed in strategic spots in a five-by-three box. He drew a smaller rectangle in the center of the box with a skull and crossbones in it—the dead box.

Larry was a whirling dervish too, but he was not quite at Chubby's speed. Street smart but reckless, Larry had the size, strength, and coordination to be a good athlete had he chosen that route. He didn't. He chose another way instead. He was just smart enough to come up with dangerous ideas but not smart enough to know which risks not to take. As a nine-year-old, he got away with being reckless; it was passed off as petty mischief. As he grew, the consequences of this flaw became more serious and lasting. Larry never made it through high school and never reached drinking age. Back then, though, he was second-in-command to Chubby.

Back then, Larry also knew how to play dead box, and I didn't.

"Now, flick your tinny around like this," Chubby said, and he demonstrated.

He formed a circle with his thumb and middle finger and then flicked his middle finger across his thumb to propel Black Beauty adroitly from box one to box two. He was lying almost prostrate on summer asphalt so hot it could melt an Italian Ivy League undershirt, which was a thinly ribbed tight-fitting white tank top.

"You have to go from box to box," said Larry.

He went on to say that if you landed in the box with the skull and crossbones, either because of your own ineptitude or more likely because Larry or Chooch intentionally knocked you in with his tinny, you had to start over.

"When you finish going through all the boxes, you have to go into the dead box. First one in wins. Got it?"

I figured that if Chooch, which I had been told was Italian for "jackass" could get it, I could get it too. Chubby and Larry said that Chooch's father had pinned that name on him early on because, as Chooch's had said, "Son, you just can't do a damn thing right." Having a wizard like Chooch in the group always gave me the feeling that I could do anything—at least anything he could do. I caught on pretty quickly. I started beating Chooch the very first day. It took me a couple of weeks to catch Chubby. He would invariably lose his concentration in the middle of the game. Larry was a bit more formidable. Toward the end of the summer, I finally caught him by surprise, knocking his Frank's Black Cherry into the dead box when we were both on our way to twelve. He responded graciously by picking up my 7 Up top and hurling it down the sewer. I didn't care. We both knew I had finally mastered the game—and him.

Dead box was harmless but vicious and time consuming. We soon learned it was best to play in the early part of the day. That was when there was no traffic on the little street and before the heat off the asphalt became suffocating.

Chubby also taught me gobagershky, a slightly more violent game than dead box. To play gobagershky, you needed a wooden spinning top and the skill and dexterity to spin your top fast enough so that you work it into the palm for your hand while it was still spinning and carry it to another kid's top that was lying in the street. If you could touch his top with your spinning top, you could take a whack at it with the point of yours and spin again. If you failed, your top went down and became a target. We called the game "gobagershky" because the object was to gobagershky—that is, hammer—your friend's top to pieces. Larry was unrivaled at this game. Although the game was the perfect duration for Chubby's attention span, Larry had both the temperament and the dexterity. After a while, not even the big kids—Petey, Frankie, Georgie, or Dominick—would play gobagershky with Larry. All of us but Larry went through a bunch of tops in those days. This greatly pleased old Jacob, the octogenarian Lebanese proprietor of the candy store up the street where we bought new tops for a few pennies and then tried to scrape up a few more cents for strips of paper dabbed with sugar dot candies of various colors—two strips for a penny.

While dead box and gobagershky were somewhat violent, nobody sustained any meaningful injuries playing them—unless you forced somebody's tinny into the dead box or you gobagershkied somebody's top to smithereens. Buck buck was another story completely. You could get seriously taken out playing buck buck. We started watching when we were about seven or eight, and we started to play when we were nine or ten. Before I played, I remember watching with envy and terror as Frankie, Petey, and the older guys shouted, "Buck buck. Number one coming. Buck buck. Number two coming."

You needed more kids for this game, and the way we played, you needed an odd number. The minimum was five kids; if you had eleven, this was better. The odd kid out had a special role. This was usually the youngest or the least athletic, and that person got to be a pillow, meaning he or she (the neighborhood tomboy, Trina, played often) would stand with his or her back to the wall and face the street. The remaining kids split up into two equal groups. These were the real contestants.

One by one, each kid in the first group would bend at the waist and hold onto the kid in front, forming a horizontal plane from the pillow that was parallel to the street. The other group would line up across the street and holler in sequence, "Buck buck. Number one coming." One kid would then run full speed and jump onto the backs of the down team. If the kid made it, number two could jump. If the kid fell off, the teams switched positions. If the down team buckled or fell, the jumpers could go again. Complicated rules determined who would jump if everyone made it.

One day when I was too young to get into a game, I learned something important. There were eight big kids around. They needed a pillow, so they drafted Chubby, the oldest little kid. This was his big chance. He'd been watching a lot. All four jumpers made it, so they went to fingers. The first jumper held up three. The down team hesitated and then guessed four. Suddenly, Chubby's head flew back and bounced off the wall. He doubled over, held his stomach, and gasped for air. I couldn't figure out what had happened. In the next round, all the jumpers made it again, and again the lead jumper held up three fingers. The down team hesitated, guessed three, got up, and smiled. Chubby smiled too, until the lead jumper looked him straight in the eyes. Chubby looked away and then started to run. I learned then that the pillow wielded great power but at great risk. You had to make some judgments to avoid a beating. As the pillow, you had to figure out which team was tougher. You had power, but sometimes you had to resist the urge to wield it. The trap was that the pillow position was the entry level into this game. We all had to go through it, and we all had to get roughed up at least a little bit. The shrewder you were, the fewer the number of body blows you took. I passed through the entry level pretty quickly, but the next year was a rough one for Cooch. For the life of him, he just couldn't figure out the code. Eventually even Chooch matured and turned into a pretty good jumper. Soon Chubby, Larry, Chooch, Skinny Lenny, and I were all playing. When we were on the same team, we were virtually unbeatable. Chubby was light, so he always jumped far. So was Skinny Lenny. Larry was strong, so he always jumped hard. Many a down team crumbled under him. Chooch was reliable, and I could usually psych out the down team when it came to flashing fingers. We loved this game, even though it resulted in frequent bumps, scrapes, bruises, and an occasional broken arm.

On the street, this quartet made it through the year and began the next in like fashion.

II

Inner city Philadelphia in the early 1960s displayed a patchwork of ethnic communities. Immigrants—first, second, and third generation Italians and Irish—dominated the demographics with small Jewish, Polish, German, and Lebanese enclaves. If you were a "2" or were a "30th streeter your names were more likely O'Hara, Sullivan, or Carroll. If you lived in the middle, you were DiPietro, Moliari, or Verna.

The two cultures mixed about the way you would expect. The Irish considered the Italians wops or dago low-life bootleggers who crushed grapes with their feet, bathed in the sink by slapping water on themselves, couldn't speak the language, and controlled the numbers racket, loan sharking, and drug traffic through the Mafia. The Italians viewed the Irish as beer-swilling micks or harps with neither intuition nor intelligence. The Italians thought the only cultural claims to fame for the Irish were that on New Year's Day they would dress up in stupid costumes and parade up Broad Street, and that in mid-March they could chug incalculable amounts of green beer, which looked disgusting on the street the next day. Despite this mutual disrespect, though, only occasionally did major problems occur between the two groups. Usually a fight would break out at the high school carnival as testosterone filled the air and swashbuckling man-children found ways to provoke a knock-down-drag-out fights until the police arrived to quell the disorder. Both sides always claimed victory, but for the most part, neither side lost these skirmishes. All that really happened was the gladiators refined their street skills for self-preservation—an essential urban attribute even then.

Early on in the street games, you were your tinny, but later on, your ethnicity provided your first real identity. Your parish and your corner formed the next two pieces of you. Prior to high school, you were either a Catholic who attended the diocesan elementary school or a public who attended the city school. The Catholics thought of themselves as smarter, better behaved, more refined, and more sophisticated. They perceived the publics as bigger, tougher, stronger, and more athletic. I grew up Catholic in the Annunciation B.V.M., which stands for Blessed Virgin Mary, parish near the Italian Market on Nint' Street. This was a seven-block open-air street market extending south to north. Neighborhood merchants sold fruit and produce from broken-down wooden stands with the wheels removed. The products came straight from the piers on Dock Street, and the prices were great, as long as the street merchant stuffed your bag. You had to pay a premium if you wanted to pick your own. Even the premium price was so low that many of us never went into a supermarket. My first experience with a chain grocery store didn't come until after I started college.

Nint' Street provided not only produce, color, and traffic to our little neighborhood, but it also provided some spending money. The street merchants used cigar boxes as cash registers, recklessly flipping their coins for later calculation. Money wasn't easy to come by, even back then, so Chubby, Larry, Chooch, and I would cruise Nint Street after hours, especially on rainy Saturday evenings. We'd retrieve the wayward coins that had bounced from the cigar boxes undetected, their escape camouflaged by the rain tattooing on the overhead canvas. We started by converting our haul into candy at Jacob's, and then we ascended to ice cream or snow cones at Stinky Pete's on the corner of Tent' and Wharton, my corner.

We were on the northern border of the parish, the tough side. The church and school, separated from one another by four city blocks, were more toward the center of the parish. I grew up feeling that the kids on the south side of the parish were richer, more refined, and more advantaged than we were. I think it was because our side of the parish housed the truck drivers, toll takers, auto mechanics, electricians, and television repairmen, while the teachers, bank tellers, accountants, lawyers, and small business owners lived on the south side. Or maybe it was just because I lived on the north side. My belief back then was that the farther south you went in South Philly, the more affluent, sophisticated, and advanced were the residents. We were immigrants and first- and second-generation Italians. They were third and fourth generation, or so I thought. They had become more Americanized—"Medigan," as my family would say. Everybody who was not Italian was "Medigan."

At the Annunciation B.V.M. Elementary School, Sisters Marita, Amabolis, Clarissa, Mary Alberta, and Theresa Marie, under the direction of Mother Maria diPrinzio, whose diminutive stature and arthritic, crooked fingers belied her stern, militaristic style, pounded us with the multiplication tables from one to twelve, the fundamentals of spelling *i* before *e* except after *c*—and the basics of our religion—God made us in His own image and likeness to serve Him in the world and to be happy with Him forever after. While the nuns pounded us in the classroom, we pounded Jimmy Olsen relentlessly, but without serious or permanent physical injury, at recess. Jimmy had the misfortune of being one of only two "Medigans" in our class. The other, Jonathan Q. Adams II, joined the class in seventh grade. Jonathan fit in right away, even though he spoke with a New England accent. It was important that he didn't have red hair and freckles, but it was more important that he could hit a baseball farther than anyone in the class, and that once, when we were shooting hoops at recess, Jonathon made 123 foul shots in a row. Jonathan was cool. Jonathan was accepted because he was cool but also, in part, because Jimmy was already firmly entrenched as class goat. Jimmy was named after Superman's sidekick, and we wanted to see if his buddy would ever come to his rescue. He didn't. Besides, Jimmy was a geeky, wimpy-faced, doughboy whose irritating allergies caused his eyes and nose to run constantly. Since he was already crying, we figured there'd be no harm in roughing him up a little. To his credit, Jimmy hung in there, and if things really got rough, he'd actually fight back a little bit. Of course, we would then laugh and back off for the rest of the day. We didn't want Jimmy to get so mad that he would transfer out of school. We liked having him around. He even achieved a level of notoriety when, one day in Sister Clarissa's class, he reeled off sixteen straight sneezes. We picked up the count at nine, and even Sister Clarissa was entertained.

Just as Annunciation was my parish, Tent' and Wharton was my corner. Tent and Wharton had many claims to fame. Notably, it was the home of Stinky Pete's arcade, and it was straight across the street from a playground where on sweltering summer nights, we would watch to see if Mario, the burly stevedore from Fourth and Shunk, could belt a fastball over the left field fence or whether Al, the star pitcher from Southern, the local public school, could strike out more than ten batters in seven innings in the local sandlot league. We thought these guys were just a step away from the Big Leagues. This was because they had clean uniforms every night, didn't have to bring their own bats to the games, chewed tobacco, and spit sunflower seeds. Al went on to be a college star and had a brief stint with the Boston Red Sox farm system, but no one from that league ever actually made it to the majors. We didn't care; they were stars to us.

The sandlot league was important, but Stinky Pete's was the essence of Tent' and Wharton. Stinky himself was a post middle age local with a potbelly and a bald head. The long, skinny stogie that naturally bounced from his left hand to his puffy lips drew a sharp contrast to his fleshy, pink face. The stogie smelled like a burning pigeon. The smell had thoroughly infiltrated all of Stinky's clothing--all four once-white short-sleeved dress shirts worn twelve months a year, regardless of the weather, and two pairs of gray, pleated not-quite wool slacks. He was Stinky Pete long before I started hanging at Tent' and Wharton, and only at his funeral years later did I learn his real name was Alfred Peter Thomas. It never occurred to me that Stinky was Lebanese, not Italian. After all, only Italians ever came into the store. Miraculously, the smell in the store moved with Stinky. For the most part, the rest of the place had a neutral smell. Perhaps the sawdust constantly covering the floor removed the scent. I was accustomed to seeing the sawdust on meat market and taproom floors in the Italian market, where sometimes my mother would send me to find out what number came out that day, but Stinky's was the only arcade I knew of where sawdust covered the floors.

Stinky Pete's housed two Italian slate-topped regulation size pool tables. While the ball field produced no Big Leaguers, those pool tables spawned two national nine ball champions over the years. You had to be good to win a game of nine ball at Stinky's. The electronic miniature shuffleboard game and close to a dozen pinball machine provided diversion for those of us who lacked the eye-hand coordination or the steely nerves to excel at pocket billiards. On the Tent Street side of the store sat the candy and cigarette case, which formed the front counter. The counter held Stinky's cash register—a real one formed of ornate gilded metal. It was nothing like the cigar boxes over on Nint Street.

Stinky's was an inside business. The snow cone maker and ice machine were behind the counter. In the heat of summer, we would sit on Stinky's step and eat crushed ice with grape, root beer, pineapple, or anisette (really licorice) syrup. This was a viable alternative to the Italian water ice we routinely got up the block. We would slip away and listen to Johnny, Frankie, Kenny, and Fat Dominick, the older kids who lived on Wharton Street, sing a cappella for hours on end after the ball games. When it was too cold to sit outside, we would watch the aspiring pool sharks. The real players didn't come in until much later. If we were lucky, we could mooch a few nickels or dimes to bang away on the pinball machines.

We didn't spend all our time at Stinky's—only summer nights and winter weekends. Mostly we played the street games I talked about. For some reason, though, I'm not sure why, between seventh and eighth grade, with the sixties barely out of the box, I decided I wanted to be an athlete. Chubby, Larry, and Chooch had no interest in real sports. In fact, none of the kids in my neighborhood played any organized sports, so I journeyed to the south and west of the school to hook up with some of my schoolmates who played basketball every day at the playground at Twelfth and Wharton, not pronounced Twelt'.

Although the playground was only two blocks away from my corner, it was in a totally different world. It was separated from our neighborhood by our school and the local police station. It had four full-size basketball court with regulation height baskets but no nets, so the basketball thundered through the hoop and smashed you in the face if you weren't attentive. I almost broke my nose a half a dozen times before I caught on. At this playground, I practiced every day that summer between seventh and eighth grade. I played with some of the guys from my school and a few older kids who loved to play hoops. I had just experienced my most impressive growth spurt, and I reached a towering height of five foot eleven, making me the third tallest in the class. Little did I know I would almost stop growing right there.

As a result of my summer of basketball initiation, come fall, I was able to play for our elementary school team. We played in the Catholic

Youth Organization (CYO) league against the other Catholic elementary schools in South Philly. We were an average team coached by a knowledgeable bald mailman who had played basketball in the US Army. He told us he had washed away all his hair taking three showers a day in the heat of South America, which we figured out was even further south than South Philly. He taught us the basics—making two-hand bounce passes, executing the give-and-go, boxing out for rebounds, following your shot to the basket, and keeping between your man and the basket on defense. For the most part, I don't remember any of the games, except one against Saint Thomas Aquinas.

Saint Thomas Aquinas was a parish deeper into South Philly than Annunciation. It was at Seventeenth and Morris. I thought of it as one of those rich parishes. Almost all the kids at Saint Thomas were Italian. They hung out at Fifteenth and Morris, a tough corner with a playground having only one basketball court. Their court had hoops with chain nets. They didn't have to worry about getting pounded in the face. Because they had only one court, the competition to get in and stay in a game was fierce. Game winners kept playing; losers had to sit out, unless there was no one waiting to play. With only one court, every game was an *A* game; on Twelfth Street, we had *A*, *B*, and sometimes *C* games. The overall park at Fifteenth and Morris was small. It had a kiddy area with swings, a seesaw, a sliding board, and monkey bars; it also had a geriatric section with a boccie court and a card table but no ball field and virtually no grass. It occupied less than a quarter of a city block. Adjacent to the playground on the east side, the Broad Street side (there is no Fourteenth Street in Philadelphia), was a branch of the Free Library of Philadelphia. Across the street was a real diner. I never figured out why they named it King Arthur's Diner—maybe because it was on Castle Avenue. I knew about Fifteenth and Morris because occasionally, when I was little, my mother would walk me to that library on the way to paying our electric and telephone bills at Broad and Passyunk. I always wanted to watch the big kids play basketball, and while she would always indulge me for a few minutes, our primary destination was the electric company;

the library was a secondary stop; basketball barely made the list. It was a far distant third.

I remember our basketball game against Saint Thomas Aquinas because it took place in the Neumann Tournament. Each year, the local Catholic high school in South Philly, Bishop Neumann, hosted a double-elimination basketball tournament for the Catholic elementary schools that would send in their graduates the next year. The high school freshmen team coach attended all the games, and the JV and varsity coaches hung around for the semifinal and final rounds. It was by far the highlight of our season. It was even more important than coming in first in our division. It was our equivalent of the NCAA tournament, except it was double elimination and all you had to do to participate was to have a team. The CYO league was divided into a north and south division. We were in the north. During the regular season, you played only in your division. We finished second, but that didn't matter to us. It was a new season, and we thought we could beat anybody. There was no reason why we couldn't win the whole tournament, and, if we did, the coaches would see us, and we would have a better chance of making the freshman team next year. We talked about it over and over before and after practices. We were a little worried about the size of the Neumann court. It was big—a regular full court. We never had the chance to practice on a court like that. In fact, the only time we played on a full court was when we played games. At Annunciation, the school had set up a little practice area in the school basement in a room next to the boiler. It was considerably smaller than half of Neumann's court. It had a low ceiling and a backboard and a hoop nailed precariously to one wall. We constantly hit the ceiling on outside shots and ran into the wall after layups. It was inside and warm, though. All games we played were on the other teams' courts. Our coach said, because of this, we could adapt to any situation, including the Neumann court. Never had we been more excited or anxious before a game.

We played a basic man-to-man defense. Our coach said this would teach us the fundamentals of the game. Our first game was against Saint

Phillip's, another north division team. We had beaten them once and lost to them once during the regular season. In a close game, we eked out a last-second victory, and I had a pretty good game, scoring our team's last six points. Next, we played Saint Thomas, a south division team. In the Saint Thomas game, the kid I guarded was skinny and had a couple of inches on me. He looked a lot older, and at the beginning of the game, he was easy to guard. He looked to be just going through the motions. He ran up and down the court with such apparent casualness that I was surprised to discover late in the game when we were losing and went to a full court press that I was having a hard time keeping up with him. Earlier on, he passed the ball more than he shot. Late in the game, he was shooting and scoring more. As the game wound on, we got more and more tired, but we continued to play as hard as we could. For one brief stretch, Anthony Alphonso caught fire, and we closed the gap. Then I went through a hot streak and hit three baskets in a row. We were leading by a point with less than a minute to go. Saint Thomas had the ball. It went to my man on the right side of the foul line extended. He sized me up, holding the ball with both hands just above his head. He stopped and looked me straight in the eyes as I inched close enough to smell his chewing gum—Doublemint. In a sudden move, he brought the ball straight past my head and took a half step back. When I relaxed and turned to see where he passed the ball, he brought it back over my head and dribbled around me for an easy bucket. It turned out to be the game winner. I was crushed. Embarrassed and crestfallen, I sat on the bench and fought back tears as my teammates tried to cheer me up. Though I had led the team in scoring, I knew I'd lost the game. Traditionally, after the game, the teams shook hands at half-court. After several minutes of coaxing me, the coach physically picked me up and walked me to the end of the line. Anger began to well up. I wanted to lash out, but I didn't know what to do or what to say. When I reached my opponent, he extended his right hand, he placed his left hand on my right shoulder and leaned toward my right ear. He said, "Sorry. I've had that done to me too. You were playing me so tight it was the only thing I could do. Good defense, and good luck in the rest of the tournament." He said it without sarcasm or arrogance, but he said it strongly and with confidence.

I heard myself mutter, "Yeah. Thanks. Good move. Good luck to you too."

I walked away, feeling beaten but a little less humiliated. That was my first contact with Paul Casabella.

III

Casabella means "beautiful house" in Italian. The Casabella family settled in South Philadelphia from Abruzzi in the early 1900s. Paul, born midcentury, was second generation—like me. Both of us were unsure why our families settled in Philadelphia, but we both learned dramatic lessons on the streets and from our parents. Paul seemed to have learned in other ways as well. Imbued with an enormous native intelligence, cleverness, and perspective, he acquired a thirst for learning from his parents. Like many first-generation Americans back then, they vowed that their children would obtain the tools required for success in the promised land. Education was essential. Paul seemed to have read everything. Either before or after b-ball games at Fifteenth and Morris, he obviously made frequent visits to the branch library. With his intellectual attributes, he combined an intoxicating likeability, charm, and charisma in a most understated way. Everybody wanted to be Paul's friend.

After graduation from elementary school (Jimmy Olsen made it too), a whole new world opened to us. In September, we began taking the bus west to Twenty-Sixth Street and Bishop Neumann High School, a butterscotch-colored brick building that was the daytime home to almost four thousand Catholic teenage boys. I would walk a few blocks south to the bus stop at Tenth and Tasker, and I would duck into the candy shop for a breakfast snack of Tastykake cupcakes while waiting for the bus. Actually, it was a bus only from the neck down. From the neck up, it was a trolley. That is, it was electric powered like a trolley, and it had a long rod extending from its top to an overhead power line. The vehicle itself, though, was a bus. It had wheels with rubber tires, not steel wheels that rode on a track. We called it a trackless trolley. It was old, it was green, it was ugly, it was overfilled, and we, its contents, were largely out of control. The trackless started on the east side of town, and by the time it got to us on Tenth Street, mostly Irish kids from 2 Street filled it. There was always a lot of diving and pushing for seats. The upperclassmen dictated the activities on the bus. We chose to board at Tenth because the Irish girls from "2" Street got off the bus there to attend Saint Maria Goretti, our sister school at Tenth and Mifflin. By boarding at Tenth each day, we got to see those girls climbing off the bus with coltish legs hanging deliciously below their blue serge uniforms hemmed an inch or two above the knee by the more daring ones. We begged for a slight breeze to tickle their dresses and tease us by revealing something more than knee socks. A few of the contacts originally made at Tenth and Tasker grew into lifelong relationships and another generation of Catholics for Neumann and Goretti. We also chose Tenth so we would have a better chance of getting seats.

When we reached the school, we were shepherded around by a faculty of lay teachers and priests from various religious orders—Franciscans, Augustinians, Dominicans. All were under the administration of the Norbertine fathers, who also made up the majority of the religious faculty. Many of the Norbertine priests had been educated near their main abbey in De Pere, Wisconsin. They were primarily white-bread Medigans whose lineage stemmed mostly from Germany, Poland, Scandinavia, and France. This was in marked contrast to the largely Mediterranean and Irish nature of the student body. We never understood where Father Weinberg came from. There were a few Irish and Italian Norbertines who originated in South Philly, went to Neumann (South Catholic, as it was previously called), found their vocations, and entered the priesthood. They had instant credibility. The others had to earn it, and in most cases, they did so with strong discipline, strong teaching skills, or both.

The building itself looked and smelled new. Compared to our beat-up, decrepit elementary school, it seemed almost elegant and palatial. Everything was bright and clean, and it had greenboards with chalk and erasers, rather than blackboards in each classroom. More than anything, the school had a distinctive smell of disinfectant laced with shellac. On those rare occasions when I went back, that smell grabbed me by the nose, twisted me at the neck, and shouted, "You are back at Neumann. We're in control here. Don't forget it." I would immediately remember I was an Italian kid from South Philly whose transition from childhood to young adulthood started at Bishop Neumann High School in the sixties.

My freshman year was wasted as far as extracurricular activities were concerned but not so with academics. The delusion that I was an athlete found its final resting place on the Neumann basketball court. More than 150 all-stars vied for twelve places on the freshman team. I looked for the skinny kid from Saint Thomas, but I never found him at the tryouts. The first couple of sessions started out the same way—ten minutes of stretching and loosening up followed by three or four laps jogging around the gym. We then ran sets of suicide sprints. We started at one baseline, sprinted full speed to the closest foul line and back, to half-court and back, to the far foul line and back, and then to the baseline and back. Everyone gasped feverishly for breath. They sent us in waves, so we always had a few minutes to catch our breath before setting off again. At first, my goal was to win my wave. After the first set, I revised that to wanting to be competitive in my wave. When we finished the second set, I reevaluated again and sought merely not to be last. Only my second revised goal was realistic.

Finally, after they softened us up, the basketballs came out, and we had to dribble the length of the court right handed and shoot a right-handed lay-up from the right side of the basket, and then we dribbled left handed down the left side of the court and made a left-handed lay-up. Finally, we went down the middle with a spin dribble at half-court and a jump shot from the foul line. Based on these simple drills, the coaches whittled the aspirants to twenty. I survived. Then the next level of competition began: half-court drills. There was one on one, two on two, three on three, four on four, and five on five—all at half-court. I felt I was doing okay. Then the full-court skirmishes began, and my fortunes began to sink. Over the length of the court, I was at least a step slow on both offense and defense or a bit sloppy making or catching passes. My shot was always just a bit short. I couldn't buy a bucket. So, when they made the next cut from twenty to fifteen, I became a full-time student.

Academically, my progress sped on. At Bishop Neumann, like all the other large diocesan high schools then, the administrators grouped the students homogenously by ability. This was an attempt to accelerate the educational process. They slotted us based on a standardized test given in the eighth grade. They put us into "books." The first six books were the academic tract, and book one was considered the honor group. Books seven through twelve were called the commercial and vocational group. Chubby, Chooch, and Skinny Lenny were in this group. Larry wound up in the next group, books thirteen and up, even though he was smart enough for book six. For the life of me, I can't remember what they called this tract—something like Cassocks or Visigoths, or maybe it was Hell's Angels or Warlocks. It wasn't so much that they were stupid; they were bad, tough kids who didn't give a shit about school. Some of them actually graduated, but many dropped out as soon as the law allowed. A few never made it to their sixteenth birthdays.

I was slotted into book three, which really aggravated me because I was one of the top three boys in my elementary school. The girls from my elementary school were in a different stratosphere completely. Half a dozen or so girls were ahead of me at graduation. When I discovered two of my Annunciation classmates were in the honor group, I became infuriated. I was certain the powers to be had made a mistake, but I didn't know what to do about it, other than to get the highest grades in my book so I could be moved up to the honor group for sophomore year.

My strategy worked, and the next September I moved up. It was there I first really met him. We were both fifteen; Paul had been in book one from the beginning.

We had not yet conceded that summer had ended as we trooped to the bus stop for our first day of classes in our white short-sleeve dress shirts and loosely hanging ties. We didn't have to wear suits or sports jackets the first week because the dress code would not be fully enforced. Afterward, however, it would be enforced to the letter: suit or sports jackets, shirts with collars, ties that were actually knotted, dress slacks, no sneakers, and no denim (dungarees, as we called them). As the year wore on, we would find creative ways to trash the spirit of the code while complying with its letter. Soon, three-button Ban-Lon shirts were the order of the day. They had collars, so they complied, but they were knit and more comfortable, and they were easier to run around in. Corduroy could be just as messy as denim, but the code permitted cords, so we wore them. Black shoes with rubber soles were almost as comfortable as sneakers. Actually, some black sneakers looked like shoes and would often go undetected. We'd keep our ties and jackets in our lockers. For the most part, the dress code was a nonissue.

As usual, too many of us packed into the trackless as our driver sequentially ground his teeth and bit his lip. The noise levels and routines increased exponentially each block. Many of us had not seen one another all summer, but the verbal cut-up fights picked up exactly where they had left off last spring. The ritualistic initiation of the new freshmen began immediately. Little did they know they would stand in between the seats of the bus for the entire school year. Only if they offered resistance were they physically harassed and bodily yanked from seats so that upperclassmen or nonstudents could sit down. After a week or so, they learned, like we all had, how to keep from falling all over one another and our book bags as the trackless lurched four or five times each block.

The two-block walk from the bus stop to the school provided another opportunity for boisterous release before we were straitjacketed into homeroom for opening prayers, the Pledge of Allegiance at the flag, and morning announcements. More than anything, homeroom forced the process of settling in to germinate so that teaching and maybe even a little bit of learning could take place later in the day. We had received our schedules during orientation, so I knew introductory French would follow homeroom for first period. I had taken Latin as a freshman, and I was looking forward to see if I could learn a language that wasn't dead—one that was actually spoken by people who wanted to converse with one another rather than just by priests in a church or lawyers trying to be erudite in courtrooms.

In the first days of school, sometimes the procedures didn't go so smoothly, and the release from homeroom would be delayed for a few minutes. This was the case on the first day of my sophomore year at Bishop Neumann High School in 1963.

As we walked into our first French class, a small group of students trailed slightly behind. They entered after the bell rang.

"Gentlemen," the teacher spoke out. "Late for the first class on the first day? This is not acceptable."

There was no response from the group members. They continued their languid stroll into the sterile, cinder block classroom.

"Gentlemen, stop where you are. Identify yourself," the teacher said, looking at the class roster over the top of his Coke-bottle lenses delicately bound by thin chrome wires. The spectacles sat precariously on his shiny, abbreviated nose as he furrowed his pale, fleshy brow and peered over them. "Okay, Mr. Novelli, Mr. Kelly, Mr. Achiovini, Mr. Murphy, Mr. DiTomasso, you are late. Didn't you hear me speak to you? Why did you not respond?"

Again, there was no response. I now noticed a bit of saccharine tone in his manner of speech, even though he was trying to be stern. He spoke melodically and with a swing rhythm in a prepubescent pitch. About five foot eight with a soft, round body, he looked like he was complying with the letter of the dress code in his frumpy gray plaid suit and a tie so tightly tied it looked like a clip-on. It didn't match his suit. His white-on-white dress shirt with exaggerated French cuffs held together with gold links engraved "FR" looked ludicrously out of place. I couldn't believe he wore cuff links to designate that he taught French, and then it occurred to me the "FR" stood for Francis Ripley. He wore no watch and no rings. He's not married, I thought. He combed his wispy blond hair straight back with a perfect part. It shone like he had shellacked it with hair spray. He appeared to be in his midtwenties. He was out of shape and new to the school.

"You will all receive late slips. Be seated."

It seemed like an overreaction, and he seemed a bit uncertain; I didn't like it. A confident, experienced teacher would have just ignored the lateness and proceeded. A new guy like this could make our lives miserable for the whole year.

Novelli, the king athlete in the eleventh grade, spoke up. "Ah, it's just the first day. We just got here. Homeroom was late. Cut us a break, will ya?"

Joe had just elected to take French, so he was one of only a few juniors in a class dominated by sophomores. He was a solid two hundred plus pounds of fast-twitch muscle packed tightly on a five-foot-eight frame. He was Hollywood handsome and a pretty good guy. He wasn't one of those athletes who acted like they're above it all. He was from my parish, so I knew he was a regular guy. As a sophomore, he had been voted second team All Catholic as a running back and had received honorable mention as a linebacker. Joe had a quick smile, and when he shook your hand, the size and strength of his mitts overwhelmed you. He was friendly, pleasant, affable, and a diligent student but a ferocious, relentless competitor on the gridiron. Joe knew football was his ticket to college, so he made sure he kept his grades up.

"There will be no breaks cut in my class; not for you and not for anyone," Mr. FR-ump replied.

All of this action took place on my right. I turned quietly to the classmate on my left, and I recognized him as the tall, skinny kid from Saint Thomas. "This guy's gonna be a problem," I whispered. "He's not going to take anything."

My classmate smiled and replied, "He's already lost the class. He's got no idea what he's doing."

"Sir." It sounded almost like a whinny from across the room. "Identify yourself."

I looked at the teacher and pointed to myself. He looked to my sidekick. "No. You, sir. Identify yourself."

My friend smiled and tilted his head ever so slightly. "Cyrano de Bergerac," he said firmly.

I looked at Cyrano with surprise. I thought he looked Italian, but de Bergerac didn't sound Italian. I knew his name couldn't possibly be Cyrano de Bergerac, although we did have a Serro d'Aquanti in elementary school. All eyes shifted from Cyrano to our teacher, back to Cyrano, and back to the teacher.

The teacher blinked and then spoke. "Gentlemen, it seems we have a prankster in our midst. Sir, rise."

Cyrano stood. He had grown to a lanky six foot two, and he towered over FR. His healthy head of chestnut hair accented a classically Roman face. He had high, elegant cheekbones. Dark green eyes encased in olive skin gave way to a medium-size nose, making his overall appearance aquiline in a distinctly European way. He looked even more striking than Novelli. Clearly Mediterranean, he didn't present the caricature of an Italian from the north or south. His sinewy thinness signaled strength and agility rather that frailty, as was sometimes the case.

"What is your real name, Mr. de Bergerac?"

"Oh, you want my real name? My real name is Paul Casabella. I'm from Fifteenth and Morris, Saint Thomas Parish. What's your real name?"

The room exploded with laughter.

"Mr. Ripley," he replied instinctively.

"Believe it or not," someone chimed out in a stage whisper.

This time, the room really erupted, paralyzing Ripley for several seconds, while Paul stood straight but relaxed. He donned a neutral expression. He was poised and in control.

When the room subsided, Ripley eked out a faint question. "Why did you call yourself Cyrano de Bergerac? Are you trying to make sport of me?" Ripley clearly looked disoriented.

"Me? Of course not. You didn't ask me my name. You asked me to identify myself. I'm taking up acting, and I've been fascinated with the character of Cyrano de Bergerac. Romantic, ideological, heroic, tragic. I've been trying to imagine what it would be like to be Cyrano."

Ripley looked dazed. He stood silently, so Paul continued.

"We hadn't started class yet because homeroom let out late. I didn't want to waste time. This is French class, so I put myself in Cyrano's persona. I was just working on my de Bergerac. I'm hoping I can learn enough in this class that I can think in French. Then I'll really be able to do Cyrano."

I had no idea what he was talking about, but I was in awe. He had this Ripley, believe it or not, back on his heels. Ripley stood catatonic for an interminable fifteen seconds. The class remained silent, choking back the laughter. Paul remained standing. Again, Ripley caved in.

"Be seated, Mr. Casabella, and don't speak in my class unless recognized. Do you understand?"

"Yes, sir. But I hope you'll recognize me in the future. You can call me Paul, or if you care to, you can call me Cyrano."

Paul sat down, and the class broke out in wild applause.

Paul became a legend at Neumann that day. Word of a student victory over a teacher spread unabated through the student body. Because the class was mixed with tenth and eleventh graders and because a football star was involved, the story permeated all four classes. Paul received thumbs-ups, high fives, and slaps on the back through the corridors all day and especially at lunch, where he feasted like royalty as a guest of the first-period French class. He accepted the accolades gracefully, explaining that Ripley had been an easy mark. He said he was serious not so much about acting but about public speaking and that he did want to learn some French. "It's too bad this Ripley guy is such a joke," Paul said. "Hopefully he'll straighten out or leave."

Everyone acknowledged that Paul had gotten us off to a great start for the school year.

IV

My father grew up in a home where everyone mostly spoke Italian. My mother's household had been similar. None of my grandparents spoke English. In our South Philly row home, where we lived with my paternal grandparents and next door to my maternal grandparents, Italian was the language of choice. Nad saw how difficult it was for some of his family members to communicate with the outside world. "You have to be a good talker to get ahead here," he would say. "Speak like a professor—clear, strong, confident. They're going to judge you by the way you talk as well as by what you say. They won't even listen to what you say if you don't speak well. If you do speak well, people will notice. They'll be more likely to respect you. Make it easy for them to understand you. And learn. Learn as much as you can," he would tell me. "The way you present yourself will affect how you feel about yourself and how others feel about you too."

He lived by this advice and never stopped learning. He was forceful in all he did.

I was almost three years old before I started to speak, and then I stammered and stuttered so badly that, at times, I couldn't be understood. I whistled my *s*'s and garbled most of my words. My parents saw this early on and worked with me. They made sure I was put into a remedial speech class. At night, they would have me read to them aloud, and they taught me to parrot nursery rhymes and children's poems. Over time, their efforts paid off, and my speech problems disappeared. Dad continued his encouragement. He had been educated in a trade school, but he spoke like a college graduate. Whenever an opportunity arose for me to speak in public, he suggested I take it. When I was in kindergarten, the principal asked for a volunteer to stand up in front of a parent-student assembly, hold a school pennant, and recite a little commercial.

He thought that if a little kid held the pennant, the parents would be more likely to buy one. I volunteered. When it came time for my routine, Mom and Dad pushed me forward, pennant in my hand, and encouraged me. "Stand up tall, Nicholas," Mom said.

"Talk proud," Dad said.

Everyone smiled when I was introduced. I remembered my lines perfectly and never realized I was holding the pennant upside down until Chubby told me after school that day.

My father's encouragement motivated me to look into the high school speech and debate team, the Forensic Union. In my freshman year, the misunderstanding I had about my athletic abilities motivated me toward the gym every day after school rather than toward more academic extracurricular activities. When that delusion shattered, I knew at the beginning of my sophomore year I would join the Forensic Union. I was pretty sure I knew how to speak. I inquired at the Main Office to find out when and where the speech team met. When the first day of class ended, I wandered into room 213, the headquarters of the speech and debate team. That was where my real relationship with Paul Casabella began.

Timidly, I slipped through the back entrance. I didn't know what to expect. I dreaded that the room might be filled with ten to fifteen Jimmy Olsens peering over the rims of their glasses, wiping their sniveling noses, discussing the most appropriate way to prevent Communism from taking hold in third-world countries, and reading articles on how to fertilize soybean crops. It is very important to a fifteen-year-old not to be uncool. Forensics, I worried, would render me so uncool that I walked in prepared to do an about-face if I didn't like what I saw.

Room 213 didn't look like a regular classroom, despite the presence of sixty student desks arranged like all the other classrooms. The front of the room had been configured like a miniature office. The desk presided over the room from a raised floor—a stage of sorts. Shelves filled with both hardcover and paperback books as well as countless manuals, pamphlets, and magazines, some with pictures, lined the wall. In the far-left corner, just above the first window, I saw a seven-and-a-half-inch open-reel Emerson tape deck, a microphone, and a control unit with levels, lights, and wires. This was all connected to what looked like a powerful amplifier and what I later learned was an AM and FM tuner and a shortwave scanner. A large military-green metal file cabinet sectioned off that part of the room. In the middle of the front wall hung a notice on a white placard. It read, "Resolved: The United Nations should ban the proliferation of nuclear weapons."

The placard scared me. It sounded uncool. I later learned that, each year, all members of the National Catholic Forensic League debated the same topic, and the year culminated in a national tournament you had to qualify for by placing in the top three in the championship tournament in your region. That year, Nationals were especially alluring because they were going to be in Denver.

In the right corner of the front wall, over by the front door, stood a large glass case with awards of all kinds—trophies with speakers standing at podiums, plaques with gavels, and medals with ribbons.

The Forensic moderator was a Norbertine priest—a big Norbertine priest. He dominated the room in stature and presence. He stood six foot five with erect posture. He had a blond crew cut and a midwestern all-American look. The almost-white robes of the Norbertine order hung casually from his broad shoulders. At first, he looked more like a football player—maybe a linebacker—than a debate coach. The sight of a strong, striking, athletic figure abated, but didn't completely eliminate, my anxiety.

He spotted me taking inventory from the back of the room and greeted me with a booming radio announcer's voice, a warm smile, and an extended hand. "You look lost," he said. "I'm Father Meulen. Tim Meulen. This is the Forensic Union. Are you in the right place?"

"I'm not sure, Father. I'd like to understand a little about Forensics before I figure out whether it's for me."

"Well, first things first. Let's get started with your name."

"Nicholas, Father. Nicholas DiDominico, but I like to go by Nad or Naddie. I'm a sophomore," I forced out.

I felt that discomfort and uncertainty that usually accompanies people, especially teens, when introduced into a completely new setting.

He came to my rescue. "I recognize your name. I'm on the placement committee, and I remember you were one of the two freshmen who moved up to the honor group this year. Seems you were misplaced last year. Well, not misplaced but placed in the wrong section. Sorry about that. Let me introduce you around the room, and then one of the team will go over how things work."

His greeting immediately swelled me with pride. He knew my name. Finally, it dawned on me that about nine or ten other students occupied various portions of the room. They were obviously enjoying themselves, telling stories, talking about the summer, and playing cards. Pinochle seemed like a big-time activity, followed by chess, but horseplay clearly won out. As the father walked me around the room, Paul walked through the front door. When I greeted him as Cyrano, everyone laughed and applauded, except Father Tim. He looked at me like I had three heads. "Cyrano? Where did 'Cyrano' come from?"

Everyone laughed. Though the story had permeated the student body, the faculty, often insulated from knowledge of this sort, was still unaware of Paul's escapades.

I answered. "We had a little comedy in French class this morning. Paul was involved."

"Really? A comedy?" Father Tim responded. "Well, Nad, if you want to be a Forensicer, there's no time like now. Paul, sit with Nad. He's about to make his first Forensic Union speech. Take a few minutes and explain extemporaneous oratory. Nad, we'd like you to tell the story."

Paul informed me that one of the speech categories involved the delivery of an impromptu speech about ten or fifteen minutes after being given a subject. Thus, my first official activity as a member of the Forensic Union was about to begin. My nervousness quelled as I stood before the club members and began. "This is a story of good versus evil. Of spirit overcoming monotony. This...is the story of Cyrano de Casabella meets Ripley Believe It or Not, you're late for class."

I was a smash. Paul, in particular, enjoyed my soliloquy and gave me a robust handshake and a punch on the arm. He was then assigned to orient me to the club and its various activities and practices.

Forensics began to provide me with structure, motivation, and an opportunity for social and individual development, but French class was an altogether different matter. Each day, Ripley lost more and more control, and the class became one prank after another. Frank DiTomasso brought in a doctor's note, which enabled him to leave the room every morning at nine o'clock to "take medication." He would sneak out of the building for a quick smoke and return for second period. Ripley never stopped him, and Frank never got caught.

One day, Dan Murphy suggested we copy some freshmen's Latin homework, turn it in as our own, and respond, to the extent we could, as if we were not in French class but in Latin class. It took Ripley fifteen minutes to figure out what was going on. When he finally did, he forced the class to say the rosary in French. On another day, Steve DiSipio hid in the broom closet, and midway through the class, he banged on the door and screamed, "Let me out! Let me out!"

When Ripley opened the closet door, DiSipio jumped out, broom in hand, and he quickly swept the front of the room. He muttered in a stage whisper, "I can't believe what a mess the classroom is." He concluded by turning to Ripley and saying, "How's it look, Teach? You need anything else swept?"

Then there was the time Tony Achiovini stood up and announced that his French poodle had died the night before—blown away by a misdirected rob hit. He requested a moment of silence...for Fifi.

Despite all this, Ripley persevered—until the schoolbag scam. It finally drove him totally berserk. Novelli was the point man. At our high school, the bookstore sold these regulation schoolbags. They were identical: hard reinforced cardboard with tin edging and flimsy hinges. They were little more than black boxes with handles and two latches. Everybody had one; they were cheap and sturdy. One day, Paul ran into Novelli at lunch after Joe had had a particularly bad day in French. He got a sixty-seven on a quiz and thought Ripley was grading him harder than the others because Novelli had been the first one to challenge him, which had set the tone for the first few weeks.

"I think he's jerking my chain," Joe told Paul.

"He's a jerk all right. I'd really like to learn some French, but we'll never learn anything from this guy," Paul responded.

Novelli didn't care so much about the learning part. "I just want to make sure I pass so I don't get suspended from the team. I think he's going to give me a hard time all year, just to try to prove he's tough."

The conversation then diminished to a whisper, but it seemed to increase in intensity and focus. Later that day, the word came down: first period French tomorrow, the schoolbag scam would start. The plan spun out in excruciating detail. Everyone in class was in on it—even Jack Rondelli, who never misbehaved, always turned his homework in neatly prepared and on time, and followed all the school rules meticulously.

We all entered the classroom, promptly beating Ripley. We deposited our schoolbags in the back of the room—fifty of us—in no particular order. Ripley came in, and we sat stone silent. Our hands were folded on our desks, our heads were up, and we stared straight ahead.

He entered as frumpy as always. His "FR" showed below his jacket sleeve, and a book and some papers were under his arm.

"Gentlemen," he said with surprise in his voice. "All present and on your best behavior this morning, I see. It's good to see you so attentive. Very well then. Please open your books to page forty-three."

No response. No movement. We were like mannequins.

"Mr. DiTomasso, where is your book?"

"Sir, it's in my schoolbag, sir." He barked like a recruit to a drill sergeant.

"Mr. DiTomasso, let's get started. Get it out."

"Sir, yes, sir. But I can't, sir," he barked.

"Why not, Mr. DiTomasso?"

"Sir, my schoolbag is in the back of the room, sir."

"Why?"

"We wanted to keep the room neat near our desks, sir. DiSipio just swept the room, sir, to make it look nice for you, sir."

"Who is 'we,' Mr. DiTomasso?"

"Sir, all of us, sir."

We all looked toward Novelli. He shook his head no. We held our positions.

"Mr. DiTomasso, I said to go get your book. All of you, take out your books, and open to page forty-three."

We again looked to Novelli. He paused, paused, paused, and finally nodded. We catapulted from our desks, scrambled chaotically to the back of the room, and climbed, kicked, and crawled our way past one another to grab any schoolbag but our own. We then fought back to our desks. Ripley's eyes lit up like firecrackers behind his Coke-bottle glasses, but he said nothing. Pink flushed up his neck and formed blotches on his jowls. We settled in and sat silently with the schoolbags next to us. Everything was according to plan.

"Well, we're having a bit of fun this morning, are we? I hope you've all had a good time, and, of course, I hope you'll enjoy coming back here after eighth period today to make up this class."

No response from us.

"Now you have your schoolbags, take out your books, and open to page forty-three."

A negative nod from Novelli held us in place.

"I said to take out your books and to open to page forty-three."

Novelli nodded approval; everyone complied.

"Mr. DiDominico, do you have your book opened to page forty-three?"

"Well, I'm opened to page forty-three, but this is not my book. Hey, Frank, this is your book. I must have your schoolbag, and there's a peanut butter and jelly sandwich in it leaking all over the place. This is disgusting. Here. Who has my schoolbag?"

"I have it, Naddie," shouted Joe. The dam burst. "Who has my book?"

"I have yours."

"I have Pete's bag. Pete, where are you?"

"Jim, do you have my bag?"

"No. I have Mike's. Here, Mike."

Anarchy prevailed—total, compete, utter anarchy.

Ripley was gone within a week, replaced by Mr. Rene, a long-term substitute. A tough but knowledgeable teacher who wasn't in education to avoid military service. Novelli passed French. He, of course, garnered all the credit as the mastermind of the schoolbag scam. Paul concentrated on writing his speech for the Forensic Union, but I knew where the plan originated.

V

Father Tim, as a high school and college student, had won many of the trophies in the Forensic room display. He kept those in the back of the display case as much as possible. "When I first set up this room years ago," he later told me, "I wanted to start with a feeling of excellence and achievement. So, I put some of my own trophies up. Over the years, Neumann team trophies have far outnumbered what I brought in, but I never took the time to pack the old ones up. I will someday."

Among his awards were a plaque thanking him for outstanding service as president of the Philadelphia Catholic Forensic League and a certificate naming him chair of the Topic Committee of the National Debate Society.

Father Tim permitted great freedom in our Forensic activities. He was an excellent teacher both inside the classroom and out. When I first reached that inevitable roadblock in my preparation, he simply said, "Nad, to speak well, you must write well. To write well, you must think well. To think well, you must think."

He cajoled me into examining my own feelings and thoughts, realizing my strengths and weakness, and developing my values. He challenged me to do the right things. I wasn't a special case, although I felt like one. He gave all of us what we needed to move on. At times, we couldn't clear the hurdles on our own. So, when all else failed, he would pair us up with one or more team members and provoke dialogue. "Thinking helps speaking helps thinking," he would tell us.

The perfect mentor for a cadre of ethnic city kids in the sixties, he taught us that thought was as much a part of living as action, but thought without action spawned hopelessness. "Live your feelings" was another Father Tim aphorism.

Neumann's Forensic Union was large compared to those in other Philadelphia schools, and that was mostly because of Father Tim. There were so many of us that we could participate in all categories of speech and debate: dramatic reading of poetry and prose, declamation (delivery of someone else's speech), extemporaneous speech (like my opening presentation on Cyrano), original oratory (delivery of your own persuasive speech), and debate (orderly argument on a stated topic). According to Father Tim, original oratory and debate comprised the pinnacle of Forensics and required the highest levels of skill, discipline, intellect, and creativity. I participated in all the categories, but my specialty was declamation. My writing was intelligible, but interpretation and delivery were my forte. Paul's natural affinity, of course, was original oratory. In the first semester alone, he generated six competition-quality persuasive speeches to my one.

Father Tim's strategy to groom us as Forensicers called for many of us to write and deliver original speeches in the first semester. Through this method, he could assess our developmental needs and direct us to where we could best excel during the competitions that led to the local finals. He focused us on a tournament in mid-December. He sent five speakers into the competition, including two sophomores: Paul and me. We were supposed to start our speeches with vignettes—something to get everyone's attention. The events of one November day provided the opening story for many speeches that year.

Geometry ended each class day for us. Father Nargonski, one of the few Franciscan priests at our school, spoke from the vocabulary of circles and squares, rectangles and trapezoids, points and triangles. Nargo himself defied categorization; no theorem captured his essence.

Standing five foot six and weighing in at 180 pounds, his steamroller build matched his personality and teaching style. Nargo dominated us into learning. His English was a bit off, but I never figured out exactly why. I was certain he wasn't born in the United States. I guessed maybe Poland or Czechoslovakia. He raced around the room with a wooden yardstick in his hand, and he shouted principles of geometry at us, to us, around us, and through us. One day, when trying to drum into us that a geometric point is the intersection of two lines, he turned to Frank Credo, a notorious underachiever, and asked him to give him a point. Frank shrugged, reached into his pocket, and dripped an imaginary item into Nargo's outstretched hand. Nargo looked skyward with one palm extended and the other closed around his ruler. He shouted, "This man do what God can't do." He shook his head at Frank, raced to the board, frantically drew intersecting lines, and chanted over and over, "A point is a place, not a thing."

It took guts to mess around in Nargo's class because he could (and did on occasion) transform the ruler, or straightedge, as he called it, into an attention-getter. Sometimes he whacked it across your desk or, if he thought the offense was sufficiently egregious, across some part of you. Talking in class was a serious offense, but only failure to do your homework merited capital punishment. Credo took his own acumen for granted, and early on in the year, he seldom did any homework. Sometimes Nargo caught him; sometimes Credo skated. It certainly was not uncommon for Credo to receive a sound slap across the hands. Usually, no great harm was done, but one day, Nargo seemed to be particularly miffed, and he grabbed Credo's homework book and tossed it out the window. Credo made the mistake of laughing. Nargo came back on him like a bear defending her cubs, raised the straightedge, and swung hard. Credo, in anticipation, began to duck, slipped almost out of his seat, and dropped his arms. This exposed him to the blow. Because his position had shifted, Credo took a shot across his left cheek. The edge of the ruler narrowly missed his eye but did cut his skin. Everyone froze, even Nargo, who never meant any real harm. Frankie needed four stitches to put him back together. He did his homework for the rest of the year, and Nargo confined himself to striking desktops.

Closing announcements blared over the public-address system in Nargo's class each day. Often a Forensicer would be assigned the task of reading these announcements, but on this November day, the Principal took the microphone. "I have a very serious announcement to make," began Father Geoghan. "The President has been shot and killed in Dallas. Vice-President Johnson is being sworn in as President and has stated there is no reason to believe the country is in danger. We are not under attack, but the President is dead. All after-school activities are canceled."

Shock hit us all; the President's youthfulness and family image had provided us with a sense of well-being, trust, security, and hope. For several minutes, no one moved; no one spoke. My first reaction, that this was some bizarre prank, quickly gave way to resignation. Why would anyone kill the President? That sort of thing happened only in olden times, like with Lincoln. The assassination triggered a sense of terror and defeat. I knew I was growing up in a risky environment, but subconsciously I expected that if I made the right choices and did the right things, I could escape danger and prosper happily and safely. Then, out of nowhere, this model of civility, affluence, propriety, status, and power was struck down in an instant. The fragility of life enveloped me in that instant. My illusions of security and invulnerability crumbled like a skyscraper built on a swamp. They imploded like an eruption in its boiler room.

Even Father Nargonski sat speechless. Down and dirty, straight from the hip, fireplug-built, bowling ball–headed, staccato-talking Nargo slumped against his desk with glassy eyes and a bewildered look. We filed past him in silence. Despite the cancellation of after-school activities, I staggered into the Forensic room with Paul at my side. Many of my colleagues had come in too. Most conversation centered on our dead President and his family, the nation's loss of a leader, the assassin, and his motives. Toward the very end of the day, Paul said there was a lesson here. He sat in a corner and began to write.

By the next week, Paul had created a whole new speech. It was finished just in time for the tournament. I continued to struggle with my speech. I remember it only vaguely. It began with a boy in a canoe who witnessed a child falling into a river. The boy hesitated and failed to act to save the child, who was later rescued downstream. I was thinking about fear and how it could paralyze you if you didn't push through it. I always swam like a Chevrolet. I tried to compensate for what my speech lacked in depth and texture by infusing my delivery with sincerity and force. This was my first real tournament, but I had delivered the speech more than a dozen times to the critical eyes and ears of Father Tim and my fellow team members. They showed no reticence when offering advice. Feel what you mean; mean what you say. Relax. Project your voice and personality. Be real. Communicate. Reach your audience. Speak to them, not at them. Make them laugh. Make them cry. Make them mad. Make them yours. These and a hundred more tidbits of advice abandoned my consciousness completely as my adrenal glands worked overtime during our drive through a wet December snowfall to the tournament at Bishop McSomebody or Somebody Else High School in some far corner of the diocese. The cocoa and toast Mom had made me for breakfast gurgled in my stomach occasionally and threatened to exit the way it had entered. I closed my eyes during the ride and internally recited the first line of my speech over and over. I had somehow reached the conclusion that if I could get that first line out, I'd be okay. I had no idea the terror I felt flowed from a competitive desire to excel or, at least, to be something better than abysmal. Only later did I learn this kind of anxiety could either paralyze you or spark you to achieve, and you could choose or, at least, steer toward either outcome.

My sole objective became to survive the first round of the tournament. I just wanted to stand up when it was my turn and deliver my speech. I succeeded but entered the room for the second round with no less apprehensiveness. As I moved toward a seat in that room, I became totally distracted. I forgot for a moment where I was. I could have been at a movie, at a concert, or maybe at a ball game. She sat up toward the front on my left. She would speak first this round. She was sixteen and had shoulder-length blond hair. She was gorgeous, tall, and thin but maturely built. She coyly got up from her seat with the confidence of an experienced Broadway actress. I could see from the order of speakers written on the blackboard that Beth Patterson had titled her speech "The Growth Within." She took complete control of the room and had us all paying rapt attention to her. I forgot for about ten minutes I was in a speech competition. I listened only to Beth. She riveted me. Fortunately, I was listed as the last speaker, so I had some time to recover and remember my own talk. The judges were permitted to provide oral critiques at the end of each round, if they chose. After the second round, the judge used Beth's presentation as a model of excellence, pointing out all the things she had done right in both writing the speech and in delivering it. I was happy to have survived the delivery of my speech. I even received some compliments on my delivery and some suggestions for improving my speech. I thought I was doing okay. My Forensic career had officially begun.

Lunch separated the second and the third rounds. I entered the cafeteria and looked for my schoolmates. First, I saw Rick DiPietro, a senior; then I saw Dan Tolan and Ben Sabato, juniors. Finally, I saw Paul. He was sitting at a table with Rick, Dan, and Ben and with Beth and some other almost as attractive girls who were apparently from her school.

"Nad, over here," Paul called to me as I came into view. "How'd it go?"

Beth turned to look when Paul called my name. "Hi, I just knew you were from Neumann. He was terrific, Paul. You were terrific, Nicholas."

All the guys laughed. I felt the redness creep up my neck to my ears. "Thanks. I go by Nad," I managed to say, and I sat down across from them.

Over lunch, I learned Beth and her friends had started spending time with our group the previous year at tournaments. The Neumann guys loved them, and they loved us.

"You guys are different," Beth said. "A bit arrogant but not quite obnoxious. Strong, slick, and irreverent. I like the irreverence. You South Philly guys are cocky but delightful; serious but fun."

Beth looked like fun and mischief rolled into one, and she spoke oh so sincerely—almost seductively. She looked like she could be trouble, in the most alluring way.

After watching the conversation between Beth and Paul for a few minutes, I resigned myself to the fact that she and Paul seemed to be together. It didn't surprise me. Paul carried himself with a confidence equal to hers. They were like royalty with nothing to prove. Paul's force emanated from his subtlety. The rest of us were frontal, outspoken, and assertive—maybe even a bit rough. Paul, in contrast, appeared thoughtful and more sophisticated but not stiff. When he spoke, he commanded attention. He looked a bit different as well. His Italian heritage displayed itself clearly, but his affect was somewhat softer than ours. His Roman features were elegant and refined, while we appeared rougher and tougher. Had we not been so young, we might have been described as rugged. His hair was different too. His straight chestnut hair was thick, and it contrasted dramatically with our almost black wavy manes. Most of my schoolmates were different from the competition, and Paul, in his way, though like us, was different from us as well.

Beth was clearly captivated. Paul clearly reciprocated. Toni, Beth's classmate and best friend, paid some attention to me. I decided to get to know her. The lunch break ended all too quickly, and soon we began the next round of speeches. Toni and I walked into the same room and sat together. During this round, I began to suspect that Paul, Beth, Toni, and I would be a foursome for a while. Toni was shorter and less striking than Beth and more conventionally well built. She was almost voluptuous, even by adult standards, and she had dancing hazel eyes, a ready smile, and a nose upturned enough for style but without suggesting snootiness. Pierced earrings of striking jade cat's-eye glowed under a canopy of almost shoulder-length sandy ringlets. I knew I could do a whole lot worse than Toni Gadjas.

At the end of the competition, the top five speakers were announced, and the first three performed one more time—in front of the entire group of competitors. They announced the top five, but actually it was six because I tied for fifth with Dan Tolan. Ed DiSanto placed fourth; Rick DiPietro was third; Beth, the lone outsider, was second. The tournament host announced Paul as the overall winner.

The exhibition round had no effect on the final order of winners. Paul had won the tournament. He, Beth, and Rick, however, mesmerized the audience through three different techniques. Rich's speech addressed the horror and pain of the recent assassination. His direct, forceful style dominated us. Beth, I knew, would approach the audience from a different perspective. She was understated in her delivery but brilliant in her imagery. She focused on the struggle of a girl facing womanhood: the tension between sexual desires and doing what was "right," the tension between motherhood and a profession, and the tension between traditional values for women and more modern ones. She noted how all these began to surface shortly after adolescent girls began to experience dramatic and sometimes shocking physical changes. She explained this to the audience.

"Sorting out your identity, your personality, and your self-esteem leaves you fragile," she said. "On one hand, you hear from your family that your value as a person depends on how you think, how you feel, how you care, and how you love—all aspects over which you have some measure of control. These are areas where you can make choices. On the other hand, though, you know, you see, and you live the experience that your value as a person among your peers depends on the drape of your clothes, the fall of your hair, the structure of your face, and the size of your bra."

Beth could say things like this and be persuasive. Her beauty and sincerity combined in a moving exhortation to the girls in the audience to develop themselves as people and to the boys not to view them as mannequins.

As Paul approached the stage, the anticipation grew. Rick and Beth had been extraordinary, but Paul, after delivering his speech "Now and Forever," had won the tournament. He was a second-year speaker making his debut in the exhibition round. He began.

"A single pistol shot cracked the Wednesday dawn before young John Bentham saw the gunman's silhouette up ahead. John lived in a high-rise tenement in the wrong part of the city with his parents and four siblings, who were spaced just more than a year apart. He rose early each morning to deliver papers so he could earn some money for the family. He sensed only now that the whoosh by his head had been intended for the woman he had just passed on his bicycle. She screamed, and the sack full of newspapers shifted on his back and almost pulled him down. John began to peddle away from the danger when he suddenly turned and rode straight into the gunman, knocking him down and sending the gun flying. John and the woman escaped, and the shooter rolled helplessly in pain."

Paul's beliefs centered on the richness and fullness of life. He connected this to spirituality but not in the way we had been taught. He sounded a gospel of morality mixed with adventure and exuberance as he magically traced young John Bentham's life and the choices he had made to live it rightly and completely. He began his conclusion. "After years of struggle and fulfillment, searching and seeking with joy and devotion, John, with friends by his side, slipped from life with a quizzical look. He set off to meet his maker and to learn his destiny. He met no one. Knowledge, wisdom, and insight infused him.

"'I'm not what you expected, John. You are to pass judgment on your own life and are to value it for how you addressed your circumstances.'

"John flashed back to that defining moment when, as a boy, he had intuitively foiled a murder and assessed the choices he had made and failed to make."

Paul had to be careful because this was the Catholic Forensic League, and priests, nuns, and Catholic schoolteachers were evaluating every word. Paul was prone to cross boundaries when he could and to at least touch them when he couldn't. Here he grasped the boundary and mangled it into little pieces. He continued by advocating a life of goodness, kindness, and caring but of controlled recklessness marked by experimentation, frivolity, and spontaneity.

"Live," he implored, "because the fullness and goodness of your life is your measure...now and forever."

He left us captivated and inspired. He left the stage exhausted and to a standing ovation.

As the year wound on, the spark between Paul and Beth ignited a relationship that became as serious as two sixteen-year olds could have. Paul began to turn his Forensic interests more toward debate. Thus, there was no replication of that glorious achievement from December. We became closer and closer. He became a fixture at my house. We would go there straight from Forensics, have dinner, do some homework, and talk almost until bedtime. He became a regular member of the family. We talked our way through everything. We shared the aspiration to write, to provoke, to inspire, to have fun.

Paul paired off with Beth, and I, more casually, spent time with Toni. On weekends, we were together as a foursome and were regulars at the weekend basketball games and at Neumann's weekly Saturday night dances. The Bristol Stomp, the Mashed Potato, and various line dances acted as preludes to the Three Spots: three consecutive dreamy, romantic slow dances. During the Three Spots, you had ample time and opportunity to get to know your partner, provided you could stay out of the line of sight of the Norbertine monitors who patrolled the dance floor to discourage the violation of the commandment that stated, "Thou shalt not commit adultery," which they somehow interpreted to include most, if not all, our postpubescent inclinations. The night traditionally ended with the original version of Glenn Miller's "Moonlight Serenade," where we could again warm one another in preparation for the ride to League

Island Park, better known as The Lakes, for a half hour of unsupervised amorous pursuits prior to the drive home before curfew. It was turning out to be a great year. Paul's exuberance knew no bounds. He excelled in class and in debate, and, with Beth often by his side, Paul seemed to be living his own speech.

That summer, Paul and I decided to try to find work together. We eventually landed jobs as short-order cooks in the cafeteria at the local aquarium. We served hot dogs, hamburgers, tuna salad, and meatball sandwiches with Coke or 7 Up to runny-nosed, screeching, happy-go-lucky kids who loved to watch the dolphins soar out of the tank to retrieve fish held high by a beautiful, long haired, bikini-clad trainer with movie star affectations who never deigned to socialize with the kitchen help. We had to work every weekend, but we had nights off, so we could see Beth and, for at least part of the summer, Toni as well. My romance ended abruptly when Toni's father was transferred from the Philadelphia Naval Base to Norfolk, Virginia. By August, Paul and I were spending only work time together, and my frustration escalated as I couldn't get the trainer even to say hello to me.

In junior year Forensics, Paul returned to original oratory. He picked up where he left off; he and Beth took first and second places in the league championship, thereby qualifying for the national tournament in San Francisco in the spring. He had fun enlisting the support of the entire school to help raise money for the trip. We even talked the administration into sending a letter to Mr. Ripley to seek a contribution. We received no reply. It was a heady time for this cadre of street urchins from South Philly. One of our own was going to San Francisco. The tournament went well for Paul and Beth; there were both in the top ten, the highest ranked underclassmen in an event dominated by seniors.

When they returned, however, Paul seemed somewhat changed. He stopped coming home with me after school. His natural enthusiasm and spontaneity waned. He became distracted—almost entranced or hypnotized. Everybody noticed it. Our questions about the details of the trip yielded short, uninformative responses. We initially thought Paul was developing an aloofness from his accomplishments. In the past, Paul had been so confident and in touch with himself and his talents that accolades hadn't fazed him. It wasn't that he had expected success. He just knew himself and what he was capable of, and he had accepted success gracefully. It wasn't arrogance. Clearly something wasn't right. I was confused and at a loss what to do. Our relationship was such that Paul had always been a step ahead of me—in basketball, academics, Forensics, and girls. He obviously held the superior position in our dealings. I was his friend, though. I knew him and could support him if he needed help. I didn't know what the problem was, and I couldn't draw it out of him. After a few weeks, I couldn't stand it any longer, and I devised a simple plan. I approached him after school on Friday.

"Paul, I need to help my folks move some things around this weekend. Could I borrow your back?"

"Where and what time?" he responded. This was almost like the Paul of old.

"Tomorrow morning. Nine o'clock. My house."

"I'll see what I can do."

That was not typical Paul. Normally he would have said he'd be there at eight o'clock for breakfast—to tell Mom to make more bacon and to tell Dad we were going to embarrass him by moving more than he did.

At nine o'clock, there was no sign of him. I hoped like crazy he would show up. Finally, at about nine twenty, the doorbell rang, and there he was. He looked sleep deprived and unkempt. He mumbled, "I think I'm ready to work."

"My folks are running late. I have to pick some things up at the hardware store. Let's take a walk."

He shuffled along quietly. As we turned the corner, I had to say something. "Paul, you've got to talk to me. What's wrong?"

"What do you mean?"

"Ever since you came back from California, you've been a different person. You haven't been coming over; we haven't talked. I thought at first the trip went to your head, but that's not it. You're distant. And you don't seem to care about anything. It's like you're going through the motions. I know something's wrong."

"It's hard for me to talk about," he mumbled.

"You've got to talk about it."

"If I tell you, you have to swear an oath not to talk to anyone else about it. Not your folks. Not anybody at school. Nobody."

"It's me. Of course, I swear." I crossed by heart and raised my right hand.

"It's Beth. She might be pregnant."

I stopped walking, even though I was in the middle of the street. Paul had to pull me out of the way of a Ford Econoline. I was a teenager with a full portfolio of sexual fantasies but only superficial experience. Not only was Paul now a veteran—a man—but he might be on the verge of fatherhood.

"What's the story?"

"Beth and I had been talking about it for a while. We were out there together for almost a week. One thing led to another, and we got into it. Beth wasn't taking anything. I was a fool too. I should have known better."

Instead of asking him what I really wanted to know, I asked, "Who knows?"

"Beth's parents. My parents. Father Tim."

"What's the status?"

"She's late, and she's going to have a test this week."

"So, you don't know for sure?"

"No, but she says she's never late, and she's been feeling tired and weak."

"Is there any plan if she is?"

"Beth's call. We'll keep the baby if she wants. She'll have an abortion if she wants. We'll put the baby up for adoption if she wants. I'll support any decision. I have a problem with every choice. My folks have said they would want to raise the baby as my brother or sister, if we go that route. I'm very confused, and I'm struggling to stay stable for Beth. She hasn't slept in days, and she's not eating. She's just been staying in her room. She isn't even going to school. I know she's confused and depressed."

His guilt spilled out with each word. I couldn't help much. I had no words of wisdom, no advice, and no thoughts on what I would do if I were in his position or hers. While I felt largely useless, I had the clear impression Paul was relieved he had told me. During the next several days, we talked quite a bit about the responsibilities of fatherhood and how they would shape Paul's life, if Beth made that choice. He said he wasn't quite sure he loved her. He thought so, but love was taking on a new meaning now, and it had larger implications. He was clear that if Beth wanted to keep the child, it would be relatively easy for him to make the commitment to her and the baby. He knew his parents were there for him, although they desperately wanted Paul to continue his education. Long ago, Paul promised his dad that he would go to college.

Beth's parents wanted her to have the child. Paul said it was a Catholic thing. And, they also didn't like the thought of an abortion from the physical point of view. In a sense, Paul said, they were being pretty progressive by allowing Beth to consider the options and to make the choice herself. On the other hand, they had started treating Paul with a coldness and a disdain that penetrated to his core. He was experiencing rejection for the first time in his life. It sobered and humiliated him—partly because he could so easily justify the way they were acting.

Three days later, we knew. Beth was pregnant. They struggled to sort out their plan when she began to bleed and had to be rushed to the hospital. Paul tried to get in to see her, but he soon discovered her parents had chosen to exercise their right to exclude him. After she was released, she called to tell him she had lost the child, but she was physically fine with no permanent ramifications. Relief and remorse consumed him. He and Beth continued to see one another, but it was different now. Paul was not welcome in her home.

During the next months, the change in their relationship became palpable. Rather than dancing together, they danced around one another. They restrained themselves so much that the spark of excitement between them became starved of emotional fuel and expired. The relationship failed to survive the trauma. While we continued to see Beth and her friends at tournaments, the contacts became increasingly more formal and polite. Over time, Beth faded from our lives but never completely from our memories.

VI

As senior year progressed, Paul's self-assurance, perceptiveness, and spontaneity reemerged but ever so gradually. Our talks about abortion and responsibility continued from time to time.

"Naddie, I've been thinking about Beth. You know, I still don't know what she would have done."

"She probably doesn't know either."

"Yeah, you're probably right. I had all these conflicts. I kept wondering about what my emotional commitment to Beth was. I wasn't sure whether I was really committed to her. Whether I really loved her. Whether I really wanted to have my life revolve around her."

"You know, we probably shouldn't have to think about things like that at this stage of our lives," I said.

"I think you're wrong. If we're going to act like adults and do adults things, we have to think about these things. Anyway, I never really figured out how committed I was to her. Another thing that tortured me was that I couldn't figure out what role I was supposed to play in helping her make up her mind. I didn't want to do anything that would make her feel I was making the decision for her or that I was forcing or pushing her one way or another, but I didn't want her to think she was alone in making her decision, that I didn't care, or that I wasn't being supportive. I never quite figured that one out either."

"It seems to me you gave her the right amount of space and help."

"Well, maybe, but the basic decision about whether or not she should have an abortion was the fundamental thing I struggled over. I read some articles about it. I know the Church's position. I know about the legal and medical problems. What I don't know is what is right morally. How do you balance the moral and practical? I never really got that one resolved either."

"Did you reach any conclusions on anything?"

"Yeah, I learned something about responsibility. In the future, the commitment will precede conception. I'm clear on that."

As the frequency of these talks diminished, other topics emerged. Some were insignificant, such as how anyone in his right mind could think Bill Russell was a better center than Wilt Chamberlain, whether black high-top Converse Chuck Taylors were better than low-cut whites, and whether major league baseball should just surrender because nobody would ever really challenge the Yankees. Some topics were important, such as how we could make our marks in life and what would happen to our parents and the world we were growing up in. One week in the Forensic room before a speech tournament, Paul was preparing some research for extemporaneous speech topics, and he called me over. "Hey, Nad, I was looking at some old extemp topics. Look at this one. The city of the future."

"Yeah, what about it?"

"What do you think the city of the future will be like?"

"Pretty much the same. Dirty. Crowded. Trolley cars. Kids playing street games like we did—halfball and buck buck. You know, more of the same."

"I don't think so. It's going the change. You're going to see a big difference in who lives in the cities and who doesn't. The educated, wealthy, and family oriented are going to move out over time. Some of them will move to the burbs. Some might move farther out—to farm-like settings. They're going to abandon the cities."

"What will happen to people like our parents?"

"If our generation doesn't do something about it, as their generation dies, a whole class of people who will feel trapped and helpless will replace them. The cities will be poised for collapse. Our kids won't grow up the way we did. They won't understand street games and washing machine boxes. They won't play halfball, buck buck, or dead box. They'll play with chemistry sets and those Erector Sets with electrical motors. We can't relate to our grandparents tending to chores on farms in Italy. The cities will be as different to our kids as those farms are to us."

When we weren't talking about sports and the future of urban living, we talked about college. Both of Paul's parents, especially his father, wanted him to go to college. Dominick Casabella was a master cabinetmaker. He could do everything imaginable with wood, and he loved his work. However, he would often say, "You boys should give yourselves the most choices you can. I've learned to do things with my hands. You boys have to learn to do things with your brain so you'll have choices."

My father was equally insistent. As a skilled machinist, he could conquer anything made of metal. If it was broken, he could fix it. If it didn't exist, he could make it. He loved to make things work, but it bothered him he never had the opportunity to continue his education beyond trade school. He thought I should be a lawyer or a teacher because I always had something to say on every subject. "Education is your future. I could see you as Professor DiDominico or Judge DiDominico. I've taught you how to build an engine, but I can't teach you to be a lawyer. Go to college."

So, Paul and I talked about college. We, along with about fifteen others from our class, focused on a local school only forty minutes away by public transportation. Economics limited our choices, and this small Jesuit college had a good academic reputation, was affordable, was located in a safe neighborhood, and had a great basketball program.

Paul said we should schedule appointments with the Dean of Admissions so we would have a better chance of getting in and getting financial aid. He made the arrangements and got the directions. My father worked only three blocks from home, so he walked to work. I borrowed his car for a morning drive to the campus. We took the expressway and exited at Montgomery Drive to make our appointments, which were back to back. As we turned onto Belmont Avenue, I saw police car lights flashing in my rearview mirror. I pulled to the right to let him pass. He too pulled to the right and motioned for me to pull over.

I turned to Paul and asked him if I had run a light. He didn't think so. I froze. Officer Somebody-or-Other walked over to the car in his black leather jacket. He had his shiny badge and his holstered gun. He was Paul's height but big and black, and he had a thick moustache.

"What the hell you doing, boy?" he shouted at me.

I was speechless. Paul leaned over from the passenger side and stated, "We have an appointment."

"Get out of the car. Both of you. And bring your driver's license and registration."

We complied.

"What's the problem, Officer?" Paul asked.

"What's the problem? Can't you boys read? You've been bucking traffic for about five hundred yards. Couldn't you see cars going around you? Couldn't you hear me honking at you?"

"I...I...I didn't...." I stuttered.

"Whose car is this, and where're you going?"

Paul took over. "It's his father's car. We're from South Philly. We don't come out here much. We've applied to Saint Joe's a few miles away, and we have interviews to try to get admitted there. We didn't see any signs saying this is a one-way street."

"Every morning at rush hour we turn the traffic one way into the city, and at night we turn it around out of the city. Other than rush hour, it's two ways," said the officer.

"We didn't see," Paul said.

"You boys are lucky you didn't get killed or kill somebody."

"We're sorry, Officer," Paul said. "We're a little nervous about our interviews, and we were in a little bit of a hurry. We're just trying to get spots in college."

"You're acting like you're trying for spots in Holy Cross Cemetery. Get back in the car, and wait for me there."

We complied. After a few minutes, he returned and handed me my license and the car registration.

"You boys are damned lucky. I should shoot you for being stupid. But I won't. This time. I'm going to give you a break. Just a warning. But, if you so much as fail to put your turn signals on, you'll get a ticket, your father's insurance company will double your premiums, and your dad will revoke your license. So, don't be stupid. Follow me out of here so you don't get killed. I'll show you the way to school. Good luck."

We followed him. Paul said the interview should be a piece of cake now. He was right. We applied only to Saint Joe's, and we were both accepted.

VII

The Forensic Union activities wound down. We finished the season well. Paul won the championship in original oratory after delivering a speech he wrote based on the city of the future theme. In the speech, he urged that we wake up and do something about it now before the plight of America became irremediable. I won the declamation, interpreting a speech that condemned materialism. A predecessor wrote it a few years before. We decided not to participate in the national tournament in New Orleans for financial reasons, so our forensic careers ended in the traditional way—with a party.

Each year a few days after school ended, Father Tim would arrange for the whole team to travel out to the abbey operated by his religious order so that we city kids could experience a real picnic on spacious grounds. The place had a swimming pool, tennis and basketball courts, baseball and soccer fields, and a nearby forest for hiking. This year, he decided to arrange a stop in Valley Forge National Park for a quick tour. That way, those of us who had never seen the log cabins and Revolutionary War cannons could acquire some historic substance. So, as the school bus worked its way west of the city, Father Tim directed the driver to pull over for a short visit.

As hard as it might be to imagine, many of us had left the boundaries of the city only to go to our high school basketball and football away games or for speech and debate tournaments. Valley Forge, twenty-five miles from our school, wasn't quite in another solar system, but to us, it was almost in another country.

We pulled into the national park in the late morning. The ride had been raucous. There had been singing, joke telling, and playful fisticuffs as forty teenage males flexed their hormones. Several games of pinochle and gin rummy sprouted up in pockets of the bus. The more cerebral played chess, although the activity level didn't exactly foster concentration. We disembarked at the parking lot with explicit instructions from Father Tim. "Explore the park in any way you can, but if you are not back in ninety minutes, you'll be given up for dead, abandoned, and fondly remembered by the rest of us during a moment of silence just before hot dogs and hamburgers at the picnic."

Footballs began to fill the sky; baseballs smacked leather gloves, and miraculously a kite appeared and popped into the clear blue sky. June outdid itself on this majestic morning. Paul and I and a few others set off to find the log cabins. For some strange reason, Paul seemed obsessed with finding some cannons. As we crossed the fields, we saw a clearing with eight or nine cabins. They were neatly placed in the midst of six or seven cannons with small piles of cannonballs available next to each.

Paul's eyes twinkled like in the pre-Beth days.

Street kids in South Philly had ready access to a vast selection of firecrackers—hammerheads, cherry bombs, and blockbusters. These were no normal, run-of-the-mill firecrackers. Blockbusters, big square gunpowder-filled blocks with a fifteen-second fuse and a kick that would blow your fingers right off your hand if you were unfortunate enough to be holding one when it exploded, clearly commanded the most attention. These were the loudest and most powerful of the street crackers. Cherry bombs looked like cherries, only three times bigger. They were round and red with ignitable stems. They were loud, but their notoriety derived from their distinctive high-pitched sound. It was more like a pistol shot than a car backfire. Hammerheads were aptly named as well. The explosive part looked like the head of a hammer, and the fuse resembled a withered handle. Louder than cherry bombs but not quite as loud as blockbusters, these bad boys were more accessible and quite capable of blowing out your eye if you weren't careful.

With the Fourth of July approaching, the firecracker supply had hit the street. Paul had been prescient enough to bring a portion of his stash to explode in the park cannons. This would cause a commotion, and we would reenact a Revolutionary battle of sorts. He distributed his munitions, and we loaded our artillery. After lighting the fuses, we were supposed to run to the middle of the field and swan dive onto the grass. This was nothing harmful —just a sophomoric prank conceived by a college-bound teenage boy with an IQ over 165.

We rigged some delays on the fuses to elongate the battle scene, and away we went. Pow! Bang! Crack! We were just some city kids having fun in the suburbs.

The reverberations shook the commons, summoning our teammates to the clearing. They saw us prostrate and motionless on the grass. From a distance, the appearance of catastrophe filled the land. As our teammates approached, we popped ourselves up and startled about half the group. The other half had anticipated Paul's prank. Our laughter soon slid beneath the blare of sirens growing from the horizon. In the next instant, four state police cars and the park ranger pulled onto the knoll. Their sirens screamed, and their lights flashed. The park ranger took control, sort of, with the state police playing the role of reinforcements behind. Their hands were glued to their holstered guns.

"What's going on here?" the ranger shouted. "What happened? Is anybody hurt?"

We did the unthinkable—we laughed. This was not the best of ideas.

"It was just a joke," Paul finally asserted.

The ranger went nuts. "Joke? A joke? This is a national park. A public memorial. Joke? This is no joke. Who's in charge here?" he bellowed.

Father Tim arrived and stepped forward. "I'm Tim Meulen. These boys are with me. I'm a priest."

Father Tim had dressed in civilian clothes and looked more like one of us than our chaperone.

The park ranger's anger heightened as he clenched his jaw and furrowed his brow. He achieved restraint—barely. He coldly commanded, "Come with me, please, Father."

The ranger and police escorted Father Tim to the cars. Thankfully, the sirens were extinguished, but the lights kept flashing like the amusement piers in Atlantic City. The dialogue persisted for about ten minutes. We perceived the ranger's heightened animation, even from a distance. He was not happy. Father Tim, by contrast, was elegant in his deportment. His height and voice gave him a distinct advantage at times like this. His persuasive skills finally quelled the ranger's ire. Calm gradually set it. After the negotiation, Father Tim extended his hand. They shook. Father Tim bowed slightly from the waist and stalked toward us with a totally neutral expression pasted on his face.

"Back to the bus. Immediately," he barked.

Father Tim had never shouted at us before. We ran back. He entered last. We remained silent.

"Who wants to go first? What happened? Who's responsible?"

Without hesitation, Paul spoke up. "We were just having some fun. We didn't hurt anything or anybody."

Father Tim interrupted. "Who is 'we'?"

We all confessed.

"Let me tell you what 'we' just did." He launched into an explanation. "*We* defaced federal property. *We* engaged in disorderly conduct. *We* incited a riot. *We* created a public disturbance. *We* clearly antagonized the federal and state authorities. *We* are about to have this bus impounded. *We* are about to be taken to the state police barracks, entered into the FBI information system, fingerprinted, and issued citations and fines. After that, if there's still daylight, *we* will be allowed to find our way home without a vehicle. Now, what do *we* think about that?" He finally took a breath.

Our eyes grew to the size of small pizzas. He appeared really angry, but I couldn't quite tell whether he was playing a role.

Silence prevailed.

"Well?" Silence. "What do you think, Nad?"

I remained silent and looked straight down.

"Paul?"

Paul choked back a smirk. After a slight pause, he let it out. "I think it's ridiculous. We didn't hurt anything or anybody. I think those guys are a bunch of uptight morons. They're playing tin soldiers and trying to flex their gun belts. That's what I think. If they were back in the city, they'd be run off the force in a day and a half."

Again, silence. All eyes shifted back and forth between Father Tim and Paul. Father Tim broke his stare at Paul and then surveyed the bus. Our eyes portrayed our anxiety. Everyone but Paul felt the intimidation Father Tim imposed. Without changing his facial expression, but with a noticeable softening of his voice, Father Tim deadpanned, "I agree. Now that we have that settled, we can go. I've convinced them to allow us to leave the park and be on our way. They agreed based on two conditions. One, I must deliver a stern lecture on the value of government property and the perils of defacing it. I have just fulfilled that condition. Two, they insisted they escort us out of the park in a cavalcade with their lights flashing. On my signal, they will surround the bus with their vehicles and assure our departure. There will be silence and stillness in this bus until our escorts depart. No laughing. No smiling. No playing. Agreed?"

We all nodded. Father Tim gave the signal, and we left Valley Forge National Park.

As we drove out, Paul pointed out the window. "That's the National Memorial Arch in the distance. It was placed here in 1917 and is supposed to symbolize national freedom. I guess Valley Forge is supposed to be the archway to American freedom. Those guards overreacted. We're fortunate we're in a country where at least there are certain protections against guys like that getting crazy in a big way. It looks like Father Tim saved our skin—mine, in particular. I'd better go thank him."

When the convoy departed, Paul went up front, traded places with Joe, and began an intense conversation with Father Tim. For my part, I was relieved we were still going on a picnic.

VIII

After high school, Paul and I, along with more than a dozen others from Neumann, began our college careers at Saint Joe's. The freshman class of 450 was small, even in comparison to our high school class, which was more than 900. Paul chose Saint Joe's, also called Hawk Hill, because Jesuits operated the school and held numerous faculty positions and because the English department reputedly had excellent professors, especially in the Shakespearean and medieval literature curricula. Only Paul could come up with such reasons. I chose it because it was close to home and because of the basketball team. All the high school crowd made the daily commute—except me. I'm not sure how this happened, but I wound up with two scholarships, which together paid for room, board, tuition, books, and supplies. So, Paul was a day hop, and I was a resident.

The first week of school involved no classes. A three-day campus orientation preceded a three-day religious retreat. Campus orientation included registration, a full explanation of the library, lectures on study skills, religious services, and a comprehensive tour of the gothic buildings housing most of the classrooms. The distinct butterscotch look and antiseptic smell of high school was nowhere to be found. The classrooms were dark and damp, a bit archaic, and reminiscent of old European-leaning centers. There was a reverence about the buildings that contrasted almost diabolically with the day-ending pep rallies, where upperclassmen (mostly juniors) alternately tried to intimidate us and whip us into frenzied support for our basketball team. Junior class members randomly selected freshmen from the assembly and required them to run twice around the auditorium while flapping their arms like wings and shouting, "The Hawk will never die" or, "Go, Hawks! Go."

This esoteric exercise supposedly was fun and showed school loyalty and team spirit. I thought it was stupid. I turned to Paul and said, "This is pretty ridiculous. Let's blend in here."

"There'll be no problem," he responded.

Just then, one of the intellectuals from the junior class walked down our row. He eyeballed candidates for the next victim. He looked past me and fixed on Paul. As he began to approach him, Paul's expression turned from his normal easy, casual look to one of total superiority and control. His posture straightened even more. His eyes flashed, and he acquired the look more of a tenured professor than a lowly plebe about to be hazed. Einstein looked at Paul and gave a slight shrug as if to say, "Excuse me, sir." He walked by to pick another victim. Slowly my pulse rate returned to under a thousand, but the wooden smile remained on my face for the duration of the rally.

The next day, we boarded buses for our off-campus retreat. Freshmen with last names beginning with *A* through *D* were herded together for a ride of unknown duration to an undisclosed location for three days of religious indoctrination by priests of an unknown order. We had no idea what to expect. During the two-hour ride, we began to get acquainted. Bob Caddy lived just two miles south of the campus. He graduated from one of the two private Catholic boys' high schools in the city. An All-Catholic rower, Bob's eight-man boat had won the Catholic League Championships the past year. Bob came to Saint Joe's to row and prepare for medical school, thus following in his father's footsteps.

Tim Dillon came from Saint Joe's Prep, the other private school for Catholic boys in the city. He lived half a mile west of campus and ran cross-country and track. He started working at age sixteen in the newsroom of the television station just up the road from campus and his house. His primary reason for picking Saint Joe's was its proximity to home and work.

Wally Barth lived in West Philly. I recognized his name from our high school football games against his school. He played halfback. I soon learned he was a better baseball player and was coming to Saint Joe's on a partial scholarship.

John Cross was the other runner on the bus. He had been one of the top milers in the Philadelphia Catholic school system and was at Saint Joe's on a free ride. Since high school graduation, he had let his hair grow down his back. He played folk guitar and liked exotic sports cars, particularly the Porsche 356 Speedster.

Kurt Cannon was the most different from us. He came from New England, where his father was a professor at Boston University Law School. He was clean cut and had the look of an aristocrat and the speech of a Kennedy. He came to Saint Joe's because his father had come here many years ago.

We became friends in short order. As we coasted off the four-lane highway, we approached a "campus." There was a small stone chapel, a large brick office building, and a boxy wooden dormitory. These structures anchored a multiple-acre manicured lawn. It was complete with a walking path and a meadow behind, which abutted a forest with a stream. We were welcomed to Easton, Pennsylvania, home of the Franciscan Fathers' retreat.

The monks ushered us into the auditorium for instructions. They assigned rooms—two men to a room. Paul and I manipulated the situation so that we were together. Services began at 8:00 a.m. Breakfast would take place between 7:15 and 7:45 a.m. Lunch was from noon to 12:30, and dinner was from 5:30 p.m. to 6:30 p.m.

All the spaces in between contained designated activities, such as reading, lectures, discussions, services, meditation, and sleep. Free time extended from 7:00 p.m. to 9:00 p.m. Services and a "short but interesting" discussion followed. They ordered lights-out by 11:00 p.m. They prohibited talking, except at meals, during free time, and during discussion. The rules applied uniformly, except that Tim and John, as intercollegiate athletes, could go out for training runs in the morning and evening. I wasn't sure who had the better deal.

Friar Mark signaled the start and finish of activities by walking the corridors and clanging a gold bell that had been a Franciscan artifact for more than a century. Figures of priests and doves surrounding a crucifix with a defeated Christ adorned one side of the bell; the other displayed the triumphant savior ascending to the clouds. The bell's irksomeness overshadowed its exquisite beauty and craftsmanship. Loudly and persistently it echoed through the halls and announced meals, discussions, lights-out, and (worst of all) rise and shine. The bell offended Paul in a typically Paul way. "We're not cows," he muttered. "Or sheep. Bells should announce monumental events. Think of the Liberty Bell ringing our freedom or the death of a great contributor to the community. I hate that bell."

Though antagonized by the bell, Paul drew energy from the evening discussion. Friar Mark announced the subject matter—the role of the Ten Commandments in everyday life. He started by telling the story of Moses descending the mountain with stone tablets permanently etched with the formula for salvation. Paul interrupted. "That can't be right. For one, if you're Christian, it's contradictory because you believe salvation was possible only after Christ's death and Resurrection, which I've been taught occurred long after the trek up Mount Sinai. Second, it has to be a metaphor. Moses couldn't tell the masses he and some of his very intelligent buddies decided the society needed some rules on social order to eliminate the chaos and unify the community. The people wouldn't have followed him. But if the rules flowed from divine fiat and had eternal consequences, then he would have had something that might work."

Bob Caddy took the challenge. "That's what makes this divine. The inspiration for the rules came from God. Moses was an instrument."

John Cross next chimed in. "When people come together, they generate a spiritualism, a karma, that takes over and gains a life all its own. It's the karma that rules. People are always the answer."

Paul had successfully ignited a debate, and for more than two hours, we discussed whether there was a God, whether there needed to be one, where morality came from, where it should come from, hedonism, altruism, enlightened self-interest, Karl Marx, Ayn Rand, and, of course, Bob Dylan. Paul loved it. We all loved it—except Friar Mark, who had completely lost control. Paul had become the de facto discussion leader, catalyst, and facilitator for the evening. Finally, Friar Mark surrendered and rang the bell for us to go to our rooms. We were to spend the remainder of the night in silence. Word spread quickly that Paul and I would host a small discussion group in our room. It was to begin fifteen minutes after the lights-out bell. Paul was in his glory.

As these intellectual recalcitrants began to assemble, the notion hit me that only the most thoughtful and analytical members of the retreat had come forward for some brain stretching. The group included Caddy, Dillon, Cross, and Cannon. We left but one light on in the room. Paul stuffed the bottom of the door with towels to block the light, hoping to side-step Friar Mark's curfew check. The debate reignited quickly. Caddy and Cannon clearly and articulately represented the traditional, conservative approach, upholding the sanctity of the Bible, especially the New Testament. Dill and I steered a middle course, adhering to a belief in God, an afterlife, and the communal aspects of the Church. Paul and Cross spoke for the left. Spiritualism for them had no grounding in a Supreme Being. They embraced a human-centered theology. The debate accelerated as a cadre of males on the verge of adulthood intellectually challenged and provoked one another in the healthiest of ways. I felt the significance of the moment. This discussion signaled our emergence into a new world—an intellectual world, a world where our thoughts, ideas, theories, and beliefs would be accorded weight and significance. We ascended onto a new plateau in our journeys toward adulthood. I wondered whether any of the others shared my conclusion. Obviously, Paul did.

The time before bed check evaporated. Friar Mark patrolled the halls, sailing by our room with no break in stride. Apparently, he was unaware the evening discussion had spawned this illegal rendezvous where only good things were happening. We continued. A few hours later, Kurt left to use the communal bathroom down the hall. Kurt had become Paul's counterbalance. The polarity of their beliefs presented vividly. Yet it quickly became clear they viewed one another seriously and with respect. Kurt avoided the traditional, apologetic defense of his belief in God and the hereafter, opting instead to say he believed because he chose to believe. The principles of life that flowed from his choice to believe created a world infinitely more attractive to him than those that would have flowed from a choice not to believe. Paul could easily honor a stance so patently honest. Kurt readily conceded the logic of Paul's attack on those beliefs, but he marveled that Paul could mold his conclusion that neither God nor an afterlife existed into a positive, synergistic, almost Christian morality. It seemed to me they would become good friends.

As we grew tired, our defenses and our discretion diminished. What started as a hushed, subdued conversation grew into an animated, even boisterous debate. When Kurt went out to the bathroom, we didn't hear him return, so he had to bang on the door. Apparently, that noise echoed through the corridor, but we somehow failed to notice. We also failed to observe that we had somehow neglected to stuff the towels back under the door to block the light. We heard no doors open or close; we heard no labored breathing down the hall; we heard no footfalls on the corridor's marble floor. However, we did hear a sudden prolonged, thunderous knock on the door and the tremorous voice of the roused Friar Mark bellow, "Open up. Open up in there!"

I quietly added, "Or I'll huff and I'll puff and I'll blow the door down."

We hesitated, scanning one another in vain for some sign one of us had formed a plan. The room lacked space for our guests to hide. They were in plain view, and we couldn't keep Friar Mark out any longer.

He looked ridiculous in a knee-length nightshirt that exposed bandy, varicose-veined legs. They appeared to dangle from a stocking cap with nothing in between except a gigantic mouth that was screaming. "What's going on in here? What's going on?"

Paul took control. "We never really finished discussing the topic you raised at the last session, Friar. So, we thought we would pick it up here. We got interested and sidetracked. We didn't want to wait until tomorrow to finish the talk."

Friar Mark refused to take the bait. "*We* didn't get sidetracked. *You* sidetracked us. If it weren't so late, I'd take all of you to the train right now and send you back. I'll deal with you in the morning. When the bell rings, report to my office."

He stormed off, naïvely trusting we lacked the temerity to continue. Undaunted, we droned on for two hours more. As dawn snuck up on us, the group disbanded. Paul decided to take a shower before lying down for a few minutes. I waited by our door to ensure his easy reentry into the room.

With only a few hours before sentencing, I wrestled with the sheets. I anticipated the clanging that would end my wrestling match and aggravate me out of bed. My insomnia passed. I crashed hard and never heard the bell. Harsh pounding reminiscent of last night catapulted me into semiconsciousness. I finished rousing myself and greeted Friar Mark, who said the schedule had changed. Assembly would convene at 9:30. We should not go to breakfast first. I woke Paul and explained the new procedure.

"What about going to his office?" Paul asked.

"He said he would deal with that later. He said something about making an important announcement first. Maybe his idea is to somehow make an example of us in front of the whole group."

"I doubt it. He's probably aware enough to know he would make us heroes by doing that. My guess is he has something else in mind. Let's get to it."

We approached assembly and started to ask questions of other students. No one knew what was going on, but Paul and Kurt engaged in a whispered conversation on the way in.

Friar Mark addressed us. “Good morning. Two unfortunate incidents have taken place in the past twelve hours. First, last night, I found a roomful of you violating curfew.” We rolled our eyes. “I will deal with these delinquents later. More significantly, as you know, we woke you individually this morning without the use of the abbey bell.” Paul and I exchanged glances. “The bell is missing. That bell has been part of this religious order for more than one hundred years. It was brought from Europe when the abbey was founded. That bell is part of our tradition. It has been blessed by several popes and is an important treasure that links the abbey back to our heritage in the old country. I will leave you for precisely thirty minutes. When I come back, I expect the bell to be returned. You are to sit in silence.”

He left. We sat. The atmosphere was oppressive. I tried to play back yesterday’s events. The bell had released us from discussion last night, and I was sure it rang for lights-out. There would not have been an occasion to hear it between then and wake up this morning. Not much happened for the next several minutes. Paul and I suspected the remainder of our group took short naps.

A soft nudge from my right side alerted me to the sound of footsteps entering the assembly. I turned to Paul and whispered, “What do you think he’ll do?”

“First, he’ll try more intimidation. But it won’t work.”

“Why not?”

“If one of us took it, how can it be returned? We’re all here. If none of us took it, how will it help to intimidate us? He’s not very good at this.”

Friar Mark assumed the control position at the front of the assembly. “Okay, gentlemen. Where is the bell?”

Silence. No coughing. No shifting back and forth. I remembered Mr. Ripley. Friar Mark merely stood and stared. After an interminable three or four minutes, he commanded, “Go back to your rooms. If the bell doesn’t appear in thirty minutes a search will begin. You are to remain silent.”

He dismissed us with a clap of his hands. We queued up and shuffled back to our rooms downtrodden. Once safe, I began to investigate. "Paul, what's going on here?"

"Be cool," he replied. "Let's play chess."

I knew Paul was involved. I also knew he had a plan, that he was protecting me, and that he would beat me in chess. We waited, and he did. An hour later, our room was searched. I broke into a sweat as Friar Mark went through every possible hiding place. Paul offered to help him. Friar Mark declined. Paul beat me in chess again. Miraculously we didn't have a bell. Friar Mark stormed out in frustration. We waited some more. Paul beat me again. Finally, there was a familiar pounding on the door. I opened it to Friar Mark's mouth, which spit out, "Assemble now."

We marched single file and took seats silently.

"We have completed a thorough search of your rooms. We have not found the bell. You will not leave this abbey until the bell is retrieved. I'm going to dismiss you from assembly. You will have free time for one hour. You can do whatever you wish. The ban on talking is hereby removed. You must return here in one hour. By that time, we expect the bell back. Are there any questions?"

This was a shock. He was going to allow us to ask questions. Kurt Cannon raised his hand.

"Yes?" Friar Mark said.

"I have no idea where the bell is, Friar, but what happens if it turns up? What happens if somebody finds it and turns it in? What if someone knows where the bell is but isn't the person who took it?"

Before Friar Mark could answer, Paul spoke up. "Friar, what about the curfew violation? What's going to happen with that?"

Friar Mark hiccupped. "I don't see any connection between the missing bell and the violation of retreat rules last night." He paused. Quiet permeated the room, and then he continued. "However, in a show of good faith, if the bell appears during the next hour, no action will be taken against the rule violators last night, and no action will be taken against whoever returns the bell. If there are no more questions, you are dismissed. Please return in one hour."

We ran out to the grounds behind the abbey. I noticed Paul and Kurt make eye contact. They drifted apart to opposite ends of the field. Bob Caddy gravitated toward Kurt. I gravitated toward Paul. As I caught up to him, he turned and said, "Try to find Tim Dillon. Ask him to slip away to the kitchen door behind the abbey. Tell him to bring the brown bag behind the trash bins to the front of the assembly and then come back out. Oky?"

"Okay."

Just then, I noticed a crowd had formed around Kurt and Bob on one end of the field. The remainder of our mates were approaching Paul. They were shouting questions that blended indistinguishably together. Paul merely put them off and hollered across the field. "Cannon, let's play some football."

Kurt shouted back, "You got it, Casabella?"

A football materialized. Paul tossed it to Kurt. "You guys kick off."

In the meantime, I found Dillon and then slipped into the game in progress. Well, it wasn't exactly a game. Each team had about twenty players, and everybody was eligible to catch a pass. The exercise quickly deteriorated into a quick pass, which, if completed, led to an unbroken string of laterals. This ultimately resulted in a touchdown on almost every play. It was fun, but it was silly.

In what seemed to be no time at all, Friar Mark appeared on the field, and he shouted for us to return to assembly. Everyone complied, but almost no one had any idea what was about to happen.

Friar Mark opened with a smile—good news. "Gentlemen, I have a brown bag here on the stage."

He held it up, and I looked at Paul. He did not look back.

Friar Mark opened the bag to reveal the bell. "Inside the bell someone stuffed a note. I'll read it to you. 'If you seek truth, you cannot curtail thought. To permit thought, you must encourage discussion. Rules that eliminate chaos are good; those that retard openness are bad.

Bells are for animals, not for people. Think about it.' Well, I've thought about it. There will be a discussion after lunch. We'll start the discussion with suggestions on what our topic should be. I'll make some suggestions, and then you can make some. We'll go from there. Free time now. Thank you."

The assembly broke into wild applause. Paul, however, just smiled as we charged back to the football field, where the standing rules were insufficient to eliminate the chaos.

IX

After the retreat, we settled into the rigors of freshman year. At Saint Joe's, one dormitory housed about 35 percent of the resident population. Most residents were scattered throughout the campus in homes that had been purchased by or bequeathed to the school over the years. They were small houses which could accommodate between twenty and thirty-five students each. There were single rooms, doubles, and triples. One of the rooms in my dorm actually was two rooms merged into one. It slept five. Typically, each residence had two resident assistants, a faculty resident, and a priest or brother who was supposed to provide stability and order to the environment. I was assigned to a two-man room in Xavier Hall, a twenty-five-man house with two RAs who went to a nearby law school and a faculty advisor named Clearly. I met him during the hall picnic that began the year, and I didn't see him again until our Christmas party. My roommate was a good guy from another state, but in the beginning, I spent most of my time trying to maintain contact with my high school mates. I tried to have lunch with some of them as often as possible and to play some b-ball with them in the gym after classes. After a short time, these contacts diminished, but I continued to see Paul at least three times a week in English class. Kurt was in that class too, and because he lived in the house right next to mine, he, Paul, and I formed something of a trio as I slowly began to forge new friendships.

Kurt and Paul shared a chemistry. They provoked one another intellectually through their penetrating insights. Yet, they came at almost every issue from incompatible positions: Kurt was conservative and traditional; Paul was liberal and avant garde. They shared a common sense of integrity and honesty, but their discussions were almost always intense debates. Neither ever gained a clear advantage, and both walked away shaking their heads but smiling. I learned as much from being with them as I did in class.

One day after several weeks of class, Paul and Kurt cornered me. "I think you should run for office," Paul said.

"What are you talking about?" I asked him, and I looked at Kurt.

"Student government is what I'm talking about," Paul said. "Right, Kurt?"

"Right."

"We want to form a political party," Paul explained. "I've been talking to a few people, including Kurt. We want to sweep the freshman elections. If we can do that with one political party, we can make some changes here."

"What kind of changes?" I asked.

"Changes to the academic calendar, for example, so that way, we can have exams before Christmas. Changes in the dress code so that we don't have to walk around like boarding school high schoolers. Changes to the composition of the student body; maybe the school should be co-ed. Changes like having student representatives on the school's core curriculum committee so the student viewpoint could be heard, and the school can keep current. Changes like having student representatives on the disciplinary board. You know, changes."

"It sounds like you're pretty far along here. Are you running?" I asked Paul.

"No. I'm not going to be able to. I'm going to get a part-time job to help make ends meet at home, but I think you should."

"Why?"

"For a couple of reasons. One, I think you could keep Kurt honest. Kurt sees things one way. Right, Kurt?" Kurt smiled. "You can counterbalance him. I think you can stimulate some things and stabilize others. You have more street smarts than anybody else around here. You're Italian and will attract votes because of your last name. And you're my friend, and I think it would be fun for you to be involved. What do you think?"

During the next few minutes, I learned that Paul, in conspiracy with Kurt, had assembled a coalition of the major players in the classes from the high schools with the highest representations. They had contacted two athletes who were not only All-Catholic basketball players but also good students, and they had arranged for Caddy, Dill, Cross, and Barth from the retreat to be candidates along with Kurt and me. At a meeting the next day, we would discuss ideas, pick a name for the party, prepare our platform, slot candidates into specific offices, and strategize the campaign. Paul had the whole thing set up.

I told Paul again that he should run instead of me. He told me again he was getting a job. He went on to say, "Besides, I'm not sure I have the disposition to work though the political process. I'll get impatient. And I want to do some writing and some other things too. I think you would be good in student government, and it would be good for you too."

"How?"

"I see you needing to connect more with other people. We South Philly types can be a bit parochial. You need broader exposure. It'll bring out the leader in you."

I knew Paul wanted very much for me to be part of this, and I never felt he was trying to manipulate me. I believed he was sincere. The planning meeting began as I expected. Paul was in control, and he set the tone. He organized the agenda and facilitated the discussion. Kurt would run for president, Caddy for vice-president, the athletes for secretary and treasurer, and the rest of us for class representatives. We fleshed out a platform based on change and inclusion. Even a traditionalist like Kurt thought the school was too rigid, and he signed off on each issue. We would seek student participation on the curriculum, budget, and admissions committees, and on the disciplinary board. We would seek a relaxation of the dress code, which required us to wear jackets and ties. We would seek to change the academic calendar and the enrollment policy so we would have exams before Christmas and so women could become part of the community. We called ourselves the Target Party. Our slogan was "Vote Straight Target. Get Good Government." Paul managed the campaign and then slowed down so Kurt could pick up the mantle of leadership.

The next month sped by. We made speeches, and we made posters. We set up campaign booths in the lobby of the Student Center and in the main cafeteria. We debated with candidates from other parties. We took over campus, with Paul performing hours of grunt work.

Election day arrived, and the freshman class voted straight Target. Kurt publicly acknowledged Paul's role in bringing us together, and we began work on implementing our platform. Changes began to take place. Kurt was told he would be appointed to the disciplinary committee next year, and I was to join the curriculum committee, whatever that was. Paul stepped aside and began working part time stocking shelves at a supermarket. He also worked as a reader and an aide at a nursing home. I continued to see him only in English class. Our contact continued second semester, as we once again shared a class.

X

It took me a while to learn that, for some strange reason, Paul was getting only borderline grades. At first, I attributed it to his job and his other interests. We decided to take a course called Philosophy and Literature. Kurt was in the class too. The subject seemed provocative, and I thought I might learn something from Paul and maybe Kurt, regardless of the professor. Discussion was lively, and the reading was intense. However, Paul and the professor made no connection whatsoever. Kurt, on the other hand, seemed to be totally on top of everything in the class. He could anticipate the professor's every thought. In his first paper for the course, Paul wrote a comparison between Marx's theory of dialectic materialism and T. S. Eliot's "Tradition and The Individual Talent." When he told me about it, I was jealous. How does he come up with these ideas? I wondered. The topic was so beyond anything anyone else in the class could think of that I expected Professor King to ask Paul to teach the remainder of this class. Paul contrasted the view that matter controls mind with the theory that each individual artist has unique value and contributes essentially to the world of art. In his paper, Paul focused on the divergence between two types of evolutionary philosophies. Clearly, this was an A++ paper. It was insightful, well-written, and eminently readable. I thought it might be publishable.

I looked over his shoulder when the papers were returned. I couldn't believe my eyes. His grade was a D-. I approached Paul after class and asked him about the paper. He shrugged his shoulders and said, "Either I don't get it or he doesn't get it."

"Did he make any comments?" I asked.

"He sure did. Want to see?"

He tossed the paper at me. Across the top, King had written the following message:

> This is drivel. It makes no sense. There is no logical connection between these two works. Before your next paper, give some thought to the subject matter. If you just throw something together at the last minute, you will not pass this class.

It was clear that King had no clue. His parochial thinking had no room for real insights. I tried to reassure Paul. He threw up his hands, turned, and went to the supermarket.

The next paper called for another compare and contrast essay. Paul chose to contrast *Alice in Wonderland* with *Waiting for Godot.* He highlighted the proactive, aggressive nature that Alice displayed and the creative consequences of her conduct with the reflection, passivity, and introspection that resulted in frustration and decay portrayed in *Waiting for Godot.* Surely this time King would recognize the genius of what Paul had to say. I was wrong. Paul received another D, this time with a notation from King that said, "This paper is superficial and obvious. It lacks creativity and insight."

Before the next assignment, I pulled Paul aside and told him I though King lacked the intelligence to make any sophisticated connections. I suggested that maybe this time Paul should select a more basic topic. He agreed to try, selected a topic well in advance, and researched the shit out of it. A week before the paper was due, Paul told me he had finished the assignment. He hoped King would find it acceptable. He felt he was on the verge of failing the course. On the day the assignment was due, Paul told me he couldn't find the paper. After class, he told King he had finished the assignment but couldn't find the final version. He asked if he could have a two-day extension to recreate it from his notes if he couldn't find the original. King reluctantly acquiesced.

When the graded papers were returned, I asked Paul how it went.

"It didn't go," he answered.

"What do mean?"

He showed me his work, which was banally entitled, "Is Kant Relevant?" Across the top, King had written another note:

> I have not graded this paper because I believe it raises serious questions about your integrity as a student. I have submitted this paper and a similar one submitted (on time) by one of your classmates to the Disciplinary board for review. You will hear from them directly. I expect they will allow you to plead your case, although I am certain, beyond doubt, this is not your work.

"What is this about?" I asked.

"I don't know," Paul answered.

I consoled him by saying I would testify on his behalf and that Kurt, as a member of the Disciplinary Committee, would surely inform the other members this was a mistake.

On the day of the hearing, Professor King spoke first to the Board with Paul present. King told them that Paul was barely a D student and that he always wrote on far-out topics that didn't make any sense. He said Paul had submitted his paper late, and someone else in the class, who was a solid B+ student, had submitted, on time, a paper titled "Kant's Relevance." It was virtually identical to Paul's. Paul testified that he hadn't copied the paper. He said he couldn't find the original but what he submitted was his own work. I testified too. A few days later, the Disciplinary Board reached the decision that Paul had plagiarized the paper, but rather than dismiss him, they directed that he receive a failing grade in the course and be given a formal reprimand. When he told me, I exploded. "I can't believe Kurt couldn't convince them."

"Naddie, it looks like Kurt wasn't convinced either. The decision was unanimous." Paul sounded more hurt than I'd ever heard.

"Unanimous? What did Kurt say about it?"

"I haven't talked to him, and I don't intend to. You shouldn't either."

"What're you going to do?"

"Nothing, but I'm short some credits now."

He walked off. Paul's dejection enveloped him. Not since Beth had I seen him so disconsolate. It took me several hours to track Kurt down in the library.

"We need to take a walk," I said coldly.

We reached the path outside the library in silence. He obviously knew what was coming but was not preemptive.

"Okay, let's talk. I just heard the decision. I also heard it was unanimous. Is that true?"

"Yeah, I voted with the faculty."

"I can't believe it. This is Paul Casabella we're talking about. You know he wouldn't copy somebody else's work in a million years. Paul's innocent, and you know it." I knew I was making a scene, but I didn't care.

"Are you going to calm down and let me explain?"

"I'm dying to have you explain. I'm just not sure you can. He put you in office, and now you've stabbed him in the back."

"First of all, he didn't put me in office. The students did. And I didn't stab him in the back. I'm in a hard spot here. This is the first time a student has been on the Board."

"Is that any reason to vote the wrong way? You're on the board in order to protect student interests. You're on the board to do what's right."

"I did do what's right. I listened to the evidence. King's presentation was strong. The paper doesn't look like one of Paul's, and Paul has no real evidence he wrote it. He couldn't produce his notes, and the other guy's grades show this is the kind of work he does."

"What do you mean he has no evidence? Paul said he wrote it. That should be enough for you."

"I can't just accept it because he's my friend. I had to put it in context with the other evidence."

"What about my testimony?"

"I'm sorry to say this, but your testimony hurt Paul."

"What? You've got to be out of your mind. I said he told me he had finished that assignment a week in advance."

"But you also said he always told you what he was writing about and that you always knew the titles of his papers. You also testified that you always saw the paper before it was turned in. This time you didn't know the topic or the title and you never saw the paper.. From what you said, everybody decided this situation was different. Paul would have been better off if you'd kept out of it."

"I can't believe this. You should have been able to help him. You know he didn't plagiarize that paper. You know him."

"I did help him. I decided the evidence was stacked against him. The board would have decided he was wrong here, despite anything I might have said. I agreed with the decision on the evidence. But because I know Paul and because I don't think he did anything wrong, I thought it would be better if I saved my arguments for the penalty part of the decision. They wanted to expel Paul. I took the position that he shouldn't be given any credit for the paper, which meant he would get either an incomplete or an F, and then he should be given a warning. I had a hard time convincing them to do that, but they finally agreed."

"Why?"

"I argued that this was his first offense, that he testified he had lost the original, and that there was a little bit of doubt cast on this thing by the fact Paul takes the bus with the guy who submitted the other paper. I said that should move the Board not to expel him. Because I voted with them on the first part of the case, they went along with me on the second part. I think they wanted to support the student rep. I can tell you. If there hadn't been a student rep on the board, Paul would be out of here already."

"Okay," I said. "But we both know this is wrong. We both know he didn't do this. You know it, Kurt."

"I did what I thought was right. I hope you and Paul understand."

I never shared this conversation with Paul, and he managed to pass all his other courses. He started to work more hours at the supermarket, and he spent time with a group called WE CARE. On Saturdays and Sundays, they would go out into the community to fix up, clean up, paint, and repair houses and apartments to make them more livable. Paul worked with WE CARE before working at the supermarket on Saturdays and Sundays, and then he would stock shelves and work the cash register. He worked nights too. He was tired all the time.

Next semester, we shared a speech class, where he should have been an A+ student. His final disillusionment came when his interim grades indicated he was either failing this course or on his way to another D.

Toward the end of the semester, he grabbed me after class. "You're going to be on your own now."

I asked what he meant, but he just walked away. At the end of the semester, he left school with no real plans. We made some attempts to keep in touch over the summer, but Paul was always working when I was free, and I was working when he was around. We drifted apart.

XI

My junior year started uneventfully. Because of my involvement in student government, it was expected I participate in freshman orientation. I did, but I attempted to prevent any real embarrassment or humiliation to the plebs by acting as a de facto sergeant at arms. As the semester progressed, Paul became a phantom. Then one night, there was a cameo appearance in the student center. I was walking through, and I sensed a familiar aura. Then I heard the caustic question. "Nicholas Amadeo DiDominico, have you saved the world yet?"

I turned to Paul, who bear-hugged me on the spot. He looked like the Paul of old: elegant and almost regal. After some initial verbal jousting, he suggested, "Hey, Naddie, let's go get a drink."

We headed the few miles up the road to the Narberth Pub, and Paul continued with the mundane. "What's going on with the Target Party? You guys change the school yet?"

"We're making some progress. I'm learning a lot more about bureaucracy. Nothing officially changes quickly. What about you? You still feeding the world?" I asked.

"Absolutely," he responded. "The supermarket is great. You see a real cross section of the world there. I see a lot of older people. Their days revolve around trips to places like the supermarket. For the most part, they're alone, so they look forward to their forty minutes out shopping. I've gotten to know quite a few of them. Bert carries her own shopping bags with handles like your mom does on Ninth Street. She has two children and three grandchildren. Her husband's been dead for five years. He was a pain, but she misses him desperately. Stephanie has gout and arthritis. She has a hard time getting the change out of her purse. She doesn't like to complain, but some days can hardly move. They all tell me about their spouses. Some are gone; some are going. They all have their aches and pains. And they never fail to complain about the prices. Then I see some young mothers with their babies. They don't talk to me very much. Their carts are always overfull, and their tempers are always overly short. They are right in the middle of life as we know it. But that's not what I want to talk about. How are your grades? Still getting all As?"

I couldn't avoid telling him I was doing very well, although I felt embarrassed about it. It never made sense to me that I was doing so well in school, but he, whose perspective was broader and whose insights were deeper, did so poorly.

"So, are you seeing anybody?" he asked.

"Sure. Remember Jan from the admissions office? I'm seeing her, but I'm not sure it's going anywhere. What about you?"

"No. I'm working a lot of hours and spending some time at a nursing home. But I've been doing some reading and thinking. Have you ever thought about art?"

"Art who?"

"You jackass. Art, like in painting or sculpture or literature"

"No. What's to think about?"

"Nad, you do all the work but you might want to consider sitting back some. Really seeing things. Enjoying your life. There's all this natural beauty in the world. It's in nature. It's in people. It's in relationships. And there's all this natural tragedy too. There are horrors all over this world of ours. In the savagery of nature, in the brutality of people. And in the despair in relationships. I think I know what art is. It's simple. Art is nothing more than shaping the natural beauty and the natural tragedies of life, giving them order and form, and then communicating them in some way we can perceive them, embrace them, and seize them. The artist as craftsman works in his or her medium to shape beauty and tragedy in the world. That's all it is. And I'm going to be an artist someday." Paul's passion swept him away, unimpeded.

"Creativity requires more discipline than imagination. Don't you see that? I have the imagination, but you have the discipline. I'm going to borrow that from you. I can't lend you my imagination, but I don't have to. You have creative impulses. You have them; you do. But you don't do anything to release them. You're going to have to stop dabbling and dedicate yourself to the process. Stop being enslaved by the product.

I'm happy for you that you're doing so well in school. But you can do more. Much more. You can be an artist too. I know you can. But I see you trapped by all these conventional boundaries. Color without a book. I think you'll be surprised at what comes out."

He continued on this roll until closing time. We drove back to the dorm, and he disappeared for the rest of the semester. As always, I thought about what he said, but somehow my natural tendency was to hit the books. I wanted to master the subjects and get As. I would leave the real artistry to him. I had a semester to finish.

I never connected with Paul at home over the holidays, although I tried to reach him by phone a few times. I even stopped by his house once, but no one was home. By late January, I had typically settled into the routines of the school year. Then one Wednesday night around midnight, I heard an obnoxious knock on my dorm room door. This was followed by an intrusive, "Hey, South Philly, you in there? Open up before I come in through the fire escape window."

"Casabella, what happened to your couth? Wait a couple of seconds?"

When I let him in, he was all questions. "Did you write a novel yet?"

"No, but I did knock off another semester."

"All As again?"

I blushed. "Give me a break, will you? I can't help it if I've figured out what they want to hear. What are you up to? Still peddling Rice Krispies?"

"Not as much as before. I didn't tell you last time, but I was taking a few courses at a small school out by Villanova. Eastern Presbyterian. Ever heard of it?"

"No. Are you sure it's not Eastern Penitentiary? What's an Eastern Presbyterian?"

"It's a tiny, little school. There are about seven hundred of us. I just started back full time. It's a lot less traditional than Saint Joe's. I have enough space there. They think I'm a Zen master. I think I found a niche."

"Great. How'd you find out about it?"

"One of the kids from there started showing up at the nursing home. She started to tell me about it. She said it was open, freethinking, and progressive. She said it had few boundaries and a beautiful duck pond that they call Landew Pond. They took the letters of Walden Pond and rearranged them. It's pretty much frozen now, but we still take walks there and have long conversations."

"Who's 'we'?"

"Joy and I. She's the one from the nursing home. We're getting pretty close."

"If that's so, I guess you better tell me something about her."

"I haven't felt this way ever before. Her name is Dowling. She's beautiful, but that's not the best part. She's reached me. We share the same aesthetic. She can write; she can think. She sculpts and draws. She plays the piano and the dulcimer. We've read the same books, and we have the same vision. And we're passionate about each other. I think I found the missing ingredient."

"I'm thrilled. Where's she from?"

"She grew up in Oxford, Maryland, down by the Chesapeake. She started coming to the nursing home because she has a great aunt there. Now she's volunteering there when I'm there."

"When do I meet her?"

"We'll get together soon. Right now, I'm working like crazy. I want to start doubling up on courses so I can get my degree when she does."

"When's that?"

"Same as you."

"You better get in gear. You've got to get in an extra semester somehow."

"I know, but I don't think it'll be a problem. I'm on track now. Here. I want you to read this."

Paul handed me a pamphlet and vanished. I read the cover page. *Open Water and Closed Wounds.* A collection of poems, by Paul Casabella.

He was finally doing it. I opened to find what seemed like a hundred or so poems. I sat and read a few. The strange mixture of hope and despair puzzled me. Many of the poems celebrated beauty and love based on a theme of harmony and hope. But, lurking beneath the surface of some of the longer poems was a strong hum of futility—the idea that nothing much mattered. That we each would be destined to some overwhelming personal catastrophe. Some ultimate, relentless, torturing anguish. Paul frequently confused me.

We missed connecting several times that next year. In early March of my senior year, as I sat in my Medieval Lit class, I noticed a familiar silhouette furtively peering into the room and then pacing back and forth. The silhouette was agitated and impatient. When class ended, I bolted for the door. Paul grabbed me hard and pulled me aside, pinning me to the wall. His black work pants were torn above the left knee and streaked with smudges of dried mud. His black sweat shirt was in a similar state—dirty and torn in several places. His arms and face were also dirty, and he was bandaged above his right eye, on his left cheek, and on his neck. He looked like he had been jumped by a street gang out to show a college boy he didn't belong in their 'hood. Worse yet, his eyes were glazed over, and his face looked even more angular than usual. It was sunken in and almost haunted.

"I need help," he spat out.

"What the hell happened? Did you get beat up?"

"I just left the hospital, and I'm a bit fuzzy. I lost Joy. I have to find her. I don't know what happened to her."

I was even more confused than he was.

"What are you talking about? What happened? What hospital?"

"I have to find Joy. She was in the car, and then I couldn't find her."

"Where did this happen?"

"On West River Drive. I was heading back home in Joy's car. She was with me. Then there was a crash. I ran into something, and then I couldn't find her."

"What hospital?

"The one on City Line Avenue. I remember them taking me there in an ambulance last night."

"Paul, I'm not following you. You have to start over. You were driving on West River Drive last night?"

"Yes."

"Were you going home or to school?"

"Home."

"What time?"

"Around midnight."

"And Joy was in the car with you?"

"Yes."

"Are you sure? Why would Joy be going to South Philly with you at midnight?"

This stopped him. He turned his head like the household dog hearing a sound off in the distance.

"Maybe she wasn't in the car," I suggested.

"She was with me earlier," he answered.

"Okay. Let's get to a phone and call her room.

While I try to reach her, you try to remember what happened."

"It was late. It was dark and raining. I was on West River Drive. There was a car parked in the right lane, and I ran into the back of it."

"Was there anybody in that car?"

"Yes, a couple was just sitting in it. I was knocked silly. I hit my head on the steering wheel. I think I might have blacked out. Somebody called an ambulance. The other people were in the ambulance too. I lost track of them at the hospital. They kept me in for observation. When I woke up, I couldn't find Joy, so I just left the hospital and came here. I knew you would help me."

"I'll help you. Let's call Joy."

We found a phone. Paul couldn't dial, so I did. Joy answered the phone, and I told her the story.

"He's okay, but he's still disoriented. He thought you were thrown from the car. He's very worried about you."

"That's because I've been feeling sick lately," she said. "Are you sure he's okay?"

"Yeah. Here. You talk to him."

I handed him the phone, and they sorted things out. Over the next few minutes, we developed a plan. I drove Paul to Eastern Pres so he could be with Joy. During the ride, I asked about her health, and he told me she had been feeling sick for the past three weeks, but they thought everything would be okay. She was going to a doctor that week. I reunited the couple and then asked Paul to call me with an update. I heard nothing for almost four weeks.

Late one Thursday night, I was called down to the hall phone. My premonition was that it was Paul, so I answered the phone with a preemptory, "Are you still alive, vagabond?"

"Yep, Nint' and Wharton, I'm still alive. What're you doing Saturday?"

"Saturday? Like the day after tomorrow?"

"Yeah. Saturday. Like in thirty hours from now."

"I'm around. What's up?"

"I need a best man. I'm getting married. Available?"

"What?"

"Here. Talk to Joy."

"Hello, Naddie. Paul and I are getting married Saturday, and we want you to be the best man."

"Saturday? This Saturday? How long has this been in the works?"

"About a day. Will you?"

"Of course, I will. I'd be honored. Can I talk to Paul again?"

She handed the phone over.

"Casabella, what the hell is going on?"

"Joy's pregnant. We're in love. We're meant for each other, so we're getting married. Will you stand for us?"

The next day was a whirlwind. Paul and Joy had arranged for Father Meulen to preside over a wedding ceremony that contained only the basest essentials of a traditional wedding. Two of their classmates from Eastern Presbyterian played guitars and sang folk songs. They exchanged personalized vows, promising never to compromise their friendship and respect for one another. We quickly retreated to the Casabella house for a family reception with wine, roast beef sandwiches, and barely enough room for dancing. With suddenness of the wedding and emotions swirling within me, I had a little trouble with the toast. I managed to blurt out that for many the search was arduous, often endless, but we should share joy in their happiness that for them the search was over. I wished them *cent'anni* of health and happiness. Paul was his irrepressible old self, and Joy was radiantly beautiful. They projected brilliance and vitality. They spent their honeymoon in Joy's dorm room, and they arranged for an apartment after graduation. The day after commencement, Paul began working full time at the supermarket and picked up part-time work as a stringer for a national wire service. The former kept them eating; the latter kept him writing. Nicholas was born just before Thanksgiving. At my Christmas break from graduate school, I became his godfather. Paul and Joy were enormously happy, and Nicholas was a delight.

XII

Once again, time and circumstances conspired to distance us. The intensity of the reading and research in law school surprised me. Always methodical and efficient in my use of time, I discovered that organization and routine weren't sufficient. There was always more to read, and the effort of the analysis exhausted me. I chose law school rather than getting a PhD in modern American literature out of practicality. I'd even thought about the path I would have followed had I pursued a literary career. I would've focused on the different notions of fate running through Hemingway, Faulkner, Fitzgerald, and Dreiser. At first, Fitzgerald's devil-may-care, cast-your-fate-to-the-winds attitude appeared identical to Hemingway's view. Then again, Fitzgerald clearly believed you made your own destiny. Hemingway knew it was so far beyond your control that your choices became almost incidental, and he believed the misfortunes would eventually overshowed the good fortune in one's life. I hadn't yet figured out how to integrate Faulkner's and Dreiser's philosophies, but I figured I would have a few years to do so. I was passionate about the subject, but for the final choice, I went with my head, not my heart. So, law school it was.

Paul needed to work and to be a father. The Philadelphia morning newspaper picked him up, first as a beat reporter and then more recently as an op-ed writer. They evidently appreciated his insight into the moral, economic, and practical implications of the events surrounding him on the news pages.

Paul, Joy, and Nicholas moved into a rented house just north of the city. Paul was adamant that Nicholas would have a backyard to play in. By phone, I reminded him the court at Fifteenth and Morris had been his backyard. He laughed and told me about the latest stabbing and drug overdose in the old neighborhood.

During my infrequent visits home, I would have dinner with the Casabellas and read to Nicholas. At two years old, he seemed well prepared to read to me instead. Law school consumed me for interminable blocks of time. Finally, two Christmases later, I paid Paul, Joy, and Nicholas a visit, and I dropped off Nicholas's present. Paul was upbeat, but he wore a more angular look than ever before. He was gaunt, scooped out, and almost hollow. His appearance dramatically opposed his disposition, which was marked by full animation and exuberance. Nicholas clearly brought him unmitigated joy. We spent hours over dinner, which was a great meal prepared by Joy. Then Nicholas, with his dad and me in tow, began a comprehensive demonstration of every toy in the universe. As fatigue began to envelop me, I started to signal my departure. Paul took me aside and put his arm around my neck. He drew me close and beamed. "I've been writing. I've written two anthologies of poems and a draft novel. I'm working on a publisher for the poems, but the book needs some work."

"When can I see them?"

I hoped I had concealed my jealousy. He had done what I had only dreamed of doing.

"During your next visit. I'll either have the poems in print or you'll be able to read the manuscript. I'm not sure about the novel."

"Congratulations. I'm eager to read them."

"The poems are a bit dark," he said. "I call the first anthology *The Empty Well.* The overall theme is the inevitable tragedy of life, the ultimate demise. The second set is called *No Return to the Garden.* You know how I've always been fascinated with religion. I use the Garden of Eden as a symbol through the various poems to portray my beliefs."

I had to ask. "Why are the themes so bleak?"

"Because I think these themes are the essence of life. The ultimate demise of man, of course, is death. That's why the choices during life are so important. I think we need to be scared into living fully but rightly because, ultimately, we face individual extinction. There is no return to the garden."

"You're right; it sounds dark. What about the novel?"

"It expresses the other side. It's a celebration of life. An attempt to steer between a hedonistic philosophy and a spiritual one without moral comprise. It's an attempt to show that, despite the ultimate demise, there can be richness, fullness, satisfaction, and joy in life. It's a good guy's story, centering on the relationship between a father and a daughter. It's from the father's perspective. The working title is *You Are Tomorrow.* It needs work on the technique, but the framework of the story and the definition of character is complete."

"Should they be read together?"

"No. The poems come first."

"Sounds great."

"I'll see you in the spring, Judge Nad."

I left to combat my own work, but my real quest was to write creatively. Paul's activities had inspired me.

XIII

Toward the middle of May, my trip home approached. Late one Thursday night, the phone rang shattering my concentration. It was Joy. She was crying.

"Nad?"

"Joy? Want's wrong?"

"I've wanted to call you for months, but Paul asked me not to. Just now he said it was time. He's sick. Very sick, and he wants you to know."

"Sick? What kind of sick? Where is he?"

"He's in the hospital; he's very sick."

"Joy, what kind of sick?"

"He has Hodgkin's disease; it's a cancer of the lymphatic system. It's spread all through his body. He's in pretty bad shape."

"Can I call him?"

"Not now. His condition is very advanced. He's been undergoing intense therapy. Today was a bad, bad day. For a while, we weren't sure he would survive the therapy. He started to pull back together a few hours ago. He gave me permission to call you about it."

"What hospital?"

"He's not going to be there long. They're sending him home."

"When?"

"As soon as he can be moved. Tomorrow or the next day."

"I'll call tomorrow. I'll be home on Saturday, but I'll call tomorrow."

Hodgkin's disease. Cancer. Therapy. Radiation. Chemo. Paul is going to die. Soon. I have to be with him.

By Saturday afternoon, I had dropped off my things in South Philly, and I made the drive out to Paul's house. Paul insisted he be brought home. The hospital disoriented him more than he could bear. As I entered, the cave-like feel of the house smacked me in the face. It was damp, dark, and cool with a dominating unfamiliar smell. A strong overlay of burning incense attempted but failed to cover the scent. The odor penetrated deep inside me. More than anything, the smell—sharp without sweetness—burned the linings of my nostrils, and I struggled to maintain my normal breathing.

Joy, shoulders drooped, eyes heavy and dark, hair disheveled, greeted me with a strained smile that obviously pained her face and a stiff, exhausted hug. She wore panic, fatigue, and resignation over her natural beauty.

"Thanks for coming. It's so nice to see someone who looks healthy. Paul's been asking for you."

"How is he?"

"Bad. Very bad. And he's heavily drugged. They have him on morphine and gin. I think the pain is overwhelming him. He has some lucid moments, but the cancer's spread all through him. He's asked for you a lot. Let me see if he's awake."

She stole into their bedroom for a brief moment.

"He's awake and wants to see you. But I have to warn you, this has really taken so much out of him. He doesn't look the same. Be prepared."

I gritted my teeth and followed her.

The pillows behind his head and shoulders braced him so he could look over at me. His eyes were sunken into cavernous, blackened sockets surrounded by an emaciated, washed-out parchment face. Those eyes managed to show though beneath a shiny, hairless dome. My first thought was to worry that his neck wouldn't hold his head. I wondered if he'd need support to keep it from rolling off his frail, bony shoulders that had once given him such a regal presence. An incense cloud hazed the room, but the smell of his medication burned through. He recklessly waved an arm devoid of muscle. A protruding index finger jabbed toward me in a circular unsteady motion as if he were a drunk trying to hail a taxi deep in the middle of the night on a rainy street in the inner city.

"It's about time you got here. Were you going to wait for the funeral?" His weak laugh yielded to a succession of deep, wet coughs.

"Easy," Joy warned. "He's fragile," she told me before she turned and left us.

"What a mess," Paul said. "Naddie, I need some help, and I need to talk."

"Are you up to it now?"

"I think so. We'll have only couple of opportunities to talk. We'd better take one now."

"Do you have much pain?"

"I'm taking medication all the time. Most of the time, I'm fuzzy. Like I'm a cloud. Not in a cloud but actually a cloud. Not grounded, wispy, and light. Not translucent and disconnected. Like I can't maneuver. My steering mechanisms 're all gone, and I go where I'm taken. Whimsically. I feel like a child's image of an angel. Just floating. But, of course, without the wings and halo."

His delicate laugh again spawned three or four eruptive, shuddering coughs. I continued to listen in silence.

"Sometimes the pain blasts through. One of the biggest problems is my eyesight. I have tumors in my head. They're behind my eyes, and they interfere with the optic nerve. I have trouble focusing. It's like bad reception on the television. Remember sophomore biology? Rods and cones? They're all whacked out too. Even the faintest light drives me wild. The tumors have spread throughout my body. I can actually feel them with my fingers. Have you ever felt a tumor?"

"No. No thanks. What about Joy? How is she?"

"We've talked quite a bit. She's the most amazing person I've ever known. She's strong and loving, but she's weary. She's worn out. She needs a break. I know she'll have it soon."

"And Nicholas. He's grown a lot."

"Yeah, he seems so mature yet so fragile. We're both worried about him. We've talked to him together, and I've talked to him man-to-man. He has some idea of what's going on but not a clear one. I've told him I'm sick and that my body can't handle the sickness anymore, but I told him he's fine, and my sickness won't spread to him or Mom. I've told him I'll have to leave him and Mom soon and that I won't be able to come back, but Mom will stay with him. I tried to explain that I don't want to go, but I have to. I said I'm not leaving because of him but because I'm too sick. I've written him some things that Joy can read to him on each of his birthdays until he's twenty-one. My thoughts and feeling for him and about him. Trying to pass on what I think he might need to know as best I can with time so telescoped. When I talk to him, he cries, and I cry too. But I've got to let him know I'm leaving and that it's not his fault. Nad, when I have these talks with him, somehow I don't seem to feel my physical pain at all."

I couldn't stop my tears. He continued.

"Nad, I want you to help out with my burial. I don't want to be buried in a cemetery. I want to be buried at sea. Can you take care of that for me?"

"Yes."

"It's important to me. Okay, Nad?"

"Yes, but help me understand why."

Paul heaved. He was obviously exhausted. "I feel like I'll be more a part of the universe that way. I don't want people to feel they have to come to one particular place, like a graveyard, to remember me. All life comes from the sea. I want to be part of that cycle. You should have expected that I wouldn't make things easy for you."

His voice began to trail off.

"Why don't you rest a bit? We'll talk more later, OK?" I asked.

"Are you staying here or going home?"

"What would you like?"

"If you could stay for a couple of days, that would be good."

"I'll be here. Now get some rest."

That night, Joy and I talked into the morning. Paul's illness came on suddenly and spread rapidly. They had a modest amount of life insurance and adequate medical coverage, so she didn't have short-range financial concerns.

"I feel so defeated," she said. "We've fought this with all our might, but we just couldn't beat it back. Finding Paul opened my life. He reached deep into my being and surfaced all that was good within me. Now life has betrayed me. I love him so much."

Her speech was modulated, but tears streamed steadily down her cheeks. They united at her chin and escaped to the forming pool on her lap. No words came to me, but Joy had more to say.

"Paul has been an inspiration to Nicholas and me. His resolve and grace permeate all he says and does. He's shown us dignity, but he hasn't withheld even the slightest measure of emotion. He's shown us strength and vulnerability. I wish he didn't have to die. Then he could show us how to live."

She paused to dry her face. "Nicholas adores Paul. Can you see it?" she asked.

"I can see it. Paul's as brilliant as a father as he was dismal as a student..

She laughed ever so slightly.

"He was only dismal at Saint Joe's. At Eastern Pres, he became almost a legend overnight. As a father, he's uncanny. Every instinct is perfect. His intuition almost scares me. I'll never be able to replace him."

"Don't try. You be Nicholas's mother. Paul will always be his male role model."

"I don't know how I can possibly carry on without him."

Fatigue finally prevailed, and she went off to sleep in Nicholas's room.

On the couch, I raced through my senses. The darkness of the house and the smell of incense and medicine numbed me. It was only in retrospect I noted something. Despite the presence of a lovely, healthy, effervescent child, solemnity muted all sounds. Joy tried to maintain quiet, allowing Paul to drift into and out of sleep. Despite his total exhaustion and failing vision, his hearing was fine so far.

The next day, I helped Joy with the house and with Nicholas as much as she would allow. Paul was slow in regaining any strength. It wasn't until early evening that he asked for me.

"I'm not even gone, and I miss my boy already," he said. "The worst part of what I'm feeling is not the pain, although I do hurt quite a bit. Mostly I'm angry I won't be able to play catch with him, to read to him, and to talk to him about his first date, his first love, and his first heartbreak. I won't be there to holler at him when he wrecks my car. I'm seething, but I'm helpless. I've lost this one. All I can do is try to show him I'm sorry to be leaving him, that I'm angry about it, and that it's okay to be angry. I hope, though, I'm showing him courage and dignity. I guess I have quite a few ambitions for these last days. Thanks for staying."

He passed into listlessness. I went into the living room.

Several hours later, Joy signaled that Paul had called for me.

"Remember at Saint Joe's," he started, "we studied a few poems by Emily Dickinson?"

"Yes. Freshman year. Dr. Olin. We sat next to one another."

"When I float in and out of consciousness, I play two of them over and over in my mind. The first one makes me laugh.

> 'I heard a Fly buzz—when I died /
> The stillness in the Room /
> Was like the Stillness in the Air /
> Between the Heaves of Storm.'

"I don't remember the middle part, but I do remember the end.

> I willed my Keepsakes—Signed away
> What portion of me be
> Assignable—and then it was
> There interposed a Fly—
>
> With Blue—uncertain stumbling Buzz—
> Between the light—and me—
> And then the Windows failed—and then
> I could not see to see—

"I've been thinking about that poem. It's ridiculous. Dickinson was either one very together lady, or she had no idea what the imminence of death feels like. I've turned it over and over in my mind. Was she that cavalier about life? Was she that much at peace with herself that, calmly, poetically, she could scoff at death? What an image to link with death! A fly-- buzzing! I've been buzzing myself lately. I think it's all that gin and morphine they're feeding me.

"I think she had both a great sense of humor and an overwhelming sense of serenity and peace. I suppose it helped her to have such tenacious religious beliefs. I guess they would come in handy for me now. Somehow, though, I don't think I'm going to need them. If there's something hereafter, it's too late for me to relive my life. I think I'll just rely on what's gone before. If there's some standard for judging me, I hope it turns out okay. If there isn't, well, then I have nothing to worry about.

"I've lived. I've been as human as I can. That'll have to be enough. The unknown doesn't scare me. It is what it is. I'll find out about that all too soon. My biggest problem is leaving here. Joy and Nicholas, in particular. That's the part that's stripping the layers of strength from me."

I listened but had nothing to offer. I had no words of comfort or hope. Paul wasn't seeking advice. He just wanted to vent. I kept silent.

"The other poem that keeps dancing around and dodging these tumors in my head is this.

Because I could not stop for Death—
He kindly stopped for me—
The Carriage held but just Ourselves—
And Immortality.
We slowly drove—He knew no haste
And I had put away
My labor and my leisure, too,
For his Civility.
We passed the School, where Children strove
At Recess—in the Ring—
We passed the Fields of Gazing Grain—
We passed the Setting Sun—
Or rather—He passed Us—

"She then describes a tomb. Her tomb. I'm hazy on that part, but she gives a glimpse of her eternity. 'Since then—'tis Centuries—and yet / Feels shorter than the Day / I first surmised the horses' Heads / Were toward Eternity—'

"Now, that's a poem about death. I like the endlessness of it. Yet she keeps this temporal framework. I've always thought of time as a measure of change. Does that mean when there's no change, there's no time? I think I should write a philosophy paper about it. I'd probably get a D. Is that what eternity is, Nad? Changelessness? It's an interesting question, isn't it? Does that mean that if there is an eternity, we'll have no contact with the real or the physical? I definitely should write that paper. What do you think, Nad?"

"It would be a typically brilliant paper," I answered.

"I could put together a syllogism. Physicality implies change. Change presumes time. To cut off time, you must cut off all change. So, eternity must be the absence of change. It isn't time without end. It's the end of time. I think I have it. Dickinson understood that, but she didn't quite describe it right. She should have said this.

Because I could not stop for death
He kindly stopped for me
The carriage held but just ourselves
And immobility.
We did not drive—He knew no pace
And I had put away
My labor and my leisure too
I cannot recall the school where children strove
At recess in the ring
I cannot recall the field of gazing grain
Or setting sun
'Tis centuries—and yet
I feel no time since I first surmised
The horses' heads were toward eternity.

"There, I've edited Dickinson. I think I improved her too. I guess you have to be fairly confident your death is right around the next curve to have the balls to rewrite someone like Dickinson. I feel particularly audacious. What do you think, Naddie? Is it an improvement?"

"It's definitely an improvement. I'll let Dr. Olin know," I replied.

"Maybe I'll write some more poems and finally publish my novel. Would that be good?" he asked.

His words were forward looking, but his demeanor was dejected. I could hear the exhaustion in his voice. He spoke with his eyes closed.

"It would be very good, Paul."

"Nad, please ask Joy and Nicholas to come in, and leave us for a few minutes."

"I'll send them right in."

Joy managed a weak smile as she passed me. Nicholas was not fully awake.

After several minutes, a bell chimed from the bedroom. Paul had asked Joy to signal his departure with the ringing of a bell. He had read a poem or a story where the death of a prominent man in the village was announced through the ringing of church bells. Paul said he was confused. Was it Blake? Hardy? Auden? He just couldn't remember the poem. I rushed into the room to see Nicholas holding his father's hand and Joy crying. She had one hand on the bell, and the other was shielding her face. I escorted them out and called Mr. and Mrs. Casabella.

The next days were tumultuous. I argued with Paul's parents, the Archbishop of Philadelphia, the US Coast Guard, the US Navy, and the Environmental Protection Agency while trying to arrange for Paul's burial at sea. I solved all the problems but one. The EPA's opposition proved insurmountable. A regulation prohibited burial at sea unless there were an emergency need to dispose of a body to protect the health and safety of others on the vessel. Joy finally suggested Paul be cremated so he could become part of the very air we breathe. We would then cast his fate and his ashes to the sea. Paul's parents objected at first and then relented. This was the best I could do to approximate Paul's wishes.

It took several weeks to close out Paul's affairs. I tried to help Joy as much as I could. After a while, she told me she would be leaving the area permanently. She needed to cut off all contact with Paul's past—except Nicholas would remain in touch with Paul's family. She said she would contact me if they ever needed anything. She hoped I would understand. I didn't, but I acquiesced.

From time to time, I think I see her and Nicholas, too. I see Paul more often. I pick a feature of his face out of a crowd. Or I see his hair. His stature. I hear his voice. I encounter a trace of his humor. His devilishness is unmistakable to me. His razor wit flashes from time to time. His penetrating insights are impossible to overlook.

As always, he sets the standard, offers the promise, and lends the hope, but his reminder is always that we need more life.

We always need more life.

Skinny Lenny's Front Step

It was a typical August night in the summer of 1969 when Nick DiDominico picked up the three-inch-thick sky-blue hardback volume with "Great American Short Stories" embossed in burgundy script lettering on the cover. He started the short walk across State Street, where he had grown up, to sit in the setting sun on Skinny Lenny's front step.

Some nights his makeshift neighborhood basketball team had a game in the local league at the playground, which was two blocks away and just off the open-air Italian market on Ninth Street. On most other nights, shortly after college broke for the summer, Nad started sitting there, somewhat innocent at first. Even though Saint Joseph's College was less than ten miles from his South Philly row home, Nad lived on campus during the school year because his scholarship covered room and board as well as tuition. In a few weeks, he would begin his senior year. Last year, he had fallen in love with many American short stories in a course of the same name, and he decided to reread one or two each summer night until the special ones became part of him. He expected Nathaniel Hawthorne's "Rappaccini's Daughter" and maybe even Ambrose Bierce's "An Occurrence at Owl Creek Bridge" to fill the time this Thursday evening until dusk had some quelling effect on the heat, if not the humidity, of August in South Philadelphia. He was wrong.

Of course, no one ever called Skinny Lenny just plain "Lenny." From when they first started playing on the side street around the corner, he was always "Skinny" or "Skins" or "Skin." Fat Lenny DiCampo, who lived on that same side street and played with Nad and Skinny every day, was known as Lenny. Skinny was two days older than Nick, and both were born in August. Lenny was only a year older but always several weight divisions ahead. No T-shirt could contain him. He poured out of all of them—no matter what size. Even his father's shirts were too small. He never had baby fat; he had rolls of fat. If you called him Fats or Fat Lenny, though, he would beat you up. It was a good thing Lenny Parisi always weighed about fifty-two and a half pounds and looked like the wind was about to blow him into the river. He became Skinny Lenny. Lenny DiCampo was just plain Lenny. Lenny and his family had left the neighborhood a few years before. Sometimes, but not often, Nad wondered how Lenny was doing. Nad always knew what Skinny was doing, even if he didn't always like it.

Skinny and Nad began traveling different paths as early as fifth grade. School and sports snared Nad. Skinny got stuck on the corner running errands for neighborhood bookies and loan sharks. He then graduated to copping black licorice and Bazooka bubble gum from the candy store on Tenth Street and small bottles of Frank's Vanilla Cream soda and Tastykake chocolate cupcakes, three in a pack, from the corner deli. He didn't steal from Stinky Pete's, the corner hang-out, because he was smart enough to know that if he wanted to play pool there when he got older, he couldn't get thrown out for stealing. Plus, it was his home corner. It was a respect thing. Skinny flunked out of the Catholic high school after one year, and then he quit the public school at sixteen. Even before Nad started Saint Joe's, Skinny was into hot car radios and even hot cars. Finally, it was drugs—pot, acid, speed, downers, and heroin—whatever he could get. The police picked him up regularly, but nothing ever stuck, so he'd be out on the street in a day or two. Skinny never paid attention when Nad tried to drag him in another direction. Skinny talked fast, moved fast, and lived fast. He liked Nad. Lenny respected Nad in his own way. But he never listened.

Of course, Skinny never called Nad "Nick" or "Nad." As a kid, Nad had always stuffed his pockets with old bottle caps and discarded keys. It made him feel like a grown-up—like he had money. The rattle they made ricocheted off the walls of their side alley as he, Skinny Lenny, and the other kids on the block played street games, like kick the can, hide the whip, buck buck, and dead box. Skinny named him "Clanks." So, to the handful of street urchins who played on the little street and their parents, Nad was forever Clanks. To them, Nick DiDominico simply didn't exist. Neither did Nad. Only Clanks.

Nad chose Skinny's step for reading for a couple of reasons. His own step wouldn't do; evening shadows covered his side of the street. To work on his tan and to have better light for reading, he had to go across the street. Directly opposite his house lived the Tenuti's, an elderly couple with elderly children who lived in the South and Midwest. If he sat on their step, depending on their proclivity on any particular night, they would think Nad was either a burglar or a priest, and they would act accordingly, trying to kick him off the step or asking him in to hear their confessions. Nad learned quickly to stay off the Tenutis' front step. He tried the Marellis' step a few times. The Marellis lived next to the Tenutis. The two small Marelli children always wanted him to play, though, so he couldn't read there either. He liked Skinny's step best Besides, if he sat there, he could talk to Skinny when he was around or to Shannon, Skinny's wife of five months.

Shannon played probably the biggest role in why Nad picked Skinny's step. About a year and a half ago, during Christmas break, Nad had noticed Skinny walking with a woman who appeared to be a tall, thin blonde. Winter clothing hid the details, though. On Christmas afternoons, Nad always went to the homes of neighborhood families carrying holiday greetings and some of his mother's famous chocolate chip cookies. He always saved Skinny's for last. A few years ago, when he knocked, Skinny's mother, Lucia, opened the door.

"Clanks! Merry Christmas. Come in and have anisette."

She hugged him through the doorway and into the living room.

"Merry Christmas," he managed. "Skinny here?"

"We're in the kitchen."

She pulled off his coat and dragged him into the kitchen.

"Hey, Clanks! Merry Christmas!" Skinny jumped up with a bear hug and his infectious open grin.

"Merry Christmas, everybody."

At the yellow Formica-topped table sat Skinny's dad, whom Nad thought of as Big Skinny, although he never called him that. Also at the table were Skinny's older sister, Maria (then twenty-three), his sixteen-year-old brother, Jimmy ("Little Skinny," to Nad), and some blonde. Nad smiled at everybody as he sat down.

"Clanks, this is Shannon. She's my girl." Skinny gestured toward the blonde.

Nad caught himself blushing and bumbling as they made eye contact. "Hi, Shannon. Merry Christmas."

She just smiled her hello and looked away. Nad's glance lingered for a prolonged instant in order to take her all in. Her long blond ringlets fell well below her shoulders and over delicate ears. This framed skin so fair that her deep sapphire eyes seemed almost too bright to be real. Her wire-rimmed glasses did nothing to restrain the brilliance of those eyes. They danced almost on their own. Her smile was pleasant and strong, even bold, and it raised her already heightened cheeks to an even higher level. During the next fifteen minutes, Nick divided his thoughts. He tried to keep in step with the conversation about Christmas presents, how school was going, whether the marriage and college deferments would hold so that he and Skinny wouldn't get drafted for Vietnam, and so forth, while also trying to work out where Shannon came from and how Skinny had managed to hook up with such an overwhelming beauty. Then Nad issued himself a warning. Be careful, he thought. This is Skinny's girl.

After two anisettes and a biscotti, Clanks made his farewells with handshakes and hugs around the table. He fumbled with an extended hand to Shannon, who hugged him in return. Back at his house, no one knew very much about Shannon Baker, only that Skinny started bringing her around a month or so ago. She seemed friendly and had started saying hello to Nad's mother the third or fourth time they saw one another, even without an introduction from Skinny.

For the next year and a half, Nad saw Skinny and Shannon only a few times. The summer after that Christmas encounter, Nad worked at a paper mill in Fort Edward, New York, near Lake George, so he was home only a few days between semesters. He did share some anisette with them again the next Christmas. While he saw them rarely, he thought about them often. He had a hard time figuring it out. He didn't think he was jealous of Skinny, although he thought he would be a better match for Shannon. Sure, Skinny was a good-looking guy, but Nad thought of himself as good looking too. Skinny was always in trouble. Shannon could have been a model if she weren't so well developed. It had to be something. Nad knew Skinny had this life-force raging through him—sometimes enraging through him. Sometimes it was out of control, but maybe that was it. Life and love on the edge. Good times. Fast times. Fun and games. Never a dull moment. Nad was more measured in comparison. More serious. More stable. Less spontaneous. Less brazen. Less fun.

Over Easter break, Nad learned that Skinny and Shannon had eloped in Elkton, Maryland, and moved into the Parisi house. In June, Skinny lost his real job as a butcher at the slaughterhouse off the river and was out on the street again.

After final exams, Nad moved back home for the summer. He noticed that, when he started to sit on the Tenutis' or the Morellis' steps, Shannon Baker Parisi would come over to say hello, talk for a minute, and then go back to Skinny's step to sit while he tried to read quietly alone. Over the next week, Nad Clanks DiDominico migrated one step over to Skinny Lenny's front step.

Skinny's step joined with the Parisis' next-door neighbors to form a double-width gray slab, so Nad could move around as the sun shifted. Nad witheld that Lucia would have kept a small mat on the step to cushion its hard surface for him. She hadn't. From Skinny's step, Nad had a snapshot of the neighborhood: a long row of three-story brick fronts. with three marbleized white or gray steps. Some of the houses, including Skinny Lenny's, had black wrought iron railings. All the houses matched, but there were three exceptions. His house was the only one with a bay window curving out on the second and third floors. Four houses to the west of the DiDominico home was the drab green Grace Settlement House, where he and Skinny went half days for two years before kindergarten to receive an introduction to religion and to school from a kind, gentle, nurturing spinster named Miss Elizabeth. Miss Elizabeth was so slight that even Skinny looked fat in comparison. Finally, three doors west of the Settlement House, Bocelli's Bakery filled the morning air with the smell of freshly baked Italian rolls and loaves. This provided Skinny and Nad, as kids, with late-afternoon snacks of deep-dish crusty tomato pies.

Once in a while, when Nad sat on Skinny's step, Skinny would come out and talk to him. "Hey, Clanks. You readin' that college crap again?" he would wisecrack. "All you need to know is in the daily racin' form."

Then they would talk, mostly about cars—GTOs, Corvettes, Thunderbirds, or Mustangs—or they'd talk about how Skinny was picking up some scratch hustling at Willie Mosconi's pool hall on Oregon Avenue. When he saw Skinny with Shannon two Christmases ago, Nad had hoped Skinny would get his life together because of Shannon. Now he wondered if he ever would.

The talks with Skinny were infrequent. He wasn't around much. The talks with Shannon became a ritual.

"How was your day, Clanks? Did you get to handle a million dollars again today?"

Nad had found a summer job in the security vault of a center city bank. He was transferring stocks and bonds from various fund accounts to others. He usually handled several million dollars' worth of securities each day.

"Absolutely, Shannon Baker Parisi. Absolutely."

"You going to stuff a few of those in your pocket for little old Shannon?"

"Oh, Shannon. I'd rather not get shot or go to jail. You're going to have to decide if you'll keep talking to me, even though I'm poor."

"That sound about right, Clanks. I've already got a man who might get shot, and he's seen the inside of a few cells. I'd talk to you even if you didn't have money for a cheesesteak at Pat's."

"Good thing because I don't. I'm saving my money for a car when I graduate. I'll need wheels to get to work. If I work for the bank, it'll be at a branch. More likely, though, I'll go to law school or get a teaching job. A teacher can't take the bus."

Through July and early August, Nad learned that Shannon worked as a seamstress at the Quartermaster, the US Army Defense Supply Depot on Oregon Avenue, that her father had been in the US Army, and that she had grown up all over the country. She had met Skinny outside the Penrose Diner, where she went to lunch one day, and he backed his car into her girlfriend's Buick. Well, it was not exactly his car. She found out later it was stolen, but she was impressed that Skinny had just peeled off ten twenty-dollar bills, handed them to her friend to fix the Buick, and then took them inside and bought them lunch. They had been together ever since.

During their talks, Shannon often punctuated her comments by briefly and lightly touching one of his arms or legs. It was always on a bare spot, and it sent a quiver through him that he hoped he concealed. She was Skinny's wife now. She told him how exciting it had been to be with Skinny at first—how he brought her to places she'd never knew existed, how he made her feel like a queen, how he partied hard and often, and how he took her to Vegas for a week. In the most recent couple of talks, though, she confided that she was worried about the future. Skinny showed no signs of stability. He was often on edge or over the edge. He was usually out all night, and she worked all day. They did nothing as a couple. Nothing. Plus, he never had any money. She was paying all the bills—the rent and food bills, which were small, and the car payment, which was not. She told him she loved Skinny but was worried.

Tonight, she came out early. It was just before seven. He'd not yet finished "Rappaccini's Daughter."

"Hey, Clanks. You readin' that college crap again?" She opened with her Skinny imitation, a flashy smile, and a tender lightning touch of his arm.

"You sound like your husband," he fired back.

"Please, spare me that!"

The remark surprised him. "Oh, by the way, Mrs. Skinny, if you want to—"

"Clanks, don't!" she interrupted. "Not Mrs. Skinny. I don't think I can take that."

"Okay, Shannon Baker Parisi."

"How about just plain Shannon? Or Shannon Baker? The Parisi hasn't really set in."

"Shannon Baker, if you want to have serious conversations with me, maybe you should call me Nad."

"Nad? What kind of a name is Nad?"

"They're my initials. Nicholas Amadeo DiDominico. Most people call me Nad."

"Your name is Nicholas? Like Santa Claus?"

"Same name. Different guy. So, talking about Mr. Skinny, where is that husband of yours? What's he up to these days?"

"Still skinny. Upstairs. Asleep, I think. Getting ready for another all-nighter at the pool hall. Or shooting up."

"Shooting pool, you mean?"

"No, I mean shooting up."

"Shooting up? What's going on?"

"Come on, Saint Nick. You know what's going on. He's been your friend all his life."

"When did this start again?"

"A couple of months ago. That was when I really found out."

"Have you tried to talk to him?"

"He won't talk to me. He won't talk to anybody. You know this was a mistake for me. You've known him longer than anybody. You know he'll never change. I found his needle and some stuff, heroin, in his room. One of these days, he's gonna get a bad batch. Then I won't be Mrs. Skinny anymore. Maybe, you'll still be—"

Before her next words made their way out, a shrill wail pierced them through the red brick walls of the Parisi house.

"Help! Help!" It was Lucia.

Nad jumped up, but Shannon got up more slowly and awkwardly blocked his way. He finally made it by her and ran to Lucia on the second floor. She was leaning over Skinny's comatose body. He was prostrate on the hallway floor outside the bathroom, and a syringe was dangling from his left arm.

"Help! Help!" Lucia cried. "I think he's dead."

Nad reached over, found a pulse, and then barked at Shannon to call an ambulance.

"If I call an ambulance, the police will come and arrest him," she shot back coldly.

Lucia and Nad stared back at her. Both were stunned.

"You'd rather have him dead than in jail?" Nad answered. "Call an ambulance."

Shannon just stood there with her arms folded.

"Lucia, go call an ambulance. I'll try to revive him."

Nad carefully removed the needle, ran into the bathroom, and started the cold water running in the tub.

"Give me a hand, Shannon," he spit out.

When she didn't answer, he made a quick swivel to find her gone. He gently dragged Skinny through the doorway and lifted him into the tub. He couldn't stop himself from thinking, Good thing Skinny is skinny. He propped him up to keep him from drowning. After a few minutes, Skinny's breathing became regular, and he opened his eyes slightly.

"Clanks, what's up, my man? What're you doin' here, my man?"

"You're going through a bad one, Skinny. Maybe some bad stuff. Too pure or cut with something bad."

"Can't ever be too pure, my man."

"Hang in there, Skinny. An ambulance is coming."

"No ambulance. I'm not goin' to jail."

"Can't let you die, Skinny. Worry about jail later if you have to."

"Right, man. College guy. Got all the answers. Where's Shannon, my man?"

"Too upset to deal with this now. She's standing outside and waiting for the ambulance."

"She probably called the police too."

"I don't think so, Skinny."

"Hey, Clanks. I'm feelin' pretty good now. Thanks, my man."

"Yeah, Skinny. You've got to get straight, man. You've got to get a life. You got a wife now."

"Yeah. Got a wife, my man."

Just then, Lucia rushed into the bathroom. "I'll stay with him now, Clanks. Thanks. You saved my Lenny's life."

Nad nodded and started down the steps as the ambulance roared up.

Outside, Shannon stood alone in front of the Tenutis' place. As Nad approached, she reached out and hugged him tightly. It was a whole-body hug, and she kissed him full on the lips. "Nad, it wasn't supposed to happen this way. I'm too young to have my life ruined. I want to have a family but not his. I want a nice life. A normal life. Maybe married to a banker or a lawyer or a teacher."

Nad's thoughts fluttered. Beautiful Shannon. She felt so good in his arms—soft, smooth, and warm. She smelled so sweet, like wild, lavish flowers in an exotic garden. Then his mind's eye flashed to a rickety wooden footbridge high on a country trail. He saw himself plunging into the swirling rapids of the river below. He looked up. Beautiful Shannon. Whacked-out Skinny. They were carrying him out on a stretcher. He was conscious but groggy. Nad instinctively pushed back from her. “I’m sorry, Shannon. I can’t help you. You better go to your husband.”

Nad Clanks DiDominico stumbled back to the Tenuti step to finish his reading of “Rappaccini’s Daughter.”

Seeing Heather

Sammy walked into my house to join his cousin, Nad. Nad and Sammy were two of my closest friends, even though they were both a few years younger than I was. They shared the same warmth, kindness, and concern for those they cared about, but their demeanors couldn't have been more dissimilar. Nad had gone to college, and his world had expanded beyond State Street, beyond the neighborhood, and beyond Philadelphia itself. He never rejected his roots, but he acquired a bit more polish, sophistication, aplomb. He was South Philly all the way, but he could relate to the bigger community in a way Sammy couldn't begin to contemplate.

Nad would stop by for a brief visit whenever he was in the neighborhood. Nad's presence was calming to me. Reassuring. Settling. He liked to talk about the old days on the street. Buck buck, deadbox, hot summer days cooling off under the fire plug. Sammy's presence electrified the air. All arms and elbows, he muscled his way through the day talking about the most mundane things in a way that would make it seem that the whole world would want to know about them.

When Sammy walked in, Nad gave him a big hug. I could feel Nad recede into the background probably to watch the Sammy show. I could sense Sammy was all amped up over something. I just didn't know what… yet

Then it came. He said he had seen her and that she was asking for me, except Sammy didn't speak that way. What he actually said was, "I seen her. I seen Heather, and she was dressed to the nines." I could hear Nad silently smile and he probably turned in to listen more closely.

"What did she look like?" I asked.

I excused his misuse of "seen," as I would excuse his "dees" and "doz." Sammy and I had been friends since birth. He and Nad had stuck with me through the trouble. They had even visited me in the hospital. Nad came when he could; Sammy came every day. Now, years later, he still never missed a chance to come by for a talk or to take me out for a walk. There wasn't much I wouldn't excuse for Sammy Berardo.

"Same hair," he answered. "Not really blond. Not really red. Not really brown. Same green eyes. You remember. She looks da same."

"Sammy, I've told you before. I don't remember that part of her so well," I confessed, again. "Did you speak to her, Sammy?" I wanted more.

"Sure. And she talked right back at me too. She got married to some doctor or lawyer. Got a four-year-old kid. Boy. Named him Stephen. Calls him that too. Not Steve or Stevie."

I interrupted. "Stephen? Is that so?"

"Yeah, that's so. Really," he went on. "She left downtown. Lives out in da burbs. Drives a Jag. But she din't seem so happy."

"How do you know that?"

Sammy had this annoying tendency of telling a story as if there were no limits on the day—as if time were eternal and nothing would ever change. I knew better. Everything had already changed for me. It had changed twelve years ago.

Sammy started back in. "I don' really know. She din't say too much. See, I axed her how it was going, and she sez she's got a great kid and all, and she shows me a bunch of pitchers. Good-lookin' kid, but he don' look Italian enough for me."

"Sammy! Why do you think she's unhappy?" I tried to maintain my patience.

"I din't say unhappy, Stevie. I sez not so happy."

"Come on, Sammy. Tell me."

"Well, ya see, when she had the pitchers out, I axed to see one of her old man, and she shoots back, kinda tough, 'Oh, I don' have one of *him.*' 'Why not?' I axe her. And she sez, 'Why bother?' And I sez because he's your old man, dat's why bother, and she comes right back, 'We're just goin' trew da motions for Stephen.' Except she sez it real nice. You remember how good she talks."

"Yes, I remember."

The rest played inside my head. I remembered everything about her except the way she looked. I remembered her voice—not low and resonant from deep in her throat. Happier, lighter, and quicker like a wine spritzer with a squeeze of lime. I could listen to her speak forever. Once, I thought I would.

And I remembered her touch—light enough to be called tender—like she would be able to cradle a fallen sparrow. Yet it was somehow strong and demanding too. It was a pianist's touch, seeking and always finding just the right spot. Never a missed note. Never a wrong chord. Everything had to be perfect. She once told me I was perfect for her. But that all changed in one instant. In one shattering flash. In one too-slow blink of the eye.

And I remembered her feel—soft, smooth, quaveringly alive, and exquisitely ready. Never compliant. She was more challenging than compliant. Challenging what, I never knew. Maybe me. Maybe herself. Maybe perfection.

And her scent. Oh, did I remember her scent! Not lilac. Not lavender. Not jasmine. The most alluringly provocative mixture I'd ever known—a fragrance that sent me uncontrollably wild, even before my heightened acuity. Sometimes when I concentrated to my limit, I could still smell her in my pillow.

"Hey, Stevie, you listenin' to me or what here? I'm tryin' to tell ya about Heather. You wanna hear or not?"

The air rustled. I could sense his arms waving broadly. "I'm sorry. I was just thinking. What did she say about me?"

"Dat's what I'm tryin' ta yell ya. Where ya been?"

"Just thinking."

"You're always goin' off somewhere just thinkin'. Good thing I'm your friend, or I'd think ya was snobbin' me or something."

"He would never do that," Nad interjected. "Sammy, just go on with what happened next."

I added, "I would never snub you, Sammy. I'm sorry. Go ahead. What'd she say about me?"

"Well, she sez, 'You still see Stevie? You still keep in touch?'

"And I sez, 'Sure, I still see Stevie, and he still don' see me.' I tried to make a little joke, but she shot me a look. Scrunched up her nose. Ya remember how she used to scrunch up her nose, right, Stevie?"

"Actually, I can't quite remember that either. I try, but I remember only the last time I saw her."

"Whaddya mean the last time ya saw her, Stevie?"

"The night of the accident. Before she left me. Before I wasn't perfect enough for her. We were driving home late on Delaware Avenue, down at the river by the train tracks. The semi crossed over onto our side. I could see the impact coming. I heard her scream, and as I threw myself toward her side of the car to protect her, the last thing I saw was the terror in her eyes. Her mouth gaped open in horror. The windshield shattered, and you know the rest. That was the last time I saw her. That was the very last time. And now, even when I try, I still can't see her face."

"I'm sorry, Stevie. I'm sorry."

"I know you are, Sammy. You're a great friend. You too, Nad."

"Sammy, I think Stevie needs to be alone now," Nad interposed.

"Yeah, I think I need to be alone for a bit," I said.

"Yeah, sure. See ya tomorrow, Stevie. Let's go, Nad"

"You, too. Next time, Nad."

"Bye."

When they left, I made my way into my bed, buried my head in the pillow, and concentrated to my limit.

The Plug Fight

Nad guided his Chevy Blazer up State Street to his block between Tenth and Eleventh. Actually, it was his parents' block. Regardless, he began looking for a place to park. As he maneuvered between rows of parked cars, he thought it remarkable that SEPTA bus drivers could routinely cruise up this street without taking the side view mirrors off the parked cars on either side. Twenty-eight years ago, when he last lived on State Street, no SEPTA buses rattled the windows and shook the walls roughly every thirty minutes. Back then, there was no SEPTA. Instead, PTC operated the urban transit system, and while green-and-cream trolleys with single cyclops-like headlights clattered and clanged north on Eleventh Street and south on Twelfth and smoke-spewing buses roared south on Tenth, State Street was spared the convenience and irritation of a transit route.

He drove past his parents' house toward the west end of the block. Typically, parked cars packed the street. Because it was evening, the cars belonged mostly to residents. On Saturdays, the spillover traffic from the Italian market one block away clogged the street even more. Only outsiders called it the Italian market. Nad, his family, and the rest of South Philly simply used "Nint' Street" to refer to the open-air street market where neighborhood merchants set up creaky wooden stands on wheels to sell fresh fruit and produce that came in right off the boat through the food distribution center on old Dock Street. The prices discouraged chain supermarkets from locating in the area. In fact, Nad didn't enter a supermarket until he went away to college. The Ninth Street store owners sold meats straight from the slaughterhouses and poultry that was alive when you picked it out and then was killed, defeathered, and cut while you waited. Fish on ice piled high in wooden fruit baskets sold out every Friday. The local merchants pedaled housewares made in America and everything else you could think of. Back in the days before the state lottery came into existence, home grown bookies surreptitiously hawked the daily street number.

Nad drove slowly and looked for a spot. Only the air conditioning kept the aggravation at bay. He eased the Blazer into the space in front of 1037 State Street, and he remembered that when he was growing up, this space always remained open. A fire hydrant protected the spot in front of 1037. He didn't remember when or why the plug was removed, but on this August evening, on his way to pick up his son at his parents' home, where both Nad and his dad grew up, for some reason, his memory carried him back thirty-five years to when the neighborhood stopped using the State Street plug.

That summer had been unusually hot, and so it seemed that they played under the plug more often than ever before. Nad, called Clanks in the neighborhood, and his buddies—Chubby, Jimmy, Skinny Lenny, Louie, Chooch, Stevie, Rocco, Petey, Angela, and Loraine—weren't allowed under the State Street plug. The street was too busy with traffic, and State Street ran the width of South Philly. It was too visible to the cops, who would come by and turn off the water so the city's supply could be preserved in case of fire. That was what his mother would tell him. So, during the day, the neighborhood kids were relegated to the plug around the corner up the little street. Nad (that is, Clanks) would ask his mother, "Mom, can I go under the plug around the corner up the little street? Shirley's going to open it for us."

This alternative to the urban swimming pool kept the kids out of trouble—for the most part. They took turns spraying the water by sticking their butts up against the mouth of the plug. The city had passed an ordinance requiring the use of metal tubes that attached to the hydrants.

This created a spray that reduced water usage, but his neighborhood didn't have one, and when he went under one in another neighborhood, Nad didn't like it. He and his buddies preferred the back-and-forth of making sprays and being pummeled by the powerful gushes of water that could push them clear across the little street.

The grown-ups used the plug on State Street. They would turn it on only at night, though. They sneaked out about nine or ten o'clock, after the kids were supposed to be asleep. Nad's house was on the opposite side of the street from the plug. He would frequently steal into his parents' bedroom, with its bay window, which was covered with gray speckled asphalt shingles. It overlooked the street, and he'd kneel with his chin on the sill so he, without being noticed, could watch the adults have a blast from the hydrant. From his hideaway, he saw many of his neighbors turn back their clocks anywhere from ten to twenty years to seek some relief from the city swelter. They had fun, and Nad loved watching.

Nad's mother and father frequently participated in the hydrant bathing, but the ringleaders were Ron and Marie—the Passantis. They lived at 1039 with their three daughters, including Angela, Nad's friend. Angela was Nad's age but rougher and tougher by a long shot. She could run faster than most of the boys and had a worse temper. She was one of the most mischievous kids on the block and the most daring. At eight years old, Angela led a troupe of seven-, eight-, and nine-year-olds on their one-speed, two-wheel bicycles down Broad Street. They traveled the three miles to Municipal Stadium, long since demolished, to hurtle down a steep, rocky, pockmarked dirt hill known as Suicide Mountain. Each of the kids, except Angela, was terrified. Fortunately, Skinny Lenny's broken left arm was the only real injury. It was also Angela who had tempted Nad in the darkness of the back alley by offering to show him hers if he would show her his. Nad had broken into a sweat and run out of the alley. And it was Angela who punched Cooch in the stomach with all her might because he called her sister, Arlene, a bitch. It didn't matter to Angela that Arlene had physically thrown Cooch off their front step and told him never to come back because she had tripped trying to go around him when getting into the house. Angela said she didn't care Arlene was in the wrong. She was her sister, and Cooch had to get socked for calling her a bitch.

Angela took after her father's side of the family. Ron was devilish too. He would frequently toss the neighborhood women—particularly Nancy and Helen, who were both attractive and outgoing—under the open plug, but it was always in a good-natured, playful way. No one was ever offended. They were used to Ron being the life of the party. He worked on the docks unloading cargo and had a stevedore's disposition—tough, hardworking, fun loving, and loyal to his family and friends.

Ron and Marie controlled the plug wrench, so whether or not the hydrant opened depended largely on them. It didn't take much effort to get Ron to start things up.

Often, Nad's dad would wait until well after the party started to wander over in his bathing suit. Sometimes he would just sit on the step at 1039 and talk with those neighbors who didn't feel young or adventurous enough to jump under the spray. At other times, he'd be right in the middle of things. Nad's mother never hesitated. She would be under the plug, laughing and playing, mostly with Nancy, who lived on Nad's side of the street across from Ron and Marie.

Nad's mother and Nancy were best friends, although Nancy was a few years younger. It thrilled Nad that Nancy and his mother were so close. He liked Nancy. She always took time to ask him about school or basketball or his building project. (Nad had an Erector Set with an electric motor.) Nad thought she was the prettiest woman in the world—even prettier than his mom, who radiated the best in Italian beauty. She had long, wavy dark hair and high cheekbones that slimmed to a thin but not pointed chin. Perfect olive skin encased deep-set, soft-brown eyes. Nancy took the best of these attributes—the cheekbones, chin, and skin—and added hazel eyes, a smile that could light up the night, and auburn hair, which was cut somewhat shorter than his mother's. Nad had heard his mother call Nancy's hairstyle a pageboy cut. Nancy didn't look like a boy to Nad, though. In the winter, she would wear these tight-fitting, fine-gauge sweaters that accentuated her figure. She was not exceptionally thin but not big either—something short of voluptuous. Perfect, Nad thought. In the summer, her sleeveless blouses and pedal pushers left Nad dizzy. When the plug was on at night, he would strain at the windowsill to see Nancy in her bathing suit. Sometimes it was a one-piece, which held his gaze raptly. Sometimes it was a two-piece, which set off a torrent of uncontrollable fantasies.

It broke Nad's heart that Nancy had already married Joe D'Aquilla, who was Ron's presumed best friend and frequent accomplice in starting and prolonging plug parties on summer nights. Nad thought Joe was a pretty good guy, even though he blocked the fulfillment of Nad's prepubescent dream. Joe worked at the pretzel factory down the street. He delivered soft pretzels all over the city. Every night, he brought home leftovers, and Nancy would dole them out to the kids on the block—Nad first. Back then, the larger soft pretzels in vogue today had not yet attained any popularity. The little soft pretzels, about four inches long and two inches wide, sold two for a penny. They would disappear in about five seconds with two aggressive bites.

From time to time, on particularly hot nights, visitors from other streets in South Philly, usually from farther south, would join the pool parties. Nad didn't like that so much. The outsiders brought a different feel to the street, even though they were always close friends or relatives of State Streeters. Nad felt a sense of ownership for the street.

He remembered clearly that August night when he and Angela were playing near the mailbox on the corner of Eleventh and State. A cyclops PTC trolley churned up Eleventh and ground to a stop at the concrete island in the middle of the street in order to discharge passengers. Several of these islands separated the northbound from the southbound traffic on Eleventh Street, making the oversize thoroughfare a fairly unique street in South Philly. Most of the other streets were too narrow to need or accommodate these barriers. The islands protected transit riders, but they would ambush a couple of motorists a year when their warning lights would burn out. When that happened, night drivers would maroon their cars with the front ends sticking up at thirty-degree angles. These dockings usually occurred between one and three in the morning, waking the neighborhood and provoking a round of cursing. Usually, Nad's dad, Ron, and Joe would reluctantly scurry out to help the driver, who would typically be either half-asleep at the wheel or more than a little tipsy.

This particular night, one passenger stepped off the cyclops. He was a big guy with thick, dark curly hair, a barrel chest, and blacksmith arms. He was carrying a brown paper shopping bag.

"That's my uncle Mario," Angela shouted to Nad. "My sister and me just call him our uncle. He's actually my dad's cousin. It looks like he's got his stuff to go under the plug. I love him," she said. "Doesn't he look like a movie star? Uncle Mario! Uncle Mario!" She ran off to greet him.

"Hey, babe. How's my chick?" Mario swaggered toward Angela with a toothpick sticking out of the right side of his mouth. He had a hitch in his walk. Nad remembered rolling his eyes as Mario asked her, "Who's the squirt here? He your guy?"

"This is Clanks," Angela answered. "He lives down the street. We're friends."

"Clanks, huh? You got rocks rollin' around in your head, Clanks? You be nice to my girl here, or you answer to Mario. You got it?"

Nad looked at him blankly; Mario turned and strutted over to 1039.

The crowd gathered early that night, even before dark. Bocelli's, at 1030 State, made tomato pies—big squares of dough smothered in tomato paste with large chucks of tomato. The swelling group readily consumed these Italian delights. Nad's parents, Joe and Nancy, Ron and Marie, Romeo Cameri, Clarisse Penter (from the lone Lebanese family on the block), Skinny Lenny's parents, Cooch's folks, and a few others drifted over to 1039 as the party started. After dark, when Nad was supposed to be in bed, he crawled over to the window to watch the grown-ups. They were now in their bathing suits and were standing by as Ron turned the plug on to full volume. Water cascaded across State Street. Everybody got into the act.

Ron carried Marie out to the street and placed her right in front of the gushing water. Romeo filled a bucket with water and chased Clarisse halfway down the block before soaking her. Everyone was festive. Nad's dad made a spray so that Helen, Johnny, Sue, and all could get wet gradually.

Nad searched for Nancy. Finally, he found her with Joe. She was soaked to the bone and on the step at 1039. She wore her yellow two-piece suit. She and Clarissa (at twenty-three, the youngster of the group) always attracted attention. Clarisse was shy compared to Nancy, though, so Nancy was in the middle of things, while Clarisse stayed kind of low key. After a few minutes, Nancy stood up, grabbed a bucket, and crept up behind Ron. She poured the cold water right onto his head, extracting the desired scream. She laughed and turned to run away. Ron caught her in a few seconds and carried her to the plug, retaliating by dousing her with cold water. Everybody laughed.

Mario got wet right away and then spent several minutes combing his hair. When Nancy walked by him, he made some kind of remark that made her laugh, and Nad watched as Mario followed her with his eyes as she went to sit on the 1039 step. She rested her back against the top step with her elbows out next to her ears and her hand cradling her head. Her legs extended down to the first step. Stretched out this way, she looked irresistible. Water dripped from her auburn hair down past her tanned shoulders to the yellow top of her suit. Nad kept his eyes fixed on her. Joe was under the spray.

Joe was a wiry guy. He was about five foot eight and had arms like those cables on cranes—very, very taut. He had been a star on the sports teams in high school. In football, he was a slashing, cutback scatback. He was the shooting guard on the basketball team and an All-City second baseman. His competitive days ended between high school and college when he tore up his knee sliding into home. He never came back from that injury, but he didn't seem bitter. He kept fit by lifting weights and playing ball in various leagues in South Philly with Ron. He had a great friend and a great looking wife—his grade school sweetheart. All in all, Joe was a happy guy.

Nad watched from his window as Mario came over, sat right next to Nancy, and said something again. She frowned and waved him away. He kept right on talking. After a minute, he turned quickly toward her and ran his right hand down her stomach and onto her suit between her legs. He stuck his whole right arm behind her knees. He simultaneously reached his left hand across her chest, starting at her left breast, going to her right breast, and then going around her back. He picked her up and carried her to the gushing water. She managed to free a hand and slapped him hard across the face. The laughter stopped, and everyone heard her holler, "You scum! Don't you feel me up!"

"You asked for it, bitch," Mario shouted back. "You know you like it, you tease."

Joe raced over and pushed Mario toward the left with his right forearm. He punched Mario in the face with a powerful left jab. Mario staggered and fell in a heap. Ron rushed over, blocking Joe and pushing him back with both hands. Joe's eyes glazed over. In response to Ron's push, he launched a right uppercut to Ron's stomach. Ron fought back, and the two best friends traded punches until Nad Sr. and Romeo got between them to restore some order.

"Your cousin grabbed my wife," Joe shouted.

"I can't believe you hit me," Ron answered.

"I can't believe you defended that prick," countered Joe.

"Don't be an asshole. I was only trying to keep you from killing him."

"You should have kept that asshole out of our neighborhood."

"You should have kept your wife in line."

Joe tried to rush Ron again, but Nad Sr. and Romeo blocked them again.

Rosa took Nancy back home, and Marie finally settled Ron down. Eventually, everyone dispersed. Somebody closed the plug, and the street went to sleep, restlessly.

During the next few days, the tension on State Street elevated as the summer heat scorched out new records. For days, nobody came out to sit on their steps at night. Things were relatively normal only for the kids. The next week, one by one, the families started to come out. Slowly, they began to socialize again —except for Ron and Joe. Nad couldn't remember the neighborhood ever going under the plug after that night. Joe and Ron never really patched things up, and Nad never saw them together again. At some point, the city removed the hydrant.

Nad finished parking his car, and he walked over to his parents' house to pick up his son, who was delighted to be playing with Nancy. Over the years, she had grown from pretty to beautiful to elegant. Nad thought it was too bad the neighborhood hadn't changed in the same way.

Falling Leaves

She awoke to falling leaves and the chilling realization that another summer—fifty-five in all now—had sped by hardly noticed. Bare trees and frosted grass provided irrefutable evidence. Rita DiDominico hauled an achy body from her pristine bed to the drafty hardwood floor. She reflected that she had no clear thoughts on what to do today. For the past thirty years, structure had imposed itself on her itinerary—get out of bed, do the morning routine, and commute to work by train while reading the morning paper. She feasted on a bagel for breakfast at her desk. On days when she needed a change, she had a muffin. Her work as an accountant at a major firm had sustained her but in an uninspired, pedestrian way.

Today she started her morning rituals as if nothing had changed. Then she stopped. There would be no business suit, tailored slacks, or dress. She pulled on a pair of old sweat pants and a faded turtleneck, fetched the paper, and sat with her coffee: Maxwell House, which was good to the very last drop.

It seemed like only weeks ago that, as a young woman, hope and promise had coursed through her soul and energized her life. She now knew that ephemeral spirit had fled—ephemeral, like her youth. Too many summers had since passed, and with each one, she became less aware of its departure but more settled in and more somber in her life.

By rote, she thumbed through the paper, but then her gaze stuck to a photo. It was of beautiful horses girded for riding and hitched outside a stable in Bucks County. It was a bucolic picture of both serenity and vigor. Rita had never been much for the outdoor life. She preferred the arts. Her brother, Nad, two years younger, was the explorer in the family. Several times he had asked her to hike and camp with him and his son. She always declined, typically preferring a book in a comfortable stuffed chair by a cold fireplace. She never had the energy to carry in firewood, and she feared her house would go up in flames if she did. Eventually the invitations stopped. She now wished she had accepted them and other passed-up opportunities.

She asked herself if today could be different. Could she unstick her gaze and do something about her daydream? Could today be a beginning? Rita had not had many beginnings. She stared at the photo. Could she learn to ride a horse at her age? Her thoughts wandered. Riding a bike is probably harder, and I can do that, she thought. Well, I used to be able to do that. It had been so long. Why do I struggle with every decision? she thought. Why can't I reach out?

The Blind Canyon Ranch was northwest of New Hope, Pennsylvania, and just forty-five minutes from her suburban home. It offered riding lessons and horses for hire. Will I do it? I haven't tried anything different in years. Small beads of sweat stained her brow, and she could feel her breathing accelerate. Early retirement presented these challenges. She continued to mull it over. I do have to fill my time. I really don't have anything else to do. Will I even be able to get on the horse? Will I fall off? Will I look like an old fool? After all, I'm fifty-five, inexperienced, and out of shape. Will there be anyone there to help me? Should I call in advance or just show up? Should I wear sweat pants? Should I go back to bed?

She thought of her grandparents—now gone. They had emigrated from Italy when they were barely beyond their teens. They decided to cross an ocean without knowing what to expect, and I can't decide what to wear to Bucks County. Maybe Mom will know what to wear. If she didn't, it wouldn't matter. If my mother wanted to go horseback riding, she would figure it out, and she wouldn't be naked.

Rita thought back to the old days in South Philly playing with Nad in the little street around the corner from their home until darkness set in and their mother would scream for them from the front step. As street kids, they played and played—hard and frivolously. They were searching for joy, not identities. Their identities were clear: they were full-fledged Americans. That was what their mother told them. Yes, they were of Italian descent, but they were full-fledged Americans. Neither Rita nor her brother had even been to Italy, but from the stories their grandparents told, they felt a bond to the old country.

Nad, though younger, had forged the way, excelling in school, going to college, and making a success of his life. As the first boy in the household, he broke the ice, set the trend, and made it possible for Rita to go to parties, to go on dates, and even to continue her education beyond high school. She was the firstborn, but she had to wait until Nicholas did things to do them. Had it not been for him, her life would have been even more conservative. Her parents embraced old-world principles. They believed in education, and they encouraged Nicholas to learn and achieve. Nad, in turn, rejected the then-conventional gender-based view that women should learn only to cook and sew; he reinforced to his parents that Rita should have the same opportunities he had.

She had commuted daily to a city college, where she majored in finance and devoted most of her time and all her concentration to learning. Her few casual acquaintances occupied very little of her time; instead she chose to center her social life on her family—her parents, her brother, and the extended family. Despite her appearance, she had almost no real social life. Diminutive in stature and build, her clear, perfect Mediterranean skin framed features that were not quite round yet not quite angular. Her face was appealing, but her almond-shaped, almost-black eyes and her long, thick, almost-black wavy hair clearly set her apart. She dated occasionally, but she had yet to meet anyone who excited her. As a commuter, she didn't integrate into campus life. Family, the neighborhood, and the trappings of her adolescence provided the substance for this stage of her life. Protected by this environment, she spurned adventure and experimentation. By age twenty, she had a settled life with modest ambitions.

Academics came easily, and, as a result, Rita obtained a job offer in the center city office of a national accounting firm. Her first two years there were unsettling. She was forced to interact with more people—particularly men—than ever before. The adjustment to professional activities paled in comparison to her adjustment to the social interactions of a male-dominated environment. She hadn't often worked with men and found the dealings awkward and a bit artificial. Her mother, in an attempt to protect and nurture her, cautioned her with old-fashioned views about men and their predilections and intentions. So, she reacted tentatively, and she was suspicious of their attempts to be friendly and cordial. She feared they might take advantage of her, use her, and discard her. She feared their motives might be selfish and callous. She restrained herself, building a wall of formality for protection. This ploy meant that, despite her warm, attractive physical appearance, her deportment projected a cold, aloof, and unresponsive image. After the first several months, her coworkers began to reciprocate, and work became as dull as the rest of her life.

Then Ted arrived. He had gone straight from college into the military and had just arrived from his tour of duty with an honorable discharge. He had an active face and chestnut hair. He was tall, wiry, and handsome. The spring in his step matched the energy in his voice and the smile in his eyes. Everyone liked Ted, and Ted especially liked Rita. Her coolness failed to put him off. He took it for shyness and burrowed straight through it. After several weeks on the job, he invited her to lunch. At lunch, she felt an instant connection with him. She opened herself as never before and talked freely about her fears and aspirations. Somehow, he seemed trustworthy. Time flew by for both of them.

The next week, it was a casual dinner directly after work. She started to learn about him Ted was the youngest of three sons and was from a suburban family. He was not Italian; he wasn't really anything. He was part Brit, part Irish, part German, part Austrian, and part unknown.

His father was a banker. The oldest brother was a doctor, and the middle brother was a teacher. Ted loved music—all kinds. Popular, jazz, and classical. He loved to dance. He drank but moderately. He liked fast cars and bicycle riding. He wanted comfort but not necessarily wealth, and he wanted a family. More than anything, he wanted a family.

Rita, in turn, told him about growing up in South Philly. She talked about the parochial schools dominated by nuns who taught that mastering the twelve times table provided an inside track to both success and heaven. She talked about hot summer nights on the streets, with the fire hydrant dousing relief from the city swelter for all the neighborhood folks, who danced without inhibition under the spray. She talked about Christmases with the entire family—more than fifty aunts, uncles, cousins, and whomever—gathered in their small row home to tell stories and drink homemade wine. Ted's interest in her history was sincere. He encouraged her with questions; he wanted to know all about her.

Rita decided that night that she wanted Ted, and a change swept over her. The barriers fell, and she allowed her spirit to flow. She now took her smile, always bright and charming, everywhere.

Ted and Rita became inseparable. They lunched together at work every day they could, and after work, they would often go out to eat. They saw one another on weekends for concerts, movies, and walks by the river. Their mutual infatuation deepened. Love blossomed, and their talks became more serious. They had not spent a night together, but they wanted to. Though the mores of the time didn't sanction it, their youth and love would not be denied. They arranged to travel to Washington, DC, for a weekend. Rita assured her family they had arranged for separate rooms.

As the weekend approached, Rita felt more alive than ever. She packed days in advance and arrived at work early that Friday. She was a bit surprised when Ted didn't appear for morning coffee, but she knew he'd arrive soon. At ten o'clock, her boss called her into his office. She sat there distracted and thought only of her weekend, and then she vaguely began to realize her boss was talking about "bad news." She heard "an accident" and "Ted" and "serious." She left for the hospital immediately, but she didn't arrive in time.

The next days and weeks blurred. Panic, anger, and despair merged into a numbness than began to trademark her life. Her family embraced her, but Rita couldn't respond. All her nerve endings had been shattered. She felt betrayed and abandoned. A life of promise settled into a perfunctory passage through time.

Rita continued to go into work every day, and she performed her responsibilities effectively but without interest. More and more, she retreated into family—her mother, her father, Nad, and his son. As her parents aged, she assumed more and more responsibility for their care and entertainment. Now that she was retired, she could more fully support them, although they were both robust and active. She stared at the pictures of the horses.

She called the Blind Canyon Ranch for directions and made an appointment for later that day. Robert, the owner, encouraged her. She would be welcome there. He would go through the basics with her, and before long, she would be riding. He guaranteed it.

The brilliant colors of autumn pointed the way up the twisting riverside road into New Hope and beyond. Even on a weekday, tourists dotted the streets of the artist colony. It had once been a terminal point of the Underground Railroad, where southern slaves fled to find freedom and a new hope for independent lives. Now a bustling tourist attraction, New Hope still managed to retain some of its original charm.

Blind Canyon Ranch presented itself on Upper Mountain Road. It was just a few miles out from New Hope. Rita came to the stable. An unwashed wooden fence formed a corral, and the stable was set back from the road. Beyond the stable was the old ranch house—maybe a hundred years old. It was built mostly of fieldstone but had rustic wooden shutters. The ranch didn't look like much to her at all. She expected a sprawling series of barns and stables and houses and silos. What she couldn't help but notice were the smells. The pungent aroma of manure, horses, hay, and life smacked her and slowed her approach. She stole up to the house and searched for Robert.

He wasn't what she expected either. She anticipated a gnarled old cowboy. She thought he'd be bowlegged, bearded, and wearing dirty dungarees, a torn flannel shirt, a tattered leather vest, and boots with spurs. What she found was a tall, handsome man slightly older than she was. His weathered face was clean shaven and put her in mind more of an experienced yachtsman than a grizzled cowpoke. He carried himself beyond his height, and while his jeans were blue and worn, they were clean and fit him perfectly. His plaid flannel shirt looked new, and his vest was the kind seen out in Boulder, Colorado—a down-filled variety with a tan leather yoke.

Robert greeted her warmly. "Howdy."

He extended his hand and flashed a full, open smile. He looked her over and said her outfit would do fine for now, but he suggested riding boots rather than tennis shoes.

"Let's go for a little walk before I introduce you to the horses," he suggested casually, and he pointed across the meadow. "What have you been doing by way of outdoor activity?" he asked.

"Not much of anything," she answered. "I walk a little bit a couple of times a week, but that's about it."

"Have you ever gone hiking or camping?"

"No, not really."

"How about bike riding?"

"When I was a little girl in South Philly, I did some. As an adult, I sometimes work out on an Exercycle. Not much more than that."

Just then, Rita began to notice she was huffing and puffing. She was starting to have a hard time keeping up with Robert, who still appeared to be sauntering casually. Rita was almost jogging to keep up. They continued their loop around the meadow.

"Why do you want to ride horses?" Robert asked.

"I...uh...won't be able...uh...to talk to you...if we continue...to walk this...fast," Rita sputtered.

"We'll slow down in a minute. You know, horses are very powerful animals. They're big, and they're strong. You have to work at what you're doing to be able to handle one safely."

"I'm willing to try," Rita responded, finally catching her breath. "The picture in the paper looked so peaceful. I've just taken an early retirement, and I've resolved to do more. To try to be outdoors more. To try to get in better shape. I want to meet new people. I thought horseback riding would be something I could do either alone or with others. That's why I'm interested in seeing if I can learn to ride."

"Oh, you can learn to ride. Let's meet some of the horses."

Robert took her arm chivalrously and guided her to the stables. Several horses were loafing around the corral. The four together on the left side of the paddock were overpowering. One was golden. It looked like Roy Roger's horse, Trigger, in the old TV shows she had watched when she was young. Two were chestnut with auburn highlights. The horse that captivated her, though, was a deep, deep black. It looked like her own hair before the gray had started to set it.

"These horses are beautiful," she said. "They're so big."

"Yes," Robert answered. "They're five or six years old, and all of them are good saddle horses. Would you like to walk one of them?"

"Very much so," Rita responded, "but I have to say, I'm a little intimidated by their size and power. I'm not sure I can handle any of them."

"They're all fairly docile. They're used to being around people. Being walked and ridden. Pick one out, and I'll introduce you."

Rita picked the black one. Robert introduced Rita to Creo. "Short for Creosote," Richard explained. "Black as coal with the disposition of a fawn. Creo's a great animal. Creo, this is Rita."

"He's enormous. How big is he?"

"Creo here is a Morgan. He's a gelding. About seventeen hands, and he weighs about eleven hundred pounds."

"Hands? How big is a hand?"

"A hand is about four inches. As you can see, Creo's taller than you."

"What does he eat?"

"About six quarts of oats and four flakes of hay. When he's not grazing."

Robert led the black to her. After momentarily recoiling as he approached, Rita encouraged herself to reach up and to touch the horse's neck. Creo flinched, and Rita did too. Cautiously, she gently stroked Creo's neck with the awkwardness of a thirty-five-year-old bachelor holding his six-week-old niece for the first time. The seconds passed quickly, though, and Rita's spirits lifted. She became bolder. With one hand on Creo's neck, she slowly approached his head so she could pet him from the front.

"Hello, Creo. My name is Rita. Could you let me ride you some time? You are a big one, and I'm a little afraid of you, so I'm asking you to be careful with me. Is that okay"

Creo looked blankly back. Rita turned to Robert and said, "He's wonderful. What next?"

Suddenly, Creo shuddered, whinnied, and bobbed his head. Rita's heart rose to her temples. As she turned at the waist toward Robert, her left leg buckled under the torque of her turn, and she stumbled away from Creo toward the ground. Robert reached out and caught her. With his left hand around her waist and his right hand on her opposite elbow, he stabilized her and carefully righted her. It was as if she were a small doll he was arranging on a shelf. He felt her trembling. Her face grayed.

"Slow down," he cautioned. "Horses have little habits like that."

"It was a natural reflex for me," she responded. "He startled me."

As she relaxed, she realized everything was okay. Her wooden smile gave way to a little nervous laugh. After a moment, her anxiety began to quell, and she approached the black again and stroked his neck once more. "You scared me, Creo," she whispered. Creo was unfazed.

Robert intervened. "Let me show you some of the equipment."

They spent the next hour talking about the paraphernalia of horseback riding. He showed her a bridle and bit, a saddle pad, and a saddle. He even pointed out how to secure the girth. He pointed to a crop, but she wouldn't be using one at first. He would require her to wear a helmet.

"What's that?" Rita pointed to a contraption that was mostly leather straps.

"Oh, that's a martingale," he answered. "It's used to keep a horse's head steady. Some of them have a habit of bobbing their heads. A martingale keeps it in check."

When the question and answer session ended, the tour was complete. Rita made an appointment for the riding lessons to begin. She departed with a feeling of vigor that she hadn't experienced in quite some time. She was eager for tomorrow.

In the next days and weeks, she made steady progress, although there were days when the weather, with the gradual arrival of winter, would not cooperate. At first, she would not drive in the snow; it had always terrified her. Eventually, with Robert's encouragement, she began to brave the elements. Ice stopped her, though. She didn't like bitter cold and wind. Then there were those afternoons when the sun covered everything in gold. Some of those late-afternoon lessons spilled into early-evening conversations with Robert by a roaring fireplace with hot spiced cider or luxurious glass of Chardonnay.

Robert had been living alone since his father died five years ago. He had grown up on the ranch with his parents and had never found a companion who wanted to live a rancher's life in the east. So, most of his contact with people came from riders who wanted lessons or people looking to board their horses in his paddock. He lived a simple life centered on his ranch, his horses, and the various other species of livestock around the property—some sheep, goats, pigs, chickens, turkeys, and three peacocks. That included one magnificent male with plumage to rival one of Rita's favorite string bands on New Year's Day on Broad Street. Robert liked to listen to music and to read—mostly American books. John Updike. Pat Conroy. Richard Russo. He liked folks who captured the life of the American baby boomer.

Robert and Rita talked into the evening, and then Rita finally took her leave. On the ride home, she couldn't stop herself from thinking of both Robert and Ted. Since his death, Ted had set the standard for other men she met.

The riding lessons resumed the next day. Rita's anxiety about riding had long since withered away, and she eagerly anticipated her daily treks to the Blind Canyon Ranch. As spring approached, she gained more and more confidence. She could easily go out for casual rides of sixty minutes, and she was learning more and more about horses. She particularly loved Creo, with his strong but gentle way with her. They seemed to trust one another.

One Tuesday morning in early spring, Robert had several new riders coming for lessons, so Rita said she would go out alone. She had done this from time to time when Robert was busy. She took Creo through the woods and to the part of the county where she routinely saw deer—three, four, five, or even seven at a time. In the past few years, the deer population had exploded, and animals, once considered beautiful, were now viewed as pests—irritants that destroyed crops and gardens and transported ticks carrying Lyme disease. They frequently wandered onto roads and caused accidents. As Rita rode through the woods, she thought of the deer and how she had never seen a real one during her years growing up in South Philly. Her roots seemed so foreign to her now. She had just never had any exposure to the outdoors back then. As a result, for years she felt uncomfortable with nature. Malls were more her thing. Now, though, with Robert and Creo, she found a new base, and she liked it.

As these thoughts rolled around in her mind, she heard a whoosh whistle through the woods. Turning quickly, she heard it again. This time, Creo reacted, bolting up on his hind legs and then breaking into a gallop. Rita hung on and tried to regain control. Whoosh! This time, Creo stumbled forward and then down to his left, pinning Rita. Her world went dark. Her thoughts tumbled into one another. One minute, she was laughing with Ted and eating a hoagie for lunch in

Rittenhouse Square, and the next she was struggling with the capital gains part of her tax final in college. Then she was sitting on her childhood bed with her Cinderella doll and reading a Nancy Drew book from the branch of the Free Library of Philadelphia that was a few blocks from her home.

Faintly, she could hear her mother's voice. "I think she's waking up."

"I hope so," whispered her father. "It's been so long now."

"The doctor said it might be a few days," her mother mumbled.

Rita knew there was a problem. Mother, Father, and Nad were there, and her foggy head and her throbbing left leg let her know something was wrong.

"Nicholas, please tell the nurse she's waking up," her mother said, and then she turned to Rita. "Hello, Rita. Sweetheart. How do you feel?"

"Hello, Rita," said her father, and he squeezed Rita's hand.

She was still not fully conscious when Nad and the nurse arrived. Nad leaned over, kissed her on the forehead, and asked, "Well, are you supposed to be Annie Oakley or Calamity Jane?"

Rita tried to venture a laugh, but her left leg hurt so badly that she stopped. "Where am I?"

"In a hospital," Nad answered.

"How long have I been here?"

"It's Friday," her dad said. "Your fall was on Tuesday."

"What happened?" Rita asked.

"The best we can piece together is that you were out riding when some deer hunter shot your horse with an arrow. The horse fell, and you went under him," Nad said.

"Creo was shot? Is he okay?"

"Yes," her mother said. "In fact, Creo saved you."

"Saved me?"

"Yes, he worked his way clear of you, and he limped back to the ranch. Then the owner came back for you," said her mother.

"Robert came to get me?"

"Yes," Nad said.

The doctor and nurse entered the room and cleared it so they could examine her.

"Rita, you're very fortunate," the doctor began. "You were knocked unconscious, and you've been in a coma. You lost a considerable amount of blood and are very weak."

"Doctor, my left leg is throbbing terribly, and I feel like I can't move it."

"Rita, this is very difficult to tell you. You can't move your leg because we had to remove it from just below the knee. Your tibia and fibula and many bones in your foot were shattered when the horse fell on you. We couldn't save it."

She felt a wave of heat flash through her, leaving her chilled when it passed. "But I feel my leg."

"You feel the nerve that once went down your leg. You'll continue to feel sensations there for a while. Even after those feelings pass, from time to time, you'll experience sensations there."

Rita started to cry.

"We didn't have a choice. We had to. The leg was crushed," the doctor said.

After a few minutes, the doctor left, and her family returned. Many thoughts raced through Rita's mind. The news about her leg and the phantom pair she felt disoriented her. Though confused, she managed to tell her family how stupid she'd been to think that, at her age, she could do something she wouldn't have dared when she was thirty years younger. Now she had ruined herself. She would be an invalid—dependent on her family and friends, unable to take care of herself, trapped in a room, and unable to travel or even shop. Her parents alternated holding her hand and quietly reassuring her she could still live an active life. Their words went unheeded. They sat in silence before they heard footsteps down the hall and into the room.

"Anyone named Rita here? I have some flowers from somebody named Creo for somebody named Rita."

"Robert, is that you?"

"Yes, Rita. It's me. I was just going to drop these off for you with a note, but they told me you woke up. Here, Creo sent these. He was asking for you."

"Oh, thank you. How is Creo?"

"He'll be fine in a bit. Fortunately, the arrows didn't hit anything vital. He's a little bit carved up, but he'll recover. He'll be okay when you're ready for your next ride."

Silence echoed through the room. Robert looked around for a minute and then broke the silence. "What's the matter? Did I say something wrong?"

"Robert, I don't think I'll be riding again."

"Why not? You had a fall; you can't let that scare you. You know what they say. You've gotta get back on the horse."

"Robert, I probably would be afraid if I thought I had a chance of riding again, but I don't. The accident was serious. They had to remove my left leg."

"I know," he said quietly. "I was here yesterday when you weren't awake. They told me. All that means is you'll have trouble driving a stick shift. It doesn't have anything to do with your riding. So long as we get you a horse with four legs, you'll be fine." He stopped and smiled gently.

They all smiled.

"We'll see," Rita answered softly.

When they all left, Rita felt exhausted. She fell asleep, but not before she began churning everything over and over in her mind. She had always been afraid she would get hurt if she did things—physically or (worse yet) emotionally. Ever since Ted died, she wouldn't extend herself in any way. There was too much at stake. She feared blows to her pride. Expectations would beget disillusionment. Why venture? But now, she thought, I've suffered the consequence. Where do I go from here? Could Robert be right?

She fell asleep. Again, she dreamed. As a little girl, she had loved the carousel. She sat sideways on a painted pony as her father held her around the waist. She was laughing as the pony whirled around and around, pumping up and down. Nad was on a wild white stallion two rows ahead of her. He was riding ferociously. She was laughing fearlessly in her father's grasp.

The next few days, weeks, and months were painful for Rita. She underwent physical and psychological therapy. She learned to walk with crutches and was fitted for a prosthesis. Robert visited her often, and the next summer, his offer to drive her out to the ranch were finally met with assent. On this late July day, the sights and sounds differed greatly from those that had greeted her last year. It was hot—sweltering hot. Tiny beads of sweat dotted her brow and her upper lip just moments after she pulled herself out of Robert's truck. The colors of summer were more lush than last year but somehow less distinct. They were almost muted in the haze. She stumbled across the grass and glanced over toward the paddock. She could smell manure, but more than anything, she could smell horses. Over the months, she had learned to love the smell of horses, and she imagined she could distinguish Creo's distinct smell from the paddock. Back on Blind Canyon Ranch, she once again felt alive and whole.

Robert left her for a moment, returning with Creo in tow. She smiled, and he nuzzled up to her, almost knocking her down.

"Creo, I'm happy you're okay. We had a rough time of it, didn't we?"

"Would you like to go for a short ride?"

"I would like to, but I'm not sure I can."

"Why not?"

"How will I mount him?"

"I'll lift you."

She reluctantly agreed. Robert hoisted her up and over, and off they went into the woods. Sunlight pierced the thick foliage arching the trail, illuminating random leaves and branches. Rita was captivated. Despite her initial awkwardness, she didn't feel uncomfortable. Two squirrels scurried in tandem across the trail and up a tall tree. They approached a clearing with a lush meadow, and she mused that a camping trip might still be an option. Without thinking of Ted, she turned ever so subtly toward Robert and caught him glancing at her. They smiled. It registered that Robert was wonderful, and she recognized that this summer was not slipping by unnoticed.

RESTITUTION

WE STILL CALLED HIM VINNY, even though he was well into his sixties at the time. On his first visit back after many years, it seemed like he'd never been absent. He screamed every sound and made flamboyant gestures. He devoured Mom's meatballs, chasing them with steady sips of home dago red from a tiny half glass. This year, though, he stayed beyond dinner. On his way out, after our traditional dessert of fruit and nuts, Uncle Vinny stopped halfway between the dining room and the front door of our South Philly row home. He leaned through the opened French door and into the living room, where I had taken refuge from the real adults. For the second time in my memory, I heard him whisper. He ordered me out to the privacy of the hallway. "Come here, Little Nick."

It had been several years since Uncle Vinny threw a meatball at the wall during Christmas dinner. I don't remember exactly how old I was, but I do remember it happening. It almost hit me in the ear. Actually, he was just throwing it—not necessarily at the wall. Mom's meatballs were and still are the best. Sopping wet with her homemade gravy, they require no chewing. Oh, that gravy! That's what we real Italians call it—gravy, not sauce. Only Medigans call it sauce. We call them "Medigans," broken English for "Americans," because they aren't Italian. After Mom cleaned the gravy from the kitchen wall, she had to wipe little red drops from my white shirt collar. Because it was Christmas, I was dressed in a white shirt and tie. Dad, of course, was in a suit, as was Uncle Vinny. His double-breasted, brown pinstripe suit went perfectly with his camel hair cashmere topcoat, also double breasted, and his chocolate fedora with a tiny tan feather on the side. Uncle Vinny was partial to brown.

We always ate in the kitchen, never in the dining room. This was true even on Christmas Day. Not that we could eat Christmas dinner in the dining room anyway. Back then, my Lionel 027-gauge freight train and Plasticville village fill every inch of the dining room table. Come to think of it, the meatball toss had to be after my ninth Christmas because the trains were set up, and I was nine when Santa brought them. Well, then again, it had to be after my twelfth Christmas because it happened after Grandpop died.

Dad took Grandpop's old seat at the end of the table. Uncle Vinny was sitting to Dad's right and next to Mom. I was on Dad's left. Uncle Vinny seemed to make an appearance at dinnertime on Easter, Thanksgiving, and Christmas Day, even though he was never technically invited. He wouldn't have a full meal with us because he would dine with his wife's family, but he liked to dip into the meatball pot. He would sit with us at the kitchen table and loudly criticize the most recent boxing match from the Friday Night Fights. He acted like an expert on everything, but he actually knew something about boxing because he'd spent time in the ring when he was in his teens and twenties. I had heard rumors he'd spent some time elsewhere as well—a place where they gave you three square meals and a funny set of clothes, mostly striped.

Vincenzo DiDominico, the one named after Grandpop's brother, the number four of five sons, and the one just ahead of my dad, never did anything quietly. That was why I was a bit confused when, at the meat-ball-throwing Christmas, for the first time, he leaned over and mouthed something in Dad's ear that none of us could hear. Dad gave him an odd look, with a half-cocked turn of the head and a visible squint behind his Coke-bottle eyeglasses. After a slight pause, Dad shook his head side to side-without saying a word. Dad was as quiet as Uncle Vinny was loud.

Suddenly, Uncle Vinny grabbed his meatball-tipped fork and waved it toward the wall. Pop went the meatball. Out stomped Uncle Vinny, shouting, "That's it then. If that's how it is, that's it."

He didn't call Dad "Beau," as he usually did, and he never said good-bye.

All this time, we were silent. I looked at Mom. Never the meek one, her piercing brown eyes gained fury. She blew up. "Just let it go. Just let him go."

After this quick exit, it didn't take me long to figure out, he just stopped coming around. Before the meatball, Uncle Vinny had seemed like a constant presence in the house for so long it seemed like he was there even when he wasn't. He and Dad had been so close. They always called one another "Beau," although out on the corner, Dad was always Nad, and Uncle Vinny was usually Vinny Morgan. This was because of their older brother, Amadeo. Uncle Amadeo had always had a few bucks in the old days, so they called him J. P. Morgan, and his brother Vinny became a Morgan too.

After the meatball, Dad stopped telling the stories he used to love to tell—the stories of his many adventures with Uncle Vinny. They had been inseparable. The Uncle Vinny story about City Hall was one of Dad's favorites. Just after receiving his license, Dad, at Uncle Vinny's urging, decided to go to a dance up in North Philly at Wagner's Ballroom on Broad and Olney. It was on the north side of City Hall. Uncle Vinny had some old Ford junker. He wanted Dad to drive because he wanted to give Dad the practice. The City Hall circle was the only slight bend in what has been called the longest straight city street in the country. As they came up on the circle, heading north, Uncle Vinny told Dad he should always go around on the east side of the building, so Dad turned to the right and continued on up to Wagner's.

At the dance, Uncle Vinny spotted two nineteen-year-old South Philly brunettes. Dad couldn't remember their names whenever he told the story, so he would give them different names at difference times. Often, though, he called one Blanche and the other Carmella. Uncle Vinny introduced them to his twenty-year-old twin brother, Nad, and two pairs formed as the night wore on. Vinny offered them a ride home. He suggested that Dad drive, so he could sit in the back seat with Blanche. Dad drove nervously, trying to keep the conversation going with Carmella, who was actually three years his senior. He was trying to avoid driving into the concrete islands that still separate Broad Street's northbound and southbound lanes. When he approached City Hall, he thought about asking Vinny for clarification, but Vinny and Blanche were going at it in the back seat. Dad didn't want to reveal he was only a sixteen-year-old kid with a fresh license and no sense of direction. So, he turned left at City Hall and started to make his way around the east side of the building. Well, that was where the problem came in.

The flow of traffic around City Hall went only one way—counterclockwise. About a quarter of the way around, car horns honked, drivers waved fists, and one big red Ford stopped right in front of Dad and lit up like a Christmas tree with blinking red lights. Back then, red cop cars were the thing. It was before some psychologist figured out that blue or green or white would have a calming effect. This big Irish cop jumped out, ran to the car, and started screaming at Dad. Dad jumped out of the car too. (You could do that back then without getting shot.) In an effort to save himself, Dad blurted out that he was confused. He confessed that he had just turned sixteen and had just got his license. He said it was his first night out driving, that he had a girl he had just met in the car, and he was nervous. A shriek shot out from the car. It was Carmella. "Sixteen? We thought you guys were twenty!"

When he heard this, the cop started to laugh and said, "Son, get back in the car. Turn the car around, and go the other way. Always drive around circles to the right. To the right. Be careful."

In a sweat, Dad returned to the car. Blanche fired from the back seat, "Take us straight home."

After they dropped the girls off, Uncle Vinny gave Dad holy hell for admitting to being sixteen. "If you'd'a kept your mouth shut like you usually do, we'd be down by the lakes now having a great time."

The lakes were what we locals called Roosevelt Park, also known as League Island. Nestled at the most southern tip of South Philly and just north of the navy yard, this inner-city park was dotted with once-swimmable little lakes that froze over each winter for ice skating. It was lovers' lane for indigenous hormone-ravaged teenagers.

Although Dad liked the city hall story, I liked the one about Uncle Amadeo's Lincoln. One day, Uncle Vinny suggested to Dad that they "borrow" Amadeo's brand-new Lincoln Continental to joyride deep in the heart of South Philly. Vinny drove. When they crested a small bridge, they unexpectedly came up on a cyclopean Philadelphia Transit Authority trolley that had jumped its track and was marooned broadside across the bridge. Uncle Vinny tried to turn the wheel to avoid T-boning the monster, but Dad feared they would plunge off the bridge, so from the passenger seat, he yanked the wheel the other way and pulled on the stick shift to get the car out of gear. They rammed the trolley at half speed but avoided the long fall over the guardrail. Only the trolley and the Lincoln sustained injury. Everybody walked away with only minor cuts and bruises. Because Vinny always seemed to rub Amadeo the wrong way, Dad agreed to take the rap, claiming it was his idea to take the car and saying he was driving. Amadeo's only concern was that his brothers were safe.

After the meatball, the stories stopped. Uncle Vinny stopped coming around, and we stopped going up to his place in Bucks County. At one point, Uncle Vinny owned a bar in South Philly. Then he didn't. I heard a rumor he might have lost it gambling. Dad always used to tell me that Uncle Vinny and Uncle Amadeo were opposites when it came to money. Amadeo was a magnet for it, but money flowed through Uncle Vinny like early morning coffee. Well, anyway, Uncle Vinny needed money because he decided to move up to Bucks County to run a gas station, which was hilarious. Dad was the mechanic, and Uncle Vinny's expertise seemed more suited to the nightly card game on the corner, where Dad hung out but never played. He bought the gas station, and we would go up to Bucks County on Sundays and spend a bit of time there. I loved to pump gas and check oil. Then we would head to the house Uncle Vinny was renting. It was a big, old wooden-frame home on as much land as the playground back in South Philly where we watched rough touch football and semi-pro baseball. The house was near the Delaware River and on a tract that had a couple of gigantic trees, which were great for a city kid to climb. After some time, Uncle Vinny bought a house and built his own gas station, and that was where the meatball came in—sort of.

A few years after the Christmas meatball, I mustered enough nerve to ask Dad if we'd ever see Uncle Vinny again. "I don't know," he replied sadly.

I pressed a little bit him about what had happened, so he told me. Grandpop had loaned Uncle Vinny the money for rent for the house and to buy the new gas station. During his last illness, Grandpop put Uncle Amadeo in charge of Grandpop's affairs. He instructed Amadeo to carry out the terms of his will to the letter. Vinny had to repay 80 percent of the loan to his four brothers. When Grandpop died, Uncle Vinny repeatedly asked Dad to renounce the bequest and convince the other brothers to do so as well. Though Dad had fewer resources and more children than the other brothers, he told Vinny he didn't care about the money. "Family's more important," Dad said. "But I told him I wouldn't tell my other brothers what they should do. He told me that wasn't good enough. He said I was being selfish. But I wouldn't back down. I guess he expected me to because I was younger. So, he never gave me any money, and he blamed me that he had to pay our brothers. At Christmas dinner, he asked me one last time, but I didn't agree. You saw the rest. I never thought this could happen in our family."

So, Uncle Vinny and his loud voice and his garish gestures and his brown double-breasted pinstripe suit and cashmere coat and his gas station disappeared like the old tree I used to climb on.

Until now.

Dad recently told us Uncle Vinny might make an appearance on Christmas Day. Mom elaborated and said there had been some awkward recent conversations between her and Uncle Vinny and that Christmas might be a test run. Finally, after years of absence, Uncle Vinny rematerialized in the same topcoat and feathered fedora. They somehow lacked their former luster and style. As he pulled me into the hallway with one battered, arthritic hand, he stopped, seemingly petrified for an instant, and seemed unsure of what to do.

It was unusual to see Uncle Vinny hesitate. He had always been so forceful and decisive. He stared silently at me through yellowed eyes encased in sockets surrounded by spider-web lines from years pumping gas in the sun. He looked confused. With the smell of dago red and gravy from the three meatballs he scarfed down in record time lingering on his breath, Uncle Vinny broke his silence. "Little Nick, come out to the car with me."

With a shrug, I started to follow him. He opened the back door of his block-long Buick, reached in, and pulled out an old cigar box. It must have been Grandpop's, but now heavy tan twine bound it securely shut. "Give this to your dad after I pull away. Try to do it on the sly."

I nodded assent. I walked back into the house and silently handed the box to Dad, who was still at the kitchen table. "Did he say anything to you, Nicholas?"

"Only to sneak you the box."

Dad reached for his pocketknife, carefully cut the twine, and then stopped for a moment before raising the ornate lid. I stood behind him. The smell of Grandpop's old stogies escaped when Dad peered in. There were a few things sprinkled in with the many wrinkled greenbacks—mostly hundreds and fifties, along with some twenties and tens. Dad pulled out an old city street map with the route traced in red from Broad and Olney south and then counterclockwise around City Hall to the lakes. Dad laughed slightly. Then he grabbed the hood ornament from the old Lincoln Continental. He cocked his head and looked up at me with his characteristic lack of expression. On the bottom of the box, he spotted a crudely handwritten note. "I'm sorry, Beau." It was signed "Beau." After a hard swallow, Dad looked up at me and smiled. Then a single tear leaked from behind those glasses. Dad rushed from the table to the front door shouting, "Beau."

But Uncle Vinny was gone.

The Stock Car Drivers

The gap-toothed grin still shimmered through a face now lined like well-worn linen. He shuffled toward the open coffin with both hands firmly on the walker he knew he couldn't move without. The music was gone from his step. The walker didn't feel at all like the bus steering wheel on his old stock car from years before. He snuck a look around the room. There were a few old-timers in the room, but the only guys he knew were Nad, the owner of his car, and Nad's son, Little Nick, who was now all grown up. He peered into the open coffin, and while bending over, he reached into his jacket pocket. Memories of the races at the now grassed over track started to swim through his brain.

When he first started to show up at the track, Tony Bel wore that broad gap-toothed grin like a name tag. Back then, he made you think of those old Ipana toothpaste commercials. "Brusha! Brusha! Brusha! New Ipana toothpaste!" But he didn't at all resemble Bucky Beaver in those ads. His cheeks weren't round. His nose wasn't snubbed, and his teeth didn't protrude. It wasn't as if he were handsome. In fact, he wasn't nearly as good looking as he seemed. He just had this way about him. When his seawater eyes gleamed directly into yours, you felt the you were the only two important people on the planet—the only fish in the sea. He also seemed to see three-quarters of the way around his head. If you tried to sneak up on him, he would greet you with his, "Hey, kiddo. How ya doin'?" He did this even though you were standing directly behind him.

He wasn't a tall guy, but everything and everyone seemed to form a symmetry around him. He would pulse through the crowd in the pits before and after the races as if he were the conductor of some peripatetic orchestra. Mesmerized kids followed by their watchful fathers formed the brass and woodwinds section on one side. Hopeful track groupies in Daisy Mae tops and cutoff dungarees comprised the violins. Oh, the first violin always played so sweetly! When he wasn't in the car, he was all smiles and melody notes. Only a few rival drivers, particularly Sil Mitchell, and their crews didn't like the arrangement. And they had orchestra section seats—front row, right alongside the pit.

Something changed Tony Bel when he strapped on his helmet, though. Harnessed into his seat, he'd peddle the nitro-laced fuel into the two-barrel carburetor atop the Ford V8 with carefully polished pistons and precisely lapped-in valves. They couldn't retrofit an Escadarian full-race camshaft into the stock engine. It was illegal; they had checked. Once he got the critter revved up, his eyes churned like a riptide. That smile turned into percussion behind William Tell cannons coursing through an unmufflered straight pipe spewing bombast over by the passenger side.

Tony Bel and Sil Mitchell drove at each other as if they were the only two on the track who had a chance to win. They were right. Long before Tony Bel started to show up, Sil Mitchell, whose real name was Sylvie Machollini, dominated the Saturday night races on the almost half-mile oval carved out of the woods. His '37 coupe, which was dressed up like an eight ball, would always win the fastest qualifying heat. As the winner of the last week's races, he always started last in the main event—twenty-five laps of left-hand turns on unbanked oil-stained blacktop--stock car racing back in the fifties.

Sil had a way of zigzagging through the field like a shark picking off prey so that, by the fifteenth trip around, he was ready to take the lead. Then, after a few years, Tony Bel started showing up.

Everybody laughed when they first saw the teal '39 sedan with the bright red question marks on the sides. It didn't help that it rolled in on a tow hook with out-of-state tags. "What's that sissy-lookin' sedan doin' here?" one of the locals said derisively. "They didn't even know what to call that piece of crap. Probably should have used a minus sign rather than a question mark."

Tony Bel took the car slowly through the warm-ups like a goldfish in a bowl. He carefully heated up the oversize slicks on the rear wheels and searched for the best groove on the inside, in the middle of the track, and up high. Even the cars that would run in the slowest qualifying heat passed him effortlessly. Another local picked up the banter. "Does that question mark mean they don't know what the car is, or does it mean the driver doesn't know how to drive?"

Everybody laughed. Sil Mitchell didn't even notice Tony Bel during these warm-ups. To him, Tony Bel didn't exist—yet. Then, halfway through the first heat, the one for the slowest cars and the new ones to the track, one of Sil's crew members pointed out that the new car was running twenty-three-second to twenty-four-- second laps. That was better by a bit than what Mitchell ran on a good night. By the end of the ten-lap heat, Tony Bel had begun lapping the field for a second time.

At this track, they had an odd way of picking the qualifiers and then seeding them for the main event. The top four cars from each of the three qualifying heats made it to the championship race. The top four finishers from the consolation heat also ran. A driver was slotted into one of the heats by the running point total over the season. They put the slowest and newest cars in the first heat. For the feature event, they lined all the qualifiers up in eight rows of two. The cars from the slower heats started up front, and last week's winner always started on the outside of row eight—dead last. The theory was that this would give anybody a fighting chance, and it would force the drivers of the faster cars to demonstrate some virtuosity through the ponderous heavy traffic that sometimes harmonized to slow down the rhythm of the spectacle.

On the first week, Tony Bel, as winner of the slow heat, started way up front next to the royal-blue fifteen car, which had finished second in his heat. The Question Mark hesitated when the green flag dropped so that it was gapped. Tony Bel then powered high in the groove, soloing into the first turn, straight pipe trumpeting and leaving the slower cars sounding like a high school marching band. He took a strong lead through lap one and into lap two. Sil's crew flashed him a board on the second lap that read "–7 ?." Sil intuited trouble. Seven seconds down to a driver who could crank out twenty-three or twenty-four second laps meant the Eight Ball would likely never catch him…unless. By starting up front, the Question Mark pretty much had a clear track in front of him. Sil hoped the new guy couldn't navigate through traffic. Sil hoped, but he hoped in vain. Sil couldn't see how the Question Mark maneuvered, but on the sixteenth lap, when his crew flashed "–9 ?," he knew the Question Mark had probably lapped almost the entire field without missing a beat.

After lap twenty-five, the Question Mark cruised through the checkered flag alone with the Eight Ball more than a straightaway behind. The crowd, with mouths agape, applauded wildly. No one could remember whether Sil Mitchell had ever lost a race. The pits crescendoed with speculation. Would Sil risk the five Jacksons required to challenge the winner to a teardown to make sure it was stock? Would anyone?

Shortly after the Question Mark came to a full stop in its pit, Sil and his crew walked over. Sil was the tall guy at the track, towering three or four inches over most of the other men. He seemed a little older than the other drivers too. He was maybe in his thirties. His look was grizzled and ornery—not a fun guy. Most of the drivers wore only work pants and simple white T-shirts. Al's shirt had a big *S* like Superman on the front and a black circle with a white eight in the center on the back. The helmet he cradled in his left arm looked even more like an eight ball.

"We're the Eight Ball crew," Sil announced through barely visible teeth. "I'm Sil Mitchell." He did not extend his hand.

"Everybody knows Sylvie Machollini," the voice behind the grin sang out.

Tony Bel's respect was genuine. He and his crew knew Mitchell was the man on this race circuit, and they knew he had been invincible on his home track. They had clandestinely watched from the grandstand as Sil dominated the previous weekends.

"I'm Tony Belfiore. You can call me Tony Bel." His hand shot out to the motionless Sil Mitchel.

"Whatcha got in there, Belfiore?"

"Three four-barrels on a blower," Tony Bel gushed.

"Sounds about right to me. Couldn't do what you did without a supercharger," said Sil.

"Come on now, Sil. I'm stock all the way." Tony Bel stared into Sil's churning eyes.

"Well, let's take a look then, Belfiore."

"Whoa! Gonna cost you a hundred to see how this thing is tuned up. Got it singin' real sweet now. You can listen, but it's gonna cost you to look."

The growing crowd of kids and groupies started to take their places. They surrounded the car and listened to the drivers.

One of Sil's crew walked up to the track steward, handed him five twenties, and said scornfully, "Well, let's have a look then."

Tony Bel climbed in, pushed the starter button, and the beast came to life. He slowly turned the oversize bus steering wheel and idled into the teardown pit.

The challenge process was neither complicated nor time consuming, but it was accusatory, insulting, and disrespectful. Another crew put up some money to challenge whether the winner was stock legal. If the inspectors found a violation, the crew got the money back, the winner was disqualified, and everybody moved up a spot in the finishing order. If they didn't, the challenged car kept the hundred and the victory, and the inspectors placed a seal strategically on the engine and rear to certify the car was legal. If the car won again, the challenge started with the inspection of seals. If they were intact, the challenge failed. If they had been broken, the inspectors would run through their inspection procedure. The inspection itself involved a couple of minor intrusions. They made a visual inspection, and then they pulled the flathead off the engine block to expose the cylinders and valves. They measured the cylinders to make sure they hadn't been bored out to add displacement and horsepower. They checked the compression and analyzed the fuel. They measured the lift on the valves and then moved under the car. They concentrated on the rear. Gear ratios in the rear could turn a stock V6 into a barracuda. They counted the teeth in the rear to make sure the rear was stock. All this took no more than fifteen to twenty minutes.

There hadn't been a challenge for years at Pleasantville. Sil won every week, and everybody else was running for place and show money. The crowd around the teardown pit stood with quiet excitement. The Jersey gang couldn't wait to have the Question Mark exposed. The Philly fans hoped it was legal. Silence droned on.

Whenever a challenge took place, a representative from the winning team and the challenging team accompanied the inspectors. Usually the owner or chief mechanic stepped forward. When Sil insisted to get started, Nichols DiDominico, Nad, the owner and chief mechanic of the Question Mark, pushed Tony Bel into the pit with a quiet, "You stay with them, Tony."

"Do you know anything about engines and gears, Belfiore?" Sil asked.

"I know how to make 'em go fast, and I know the difference between a single, stock two-barrel and three fours on a blower. That should be enough, I'd say."

Sil Mitchell just snarled.

As the inspection concluded, the stewards huddled together apart from the crowd and handed Tony Bel one hundred dollars and a marble-based trophy with a sparkling chrome stock coupe perched fifteen inches up on a shiny column. The crowd applauded as Tony Bel waved the trophy in the air, but Sil sneered. "We'll see what you can do next week when we start out together."

"Looking forward to it, Sil. I'm new here, and I want to run against the best. That's you. So, here we go. You have a nice week now."

A cute, big-haired brunette approached them with her midriff bare between an hourglass waist and an almost-covered chest. She navigated past Sil and sidled up to Tony Bel. They locked eyes. She handed him a sweat-soaked open Coke bottle. "Great race, new guy. I'm Vera. Your car says you have some questions. I have the answers."

She grabbed him by the arm and walked him away from the crowd. Sil just shook his head and walked back to his pit.

Anticipation swelled as the weekend neared. Would the Question Mark really return? What would happen if it did? Had it been a fluke? Could this Tony Bel really drive? Could he handle heavy traffic? How would Sil meet the challenge? The excitement exceeded even the fervor surrounding the track when it first opened.

Not yet ten years earlier, some farmers cut the Pleasantville Speedway out of the Pine Barrens in South Jersey, closer to the Atlantic Ocean than to the Liberty Bell. It was mostly locals who raced and made up the fan base. What started out as a loose-dirt track that hurled pieces of itself at anyone standing near the turns when the Fords howled by evolved in steady measure into a nicely groomed asphalt oval with neat rows of light towers evenly spaced deep in the infield and on the backstretch and homestretch well beyond the outside wooden rail. There was but one grandstand, running from the end of the fourth turn to the beginning of the first. Behind it, the refreshment counters dispensed Cokes, hot dogs, and hot chocolate. Early and late in the season, the chilly night air could shiver race fans up pretty good. There was also a little souvenir booth where they could pick up pictures of their favorite drivers or cars or both, checkered flags, and miniature trophy replicas. The most prized souvenirs were always the plastic model cars painted up like the real ones on the track—the Fifteen was a royal-blue coupe, the Ten was cherry red, and the Two was the color of scrambled eggs. The sedans didn't sell well because there were only a few in the field, and they didn't seem very competitive. Before Tony Bel started coming around, the Eight Ball black coupe was always the best seller. Tony Bel himself bought one when he came to the track to observe before he entered his first race there. After Tony Bel's initial victory, a few kids started asking for a teal sedan with a red question mark on it. None were available...yet. It would take a few appearances before they started making some up.

The next Saturday night finally rolled around. Everyone noticed when the black tow truck with Pennsylvania tags dragged the teal sedan with the red question mark into the pits. Last week's derisive comments evaporated like condensation from an exhaust pipe. The only open spot in the pits was the one right next to the Eight Ball. When Tony Bel jumped out of the tow truck's passenger seat, his vision spun directly to Sil. Tony Bel smiled and waved. Mitchell glared and turned. Vera, the blonde from last week, showed up a few minutes later, but Tony Bel spoke to her only briefly before putting on his helmet.

The heats were under way. The main heat went off uneventfully. The Question Mark won, and the Eight Ball finished second without really trying. For the main event, Tony Bel lined the Question Mark up on the outside high. He was to the right of the Eight Ball. At the green flag, the Question Mark held its line through the first and second turns and then drove high to the outside on the backstretch. The Eight Ball ducked low, zigzagging through traffic. By the time they reached the third turn, Tony Bel had made up eight places, while Mitchell was boxed in and four places back. Halfway through the race, they were running one-two, with the Question Mark up about four car lengths.

Tony Bel seemed to be able to find a fast groove anywhere on the track. Mitchell drove fearlessly in and out, climbing high when he had to and then ducking low. He couldn't hold the high line, and he couldn't close the gap. After the checkered flag, Tony Bel took an insurance lap and then pulled up next to the starters' stand. He motioned for the checkered flag. He then took a victory lap holding the flag in his left hand, steering carefully with his right. The crowd went wild. No one had taken a victory lap with the checkered flag before. In the pits, the crowd surrounded a smiling Tony Bel and the undefeated Question Mark. This week there was no challenge, so they conducted a more conventional awards ceremony. When they handed the checks and the trophies to the drivers, the Eight Ball's mechanic accepted for his team. Tony Bel and Sil Mitchell didn't speak that night, but soon after, the rumor mill started to speculate that Mitchell had a plan. This week was the prelude. Mitchell drove his own race to see how it would work against Tony Bel. The next stage would be to follow Tony Bel through traffic to see how he did it. The next step was for Mitchell to do anything he could, legal or not, to take back his rightful place in the winner's circle.

On the next Saturday night, when Mitchell darted behind Tony Bel at the start, everyone knew the rumor was true. Unfortunately for Mitchell the result was the same. The Question Mark had only slightly more power and just about the same handling. The real difference was Tony Bel. He brazenly passed high on the turns, and Mitchell blinked a few times, lifting off the throttle as he started to drift up in the middle of turn three, which was the toughest on the track. This week, Tony Bel won by half a straightaway. Nobody from the Eight Ball crew attended the awards ceremony. Mitchell's legend waned in Tony Bel's wake.

Everybody expected the question Mark to show up the next week. When neither the teal sedan nor Tony Bel was anywhere to be found midway through the second heat, a buzz started to circulate through the infield and the pits. Was the coronation a shot in the dark? Did Tony Bel think his luck had run out? Did the rumor that Sil Mitchell was angling to put the Question Mark through the rail on turn three make its way to Philly? The Eight Ball's victory seemed a bit hollow that night, but Mitchell was glad to return to the winner's circle.

The Question Mark was one of the first cars to arrive the next week, and the word quickly spread that they had missed last week because of a death in Tony Bel's family. Everybody wondered what would happen this week with Sil Mitchell starting on the outside of the last row with Tony Bel on his left. The qualifying heat foreshadowed nothing. Mitchell dropped back at the start, and Tony Bel took the high groove to victory. But when the green flag dropped on the feature event, Mitchell dropped down low, pinning the Question Mark to the track's grassy apron. Inches separated them through turn one, and then suddenly the car in front of Tony Bel drifted slightly up, and the Question Mark dug its left front tire into the grass and powered through turn two safely up the straightaway, leaving the Eight Ball in yet another fruitless chase. The race, like those before, ended with the Question Mark winning and the Eight Ball second. Even though Tony Bel had fewer races, his point total gave him his first ever track championship. With the season over, he looked forward to the next year.

Meanwhile, Mitchell looked for new angles. He and his crew tweaked the car as much as possible, staying close to the rules. They replaced the carburetor jets with bigger ones to allow a richer fuel mixture. This change would probably go undetected. They hand polished the valve seats and carefully hollowed out the cylinder head. Occasionally, during the off-season, the Eight Ball managed to get out on the oval for testing. The best laps they could turn were in the twenty-four-second range, with an infrequent dip to twenty-three. Shortly after one of those runs, a crew member decided they should focus on the gear ratio in the rear.

"We can't do that," Sil Mitchell cautioned. "We'll get caught."

Stock rears had a specified gear ratio; each had a regulation number of teeth. Part of the inspection protocol after a challenge was to mark one of the grease-covered gear teeth with a punch, turn the rear wheel and tire, count the teeth to the stock number, and wipe the tooth again.

If the centered punch was there, the rear was stock, and the challenge was defeated. This had been the procedure used on the Question Mark when it won its first race.

"I know a way to hide the change," answered the mechanic. "Let's just see what it'll give us."

They improved the ratio, and suddenly the Eight Ball was consistently turning twenty-three-second laps with a few twenty-twos mixed in. There was even an occasional 21.7 Everybody smiled and waited for spring.

The anticipation grew before the first night of racing. The Question Mark crew kept tinkering with the engine and the setup but felt confident they'd be ready. Tony Bel easily won the third heat with Sil Mitchell, driving conservatively, a distant second. At the green flag of the featured event, Mitchell let loose, hurling the Eight Ball through the pack and going from fifteenth place to first in three laps. Tony Bel picked his way through traffic into second place. The crowd watched in awe as the Eight Ball started its victory lap. The Question Mark was still on the backstretch. Fans mobbed Sil Mitchell's pit. The Eight Ball was back. Tony Bel and his crew walked over.

With his characteristic smile, Tony Bel extended his hand to Sil and offered congratulations. This time, Mitchell stuck his hand out in return.

"Great run, Sil. Seems like you got it all together for this season. I guess I have my work cut out for me."

"It was only a matter of time, Belfiore. No way you could stay ahead of me."

"I've got to hand it to you. You figured out a way to put more jump in that Eight Ball. I felt like I was on a plow horse out there, and you were on a thoroughbred."

"You sayin' I'm cheatin', Belfiore? It's gonna cost you to find out."

"No way, Sil. We don't have that kind of money to throw around. You won. That's okay with me. I'll try to catch you next week."

"I've got money for a challenge," called a voice from the crowd. It was Johnny Santo, the owner of the Fifteen car. "I've never seen a legal car go through a pack that way. My team challenges."

"Your car was way back, Johnny. A challenge can't get you into the money," Tony Bel said.

"We'll take your money if you want, Johnny, but Belfiore's right. You shouldn't even bother," Mitchell said.

"It's okay. I'm willing to throw my money away, but I want Tony Bel to be my representative during the challenge. That okay with you, Tony Bel?"

"If you want, but you'd be better off with a mechanic," said Tony Bel.

"Okay. I'll use your mechanic, if he's willing," said Johnny.

Tony Bel looked around and immediately saw Little Nick. "Hey, Little Nick, where's your dad? We need him here."

"He went to the refreshment stand. I'll go get him." Little Nick ran to find his dad.

"What's up?" Nad said when he came back with a coffee for himself and a Coke for Little Nick.

"Johnny challenged Sil Mitchell's car, and he wants you to be his representative." Tony Bel explained.

"Okay, I'll keep an eye on them," said Nad.

The stewards started with the engine. Nad kept an eye on things and noticed they didn't check the carburetor's jets. The engine checked out. One of the stewards made his way under the car to the rear. He marked the gear by striking a center punch with a ball peen hammer. He turned the rear wheel slowly and counted the teeth. When he reached the stock number, he stopped, wiped the tooth, and saw the mark. He called to Nad to pull a creeper under the car to verify the count. Nad pointed the flashlight squarely on the tooth and thought he saw the mark as grease started to drip down.

"The tooth is covered with grease," Nad called out. "I can't see a thing. Toss me a rag." Nad swiped at the tooth again, catching it and those surrounding it. He wiped again and again. "I think there's a problem here," Nad said to the steward. "I see center punches on a couple of these teeth."

"Let me see." The steward slid another creeper under the car. He wiped a couple of teeth himself and verified that each of them had a center punch mark. "You're right. We have a problem. Each tooth is marked. We have to find another way to count. Give me that hammer and punch." He added two more punches to one tooth, making a triangle. "Okay, turn. I'll count." When he reached the stock number, he wiped the grease and saw a single mark. "Let's start over."

He found the triangle and began his count again, this time wiping each tooth as they passed. When he counted to the stock number, he saw a single mark, so he kept going until he found the triangle. It was on the wrong spot for a stock gear ratio.

The steward called to the Eight Ball representative to join him under the car, and he repeated the procedure with the same result. He then asked the other stewards to verify what he found. When they finished, the men conferred and then called Johnny Santo, Tony Bel, Sil Mitchell, and the crews together for a discussion. When they finished, the chief steward turned to the crowd and announced, "Challenge upheld. Eight Ball disqualified for an illegal gear ratio. Everyone moves up one place."

The crowd erupted with a chant of "Tony Bel?" It was shouted like a question in honor of the car that got him there. The Eight Ball crew, along with Sil Mitchell, withdrew in disgrace but not without resolve.

Mitchell returned each week with a legal car and chased the Question Mark around the oval. He even managed to win a few main events—once when the teal sedan hit some debris on the nineteenth lap, puncturing its right front tire, and one again when Tony Bel couldn't avoid a crash right in front of him, got nicked by the spinning Two car, and had to retire early. Because of Mitchell's two victories in races where Tony Bel scored no points, Sil Mitchell and the Eight Ball were still in contention for the track championship going into the season finale. With diabolical determination, Mitchell began to think of a new plan. He'd need one that utilized raw muscle rather than speed and finesse. He played back all of Tony Bel's victories one by one. He thought he knew Tony Bel's natural tendencies.

Saturday night of the season finale arrived. The third heat started and ended the way they all had for the past year. Mitchell tried to shoot the gap to the high groove, but he lacked the horsepower to establish position, so Tony Bel and the Question Mark flew by on their way through the pack to another win. The Eight Ball finished a close but futile second. After the consolation heat, the pit steward began hand signaling the qualifiers out of the pits for a couple of parade laps. The pace car, tonight a fire-engine red Ford Thunderbird convertible, made sure the field was properly aligned before pulling into the infield off the fourth turn. The starter could then drop the green flag for an always exciting flying start. No matter how many races they attended, the grandstand fans could not restrain themselves and stay seated. The twitchy field began its raging stampede into the homestretch. It was as if so many electric eels simultaneously shocked the spectators to their feet. In unison, they shouted, stomped, and clapped the leaders past the starters' stand. They fixed their closest surveillance over at the back of the pack. They knew the real action would take place there. The normally stormy start took on typhoon-like features in this, the last main event of the season. The track championship was on the line. If Tony Bel finished fourth or better, the championship would be his, no matter where the Eight Ball came in. Everyone knew that.

It didn't take long for Mitchell's plan to unfold. The slower cars jockeyed for the early lead. Even before the tenth row cleared the starter's stand and even before the last row with the Eight Ball on the inside and the Question Mark on the outside made it a third of the way up the homestretch, the Eight Ball drifted high on the homestretch, pinning the Question Mark on the outside rail. Tony Bel was blocked. The fans had a clear view of The Eight Ball's maneuver. But the starter, who always looked up the track to make sure the first lap passed cleanly, didn't see it. With the pedal to the floor, Tony Bel had neither the time nor the inclination to lift in order to let the Eight Ball go by. The only route that remained was through the rail, smack-dab at the start of the first turn, where the berm dropped suddenly into a drainage ditch, isolating the pits from the track. The Question Mark dived nose first into the ditch, flipping tail over nose twice before hitting a soft spot, which spun it sideways. The final two rolls took him side over side.

The flagman dropped the red flag immediately. With no laps complete, the race would restart. As the cars slowed, the rescue team and raceway tow truck sped toward the wreck. The seat bolts and harness anchor held firm. Inverted, Tony Bel, head dangling, surrounded the steering wheel with his arms. Because the doors had been welded together, his confinement was total. It was standard practice to remove all the glass from these cars, except for the windshield, which was retrofitted with the current version of shatterproof glass. Sometimes it held; sometimes it didn't. This time, it spidered but held. The fuel tank didn't breech; there was no fire. There was no smoke, only billowing steam from the ruptured radiator. The crash was bad, but it could have been worse.

When the ambulance arrived, Tony Bel was trying vainly to free himself from his safety belt. He didn't notice the rescue crew as two of its members reached into the wreck. Startled by the first one's touch, he smacked the extending arms, letting go of the steering wheel in the process. This reaction released his entire body weight to the care of the harness. His head jolted backward, and the straps began cutting through his thin T-shirt and into his throbbing shoulders.

"Hang on, Tony! Hang on!" one member of the rescue team hollered. "We're going to roll the car back onto the wheels. You all right?"

The answer was gruff and unintelligible. By now, almost every pit crew had reached the Question Mark and was providing man power to set the car upright. They pushed in unison, and the Question Mark flopped onto its splayed, twisted wheels. Tony Bel unhooked himself and wiggled through the window. He shouted unintelligible sounds, he fell face first next to the car, catapulted up, and ran, helmet down, into the crowd, spearing one of the mechanics. All the while, he windmilled haymakers at everyone in his path, hitting mostly air. Everyone retreated. Finally, one of the mechanics in his crew, nicknamed Johnny Shoes, ran up behind him, bear-hugged him to the ground, and pinned his arms. Shoes held onto Tony Bel, saying with amazing calm, "It's OK, Tony. It's okay. You're all right."

After a seeming eternity, Tony Bel's adrenaline started to subside. Johnny Shoes relaxed his grip. Tony Bel turned to him and asked, "What da hell happened?"

"The Eight Ball put you through the fence. We're filing a protest," Johnny Shoes replied. "You okay?"

"I think so," said Tony Bel. "But I don't think that's what happened. I just couldn't get the car to turn left. Are they going to restart? Can we get back in it?"

"The Question Mark is a wreck. It can't run. We saw it all. Sil Mitchell drove you up there. He took the turn away. Mikey Eyes is filling out the paper work with the steward," said Johnny Shoes, referring to another crew member.

"No protest. This is racing. Stuff happens," Tony Bel said.

"Tony, you have to get checked out at the hospital. Your head's all banged up. You probably don't remember what happened. The team will decide what to do."

"No hospital. No protest. See if you can get me another ride."

"Tony, you can't drive. You've just been in a wreck."

"See what you can do."

While this drama unfolded, the starter waved the field back into the pits. Because the main event had run less than one lap, the track officials decided to repair the rail as best they could before restarting the race. The medical team grabbed Tony Bel from beside the Question Mark and put him through a battery of tests. They had him walk a straight line, stand on one leg, touch his nose with a finger while keeping his eyes closed, follow a finger with his eyes, and catch a stone the size of a golf ball thrown from about ten yards away. All the while, Tony Bel talked calmly to the doctor in charge. "You know I'm okay, Doc. You know that, right? You want me to recite nursery rhymes? I can do that too if you want. Want me to sing 'Stardust'? I can do that. Just don't ask me to play the piano. Never could do that. Come on, Doc. I can drive. You got to hurry up, though. They'll be startin' up soon. Got to get me a ride."

The track doctor had finally had enough. "Will you please shut up? The more you talk, the slower I get. Plus, it's irritating."

"Well, I'm glad to see you can talk, Doc. Thought you had gone dumb there for a bit. Or maybe deaf. Or maybe both. You know what, Doc? Now that I know you can hear and talk, I'm not gonna shut up until you clear me to drive. Get my point, Doc?"

"All right already. If you don't shut up, I'll walk away, and you won't drive until some other doctor clears you. If you shut your trap for three minutes, I'll know you have your senses, that you can understand directions, and that you can control yourself."

Tony Bel flashed that signature smile of his and fell silent. All he needed was a ride.

Once again, Johnny Santo came to the rescue. "Hey, Tony Bel. My driver, Tommy, he got sick. Throwin' up all over the car. Sez he can't drive. Sez he'll give up the wheel if they clear you and you want back in."

"Sick? What sick?" asked Tony Bel.

Johnny Santo leaned toward Tony Bel, putting his arm around Tony's shoulder and drawing him in for a more private conversation. "After he found out what happened, he downed five hot dogs and three Cokes in about a minute so he could make an argument he's too sick to go. He likes the way you drive. Plus, Mitchell has cleaned up here for long enough. And we never liked the way he did it. Always thinkin' he was better than the rest of us. Not bein' friendly either."

"Johnny, that's terrific. Where's Tommy. I've got to thank him right away."

"He's in the pits near the car. You can thank him over there."

Tony Bel grabbed his helmet and sprinted toward the Fifteen. When he arrived, he hugged Tommy and whispered in his ear, "Thanks. This is damned impressive of you. I owe you."

"Pay me back by winning the title. Just keep Mitchell away from the crown."

As Tony Bel started to climb into the car, the stewards, Sil Mitchell, and his crew surrounded him. The head steward spoke. "Tony, your crew filed a protest to disqualify Mitchell. They claimed he intentionally put you through the rail."

"No way," Tony Bel shot back. "This is racin'. Stuff happens. No protest."

"Too late for that, Tony. We conducted our review. The starter didn't see anything wrong. The protest is denied. Mitchell's allowed to drive."

"Good," said Tony Bel. "Then it's settled. What position was the Fifteen car in?"

"Well, that's a problem, Tony. Mitchell's team says that because you didn't qualify in the Fifteen, you can't drive it."

Before Tony Bel could respond, Johnny Santo stepped up. "That's not what the rule says. The rule says the car qualifies. Not the driver."

"Let me look it up," replied the steward. The steward took the rule book from his back pocket and Johnny Santo pointed to the rule.

"I agree. Tony, you can drive the Fifteen car. It's qualified for the main event."

"Now wait just a minute." It was Sil Mitchell. "He's at least got to start last because he didn't qualify the car. That's the way we do it here."

The steward came back. "He's got a point there. If it's the owner's decision to switch drivers after qualification, the new driver has to start last."

"No problem," Tony Bel answered.

"It is a problem, Tony," said Johnny Santo. "Here's the problem. Mitchell wants you behind so he can sail away on you. The Fifteen is not the car the Question Mark was."

"I don't care," Tony Bel said. "This is racin'. Racin' is racin'."

"I care," said Johnny. Turning to the steward, he argued. "This isn't the owner's decision. Tommy's been my guy forever. He's still my guy."

"Settled then," Mitchell shot back. "Belfiore's out."

"Not so fast, Sil. It's not my decision because Tommy can't go. Too sick. Throwin' up."

"Where?" Mitchell asked.

"There." Johnny pointed to Tommy's mess.

The stewards conferred briefly and announced, "Car Fifteen, driven by Tony Bel, starts in the tenth row outside as qualified. Tommy Lyons is too sick to drive. Let's get this race started."

Tony Bel settled into the Fifteen car and tried to get its feel. A coupe handled much differently than a sedan, so Tony Bel tried to experiment a little during the pace laps. He could feel some understeer in the turns, but he figured he could use that to his advantage. The coupe also seemed to grab better than the sedan on the straightaways. He'd manage. He also wanted to understand what the power difference would be. He knew he couldn't outgun the Eight Ball. He'd have to use finesse.

When the green flag dropped, Tony Bel had already driven the gas pedal almost through the floorboard. A small seam opened low, and Tony Bel dived for the first turn. The back end broke loose ever so slightly, forcing the driver in the outside car to lift off the gas. The Fifteen dug into the turn, and Tony Bel managed to pass five cars on the first lap. The Eight Ball was charging too, however, weaving in and out through the first of the cars in front of him. Just like the old days, thought Mitchell, as he looked up the track for the Fifteen. By lap ten, Tony Bel was fourth, and the Eight Ball was working hard in ninth. Tony Bel held the fast line all around the track. The traffic in front of him seemed to slipstream him along.

The bad news for Tony Bel was that the Eight Ball had more power. However, it seemed as if Mitchell was now having trouble with the traffic between them. It all started when the yellow Deuce, the green Five, and the cherry red Ten drove three abreast in front of Sil Mitchell. They left him only the smallest opening up high. Mitchell tried to time his move. He always felt more comfortable down low in the groove. Only rarely did he venture up high. Coming into the fourth turn, Mitchell thought he might have a chance. When he went for it, though, the Ten sealed him off and forced him to lift. The Two car stayed directly in front of him, and the Five and the Ten dropped down on either side. The Twenty-Three car saw the diamond forming and completed it by coming right up on the Eight Ball's tail. Mitchell was trapped. Jimmy D'Angelo, the driver of the Deuce, realized he was in control but wondered whether he could hold Mitchell in place. The next lap would tell. Any sudden slowdown would likely send all five cars tumbling over one another. Jim applied a little less foot to the gas pedal. He gave more gas in the turns than on the straights. Everyone else held position. Mitchell tried to break out of the box for three laps...to no avail. On the straightaway, he took his left hand off the wheel, balled it into a fist, and shook it violently. No one saw him. The diamond held. On lap twenty, Mitchell decided the only way out was by force. He tapped the Two, and then he tapped it again. He locked onto its bumper, pushed, and gradually went full throttle. The Deuce couldn't hold the pace and started to drift. In a flash, it started to spin, and the Eight Ball ducked down into the clear. Mitchell was on a mission. He couldn't see the royal blue Fifteen, though, until he came off turn four on lap twenty-three. He'd have two laps to hunt him down, but the Fifteen held a lead of seven car lengths. With superior power, Mitchell knew he would catch him eventually. He just didn't know if he would run out of real estate before he did.

Tony Bel saw the Eight Ball in his mirror. His only advantages were that he had the lead and that he would get to the white flag on the next lap. He concentrated on holding the fast groove on the straightaway and using the understeer to power through the turns. He couldn't let the back end come out completely.

Just the Ninety-Four car was in front of him. Tony Bel got the white flag in second place. The Ninety-Four drifted up high, and Tony Bel took the low road into the lead. The Ninety-Four tried to drop in behind Tony Bel, but he had waited too long. The Eight Ball slipped past him. It was now a charge to the finish. Tony Bel held the gap through turns one and two, but Mitchell ate up the backstretch. Tony Bel held the low groove through turn three and into the short chute approaching turn four. Mitchell decided to wait for the homestretch, but suddenly the Fifteen slowed up in turn four, forcing the Eight Ball up high. Midway through the turn, Tony Bel went full throttle, ripping the Fifteen's back end loose. Mitchell had nowhere to go. He lifted completely. The royal-blue coupe bolted down the homestretch, while the Eight Ball went down through the gearbox to find some power. Tony Bel took the checkered flag and then took the final parade lap of the season. The Eight Ball won the car championship, but the driver title went to Tony Bel.

After that season, Mitchell stopped racing at Pleasantville, preferring instead to run at Pitman on Friday nights and at Vineland on Sunday afternoons. Tony Bel raced two more seasons, but without the competition from Sil Mitchell, he started to lose interest. The Friday and Sunday schedules and venues were not to his liking, so he eventually parked his helmet in his living room with his trophies, a few replicas of the Question Mark and the Eight Ball, and one of the Two, the Five, the Ten, the Twenty-Three, and, of course, the royal-blue Fifteen. He placed these memories between the elaborate saltwater fish tank he maintained with scrupulous devotion and the record collection he was diligently expanding. When he sat in the room with the music on, he'd flash that gap-toothed grin at the whimsical thought that his fish were, in fact, swimming to the music.

By following the sport in the papers and through some friends, he kept track of Mitchell's success at Pitman and Vineland. Mitchell won his share of races, but he never dominated the way he had at Pleasantville before Tony Bel showed up.

When Tony's scaled right hand swam free of his pocket, it had fished out a shiny plastic car model. It was all black except for the white circles on the sides and the top. The eights inside the circles were black. The Eight Ball. He returned his right hand to the walker and then used his left hand to produce a replica from his left pocket: a teal sedan with a red question mark. He leaned into the casket and whispered, "I understood you. You wanted to win. These belong with you."

He turned and slipped out of the wake.

A Second Coat of Paint

As he packed up Angelo Avellini's clothes, Nad came across an old gray work shirt splotched with the most despicable mustard-colored paint imaginable. The tattered remnant reminded Nad of the time he walked out of his house one Saturday morning to find his car, parked in front of Angelo's house, had been splattered with the most despicable mustard-colored paint imaginable. Nad went wild. His ocean-blue Oldsmobile Delta 98 was his pride and joy; he kept it immaculate and running perfectly. Dirt never lingered on the mats for long. Dust never hazed the speedometer. The ashtrays could have been lifted out and placed in a new showroom model. Nad was usually not one for expletives, but this Saturday morning, he let them fly, spewing *f*-bombs for ten minutes. Only shallow gulps for air interrupted him. He checked off a mental list of possible villains. Frank? Nad had argued with Frank last week about whether the mayor's common sense had evaporated. His Honor had proposed changing the municipal parking ordinance in South Philly. Frank thought the money to be generated by neighborhood parking meters would benefit the city. Nad couldn't fathom having to pay to park in front of his own house. Still, Frank didn't seem the type to retaliate that way to a discussion. They discussed things all the time.

Then he thought about Little Mike from around the corner. Nad and Little Mike had a very animated conversation about boxing just a few days ago. Little Mike thought the heavyweight division had more talent and depth than any other. Nad rebutted that the light heavyweight division packed almost the same amount of power but had more speed, agility, and overall boxing skill. They argued for hours, almost staging their own three-rounder before Nad walked away. He had told Little Mike, "Someday you might learn something about boxing. Maybe. Someday. If you're lucky." Little Mike could be something of a punk, but he was probably too timid for this type of action.

Nad next dialed up Fat Dominick from Eighth and Passyunk. Nad gave Fats a hard time when Fats tried to do some number writing at Tenth and State. Nad told him to stay on his own corner. He said Tenth and State had its own bookies and that Fats shouldn't be going around raiding somebody else's turf. Fats shot back that Nad had no say. Nad wasn't writing numbers, so he had no right to protect any turf. He said he'd show Nad what he, Fats, could and couldn't do. Nad decided Fats was a definite possibility.

He swore that it he ever found out who had done this, he would use the same mustard-colored paint on him—not his car, not his house. On him, the actual person. He would paint his eyes shut, paint the inside of his nose and ears, and paint him where the sun don't shine. Nad's voice was no stage whisper. Before long, Rosa, her sister, Louise, Nad's brother-in-law, Angelo, and most of the rest of the neighborhood was standing by, witnessing the eruption. Only Rosa was effective in calming him down. At first, there were a few smirks from various neighbors, including Ralphie (from across the street), Danny (from up the block), and even from Angelo. But, when everybody realized just how livid Nad was, everybody turned sympathetic. Ralphie and Danny offered to help clean the car up, but Nad declined. "Ange'll help me. It'll take only a couple of hours."

A confused Angelo ran inside to get a sweat shirt, and by dinner, the Oldsmobile Delta 98 sparkled like the Caribbean. Nad recalled how hard it was to get the paint off without ruining the finish. They used vinegar rather than turpentine. The process fed his anger. They worked through the job with no real conversation. Angelo knew how mad Nad was, so he was afraid to open his mouth. The day ended quietly. Nad could never prove his suspicions about Fat Dominick.

Nad tossed Angelo's old mustard shirt into a box with mismatched socks and a couple of twisted belts. After looking quickly through the rest of Angelo's clothes, he told Louise they should be discarded too. Nad and Angelo dressed differently. Nad changed into a sports jacket and tie most nights after work to hang out on the corner with the guys, and he wore a suit each Sunday to church. Nad helped Louise fill boxes from the liquor store with yellowed boxer shorts and sleeveless undershirts; five pairs of shoes, which were cracked on the tops, between the toes and the laces; a few pairs of brown and gray pants sprinkled with cigarette holes; a black double-breasted suit jacket with no buttons, which he wore to weddings and funerals; and three hideous ties stained with brown gravy in exactly the same places.

When Louise asked him to help her sort through Angelo's things, Nad had agreed without hesitation. He said they could go through it little by little, as time permitted. She would do those parts of the house she felt she could do on her own, but she was worried about the cellar.

Louise and Angelo lived just next door. Louise was very much like Rosa—friendly, fun loving, and cheerful. Quiet in comparison to the two sisters, Nad was closer in personality to Angelo, but their temperaments differed dramatically. Nad considered himself fairly normal with an even temper. Angelo sometimes seemed belligerent, brooding, and even spiteful. They were different in other ways as well. Angelo liked horse races; Nad's passion was fast cars. Angelo listened to accordion music; Nad preferred Rosemary Clooney and Perry Como. Nad shunned Angelo's steak and potatoes, favoring manicotti or lasagna. Nad was thoughtful; Angelo was spontaneous, impetuous, and prone toward impulsive action. It wasn't that planning eluded him. He just didn't have the patience or discipline to follow through. When he played the horses, he'd study the race forms and analyze jockey tendencies and previous performances over various distances in all kinds of conditions—only to act rashly just before post time. He invariably picked a loser. Nad went with him once to Atlantic City Race Course. By picking Angelo's alternates, he cashed in on seven of nine races. Angelo never really fit with the corner crowd. He never hung out with the Nad, Ralphie, Danny, or any of the other guys. He didn't make dago red in his basement. He didn't have a fig tree or a grapevine from the old country growing in his backyard. Nad's corner crowd thought Angelo was a bit strange, and if Angelo hadn't been Nad's next-door neighbor and brother-in-law, Nad would have thought so too.

Despite their differences, though, they seemed to enjoy an easy relationship. Rosa and Louise got along the way sisters should, so Nad and Angelo often found themselves together at dinners, birthday, anniversaries, weddings, and wakes. They even had some things in common. Each fixed things, although Nad fixed cars, and Angelo fixed appliances. Each liked to park his car directly in front of his own house and would rush out to move his car when that space came open. They would try to save the spaces for one another, although Angelo parked in front of the DiDominico house more often than Nad parked in front of the Avellini house. Nad really didn't much like the Avellini house.

The houses were not so identical, even though they shared a wall. The brick on Angelo's house had that rough surface and a light-brown, almost beige tinge that kept it from looking clean and kempt. The faded, cracking mud-colored window frames and separating, once-white marble front steps sunken in toward the center where rainwater often collected, supported the impression that neglect had been perfected. The DiDominico home formed a stark contrast. Conventional red brick made up the first floor of the DiDominico home, although many years ago, Nad's older brothers, at their father's direction, had painted the brick a flat black up from the sidewalk and to the bottom of the bay window. Nad and Little Nick had since blasted the brick clean—even cleaner than when it was new. The bay window extended from the second floor past the third to the roof, making the DiDominico house distinctive. Although it was no taller than the other houses on the block, it seemed to reign above them. Each of the three sides of the overhanging facade housed an actual window, which was framed in glossy white. Gray shingles of various shades were flecked with black and an occasional red speck, which picked up the color of the brick below. These shingles bordered the bay window on the top, bottom, and sides and between the window and the base. The structure swept in an almost stately way over the often broomed, uncracked cement sidewalk. Rosa compulsively whisked debris of any kind from her sidewalk and frequently cleansered the three prefect front steps.

With Angelo gone now, Louise was alone. Angelo had been ailing for some time. Actually, it seemed to Nad that Angelo had always been ailing in some way or another. Nevertheless, it seemed like Angelo passed quickly and unexpectedly. Heart failure stopped the cancer from spreading further. Because he had cancer, Angelo figured the end was coming, and he formed the intention of taking some time to get his things in order. He hadn't, adding the last line to a long to-do list he would never get to.

Nad hoped that, after cleaning out the house, Louise would stay and make a fresh start without leaving the block. It was good for Rosa to have her sister right next door. Louise also seemed to love the neighborhood almost as much as Nad did. Nad's family was one of the senior families on State Street. His parents had moved there from another part of South Philly in the late 1920s. Nad had been seven. Rosa's family had a long history there too. This was Louise's second time on State Street. She lived there as a child but moved away when she married Angelo. Angelo Avellini was a newcomer to the South Philly neighborhood—compared to Nad. Angelo had moved to State Street thirty years before after quitting a decent job to start his own business as an appliance repairman. He, with Louise and their three children, gave up their house in North Philly to move in with Genevieve Girardo, his mother-in-law, next door to the DiDominico home. Genevieve, now long passed, had occupied the house alone ever since her husband died and Rosa made the trek next door after marrying Nad.

The neighborhood was colorful. The ten hundred block of State Street housed Bocelli's Bakery, one of the best in all of Philadelphia for Italian bread and rolls and tomato pies. It was just one block from Ninth Street, the open-air Italian market bracketed on the south by Pat's Steaks, where the cheesesteak was born, and on the north by Isgro's Bakery, where locals and visitors could find cannoli stuffed with cheese or cream (the best in the world); an incomparable Italian rum cake; and a wonderful angel food cake with nuts on the side, sugar icing on the top, and a rich layer of rum-laced cream in the center. The Italian market itself was made up of rickety once-moveable wooden fruit and produce stands, stores with live poultry, butcher shops, fish markets, and two rival cheese shops. One specialized in provolone aged for years and hung from its ceiling and a mystery cheese called tuma persa; the other was known for the cheddar sharper than in Vermont and opulent string cheese soaked in oil and garlic. Shoppers could stop to buy toys, appliances, household goods, and furniture. If you lived on Tenth and State, you never went to a supermarket.

Nad and Louise started to go through the house from top to bottom. She had already attacked the bathroom on her own. All traces of Angelo were already gone—his toothbrush, the comb he had had little use for in recent years, his Gillette double-edged razor, and his flimsy, once-white terry cloth bathrobe. The bathroom was easy. She wanted Nad to help in the bedroom because she thought he would have some idea about what to do with Angelo's jewelry and clothes. Her children were evenly dispersed throughout the county and showed no tendencies toward sentimentality. She offered Nad Angelo's old pocket watch. He wasn't sure why he accepted it. Maybe it was to avoid hurting her feelings. He knew it would help her feel she was giving him something for his efforts. He appreciated the gesture, but it wasn't necessary. He thought the rest of the things—old cuff links, a Lord Elgin wristwatch with a broken leather band, and a neck chain with a Saint Christopher medal—should be discarded.

With the upstairs complete, Nad knew he couldn't avoid the cellar any longer. He moved cautiously toward the door. Whoosh! The cellar smell smacked Nad in the face even before he had the door fully open. He took a step back, trying to clear his sinuses. He knew all too well he'd have to push through the odor; there would be no acclimating to it. Coal residue from the days when anthracite chuted through a carved-out opening, which was later converted into a casement window, coalesced with ammonia from countless futile attempts to disinfect the oil-stained concrete floor. He could smell Clorox too. Well, it probably wasn't Clorox. More likely it was Ghirelli water previously vendored around by a street huckster in a horse-drawn wagon for use as bleach by neighborhood housewives who hand-washed the laundry in the years before the first primitive washing machines. All this had fomented for years and combined with dampness and mold to add a harsh bite to common basement dank. It burned—eyes, ears, nose, mouth, throat, and lungs. Everywhere! He'd never experienced smelling salts or tear gas or pepper spray, but he couldn't imagine they'd be any more toxic than the Avellini cellar.

Nad's eyes—but not his nose—started to adjust as he stepped carefully on the first of the creaky, barely painted steps down to the dungeon. He anticipated standing water and wondered whether he'd need galoshes and rattraps in addition to the thirty-gallon trash can he was maneuvering on his hip. He also worried a barrelful of Angelo's life might collapse one or more of the steps on his way back up. Well, he'd figure that out once he started to clear out the debris.

Nad was relieved to discover that the cellar floor, though wet and slick with accumulated dirt and spilled oil, contained no standing water. If there were rats, they were hiding silently behind the oil tank and heater. He couldn't see or hear any. He decided to start in the back of the cellar on a workbench. He poured three half-full quarts of motor oil into a bucket he found in the corner. He should have remembered to bring a container for liquids. Next, he poured in the antifreeze from a yellow can with no top. He started to clear the random wires, washers, and cotter pins from the top of the workbench. He realized he would soon have to drag the trash can up the steps and bring back an empty one.

The bits and pieces Angelo left behind stimulated Nad's memory. As neighbors and relatives, they had tried to help one another out whenever the need arose. Angelo would come over to fix the television or the washing machine. Usually, the repair took only an hour or so, but Nad remembered vividly the one time Angelo almost embered the DiDominico house when his soldering iron recklessly ignited some fabric covering an audio speaker in the mahogany television console. The flames blasted through the entire cover, filling the living room and the rest of the first floor with thick smoke that teared everybody's eyes and tasted like an alchemist's mixture. That repair lasted much longer. Angelo knew how to fix appliances, but he wasn't the most careful technician Nad had ever met. Nad, on the other hand, was meticulous when fixing cars. Angelo never had a new car or even a good one. So, from time to time, Nad would replace a starter, water pump, or generator. He would change a head gasket or repair the carburetor linkage or dashpot on one of Angelo's junkers. They seemed willing to help one another without resentment. It was never a burden, and they didn't keep score. Helping out was what neighbors—and relatives—did.

Nad lugged the full trash can up the steps and returned with a couple of empty boxes. He decided to turn his attention to the front of the cellar. This was where remnants of wallpaper rolls, swatches of carpet, and chunks of linoleum surrounded a pyramid of gallon paint cans. This rose almost to the casement window. The wallpaper, carpet, and linoleum went first. Nad piled everything but the paint into boxes and pondered what to do with all those cans. Where did they all come from? he wondered silently. He couldn't remember the house ever looking freshly painted. He decided to relocate them to the yard so he could get rid of a few of them at a time. After traipsing up and down the flimsy steps several times, he felt the end of his task was near. Only five gallons remained. He grabbed the two in front, but then he shuddered as he stepped back. The gallons he had lifted slipped from his hands and crashed to the floor. He saw it in the center of the three remaining cans, at the very bottom of the heap. He leaned over to pick it up. Unlike the other gallons, this one had no weight; it was totally empty. One side was completely covered with the most despicable mustard-colored paint imaginable, but the lid was secure. Next to it was another gallon of paint that had never been opened. Nad used a screwdriver to pry the lid off. The paint had separated, but he could clearly see the pigment matched the drippings on the empty can. He carried both cans up from the dungeon.

"Louise, do you know anything about the paint cans in the cellar?" he called out to her.

"No, Nad. I didn't know any paint was down there. Is it any good?"

"I don't know. Maybe."

"You can take what you want and throw the rest away."

"Thanks, Lou. I think I'm done for today. See you next time."

"Thanks, Nad. Bye."

He carried the two cans to his front steps and sat next to them for several minutes. He walked through his house to his basement. The tools were all neatly arranged. Wrenches were on the left; power tools were in the middle. Paintbrushes, sandpaper, and paint rollers were on the right. He picked up a five-inch paintbrush. It wasn't new, but it looked that way. As he walked to the front door, he called to his wife. "Rose, I'm going out. I'll be back."

"Where are you going?"

"I have to get rid of some things from next door. Angelo's things."

"Okay."

The Oldsmobile Delta 98 had retired years ago. A silver Cadillac Nad had bought and restored to mint condition replaced it. During the drive, Nad's insides churned, and his anger bloomed. He fumbled his way to the cemetery and located the grave site. The marble gravestone stood two feet high and three feet wide. It was a good eight inches thick.

Avellini
Angelo
Beloved Husband of Louise
May He Rest in Peace

Nad opened the full can of paint and stirred it to a consistent texture. He dipped in the brush, saturated the bristles, and then dabbed harshly on the side of the marble. He stopped. His anger quelled. He slowly carried both cans to the head of the grave and left them directly under Angelo's name. He took the brush and buried the dripping bristles deep into the ground. Only the handle showed. It was splotched with the most despicable mustard-colored paint imaginable.

"Good-bye, Angelo," Nad mumbled.

He shook his head in total bewilderment and walked slowly back to his car.

Forgetting All Over Again

Rita closes her eyes in silent nonprayer. She tries replacing the traces of irritating ammonia smell with warm memories of the intoxicating aroma of chocolate melting in her mother's cookies as they shifted from the oven to cool on their kitchen counter. She can't. Her dad's room is neat and comfortable, but it has hard accents on its corners, and the wall is colored closer to alabaster than to eggshell. Though it is where he sleeps now, it is not his home. Not their home.

Nad speaks his next thought aloud. "It's time to go to church, Rosa. Are you ready? Where is she now? I wonder about her lately. She seems to just disappear without telling me where she's going. Maybe after church I'll have a little talk with her."

"Please, Dad. Don't call me Rosa again. Please. It's me, Rita, your daughter. Rosa was your wife. Mom. Dad, Mom has been gone for many years."

"Rita, when did you get here? It's nice to see you. Where did Mom go? I could've sworn Rosa was here a minute ago. We have to go to church. She's always wandering off like that. It makes me so mad I could scream. Rita, you look very nice. I wonder if Mom remembers how you looked in pigtails with your plaid uniform and white blouse. I do. The gold crucifix we gave you for your First Holy Communion used to bounce around your neck when you squirmed at breakfast. We used to have the same breakfast every morning—buttered toast for dunking in hot cocoa. Do you remember?"

"Yes, Dad, I remember."

"I hope your mother comes back soon. She'll be upset if she misses you."

"Mom's not here, Dad. How are you feeling today?"

Rita hopes he will be able to follow the conversation. Lately, he can muster only a few moments of clarity at a time.

It's like this every visit. Every week. Sometimes, she can visit several times a week. She would come to see him every day, but the smell always bothers her—and the sterility too. Once, she brought framed family pictures and set them on his bedside table. On her next visit, though, they were folded into a drawer, so she removed them. On another visit, she brought his twenty-five-year service award from work, his old war mementos, and one old stock car trophy. When they too were put away, she asked him about them. He told her he was just passing through here, and he didn't need his memories on display. He had them stored in his head. On that visit, she waited until she left to begin to cry.

"Mom will be disappointed she missed you. Can you stay for a while? I'm sure she didn't go far. Maybe to the store. I wish she would tell me when she's going out."

He thinks Rita looks different today, like she's playing dress-up or something. Maybe she's going out to dinner with Frank or to a job interview, he thinks. He remembers how she looked for her senior prom. Her hair was all done up like an adult, and she wore a long maroon dress, almost the color of the wine they made in the cellar. She could have been a movies star that night. Any night.

"I can stay, Dad. I'm here for a visit. How are they treating you? How's your back feeling? Do you remember? It was bothering you the last time I was here."

It pains her to see him living in this glossy shoe box of a room. Though the home has the best reputation in the city, she wishes he could live with her. With her leg, though, she couldn't really take care of him properly. Deep down, she knows he's receiving better care here. There are long stretches of time when he needs more attention than she and Robert or Nick could give.

"Back's fine. Strong like bull. How's school? Ever since you started college, I know it's hard for you to come over. I'm glad you talk to your mother all the time. She tells me. But I miss having dinner with you and holding your hand when we walk to church. I always appreciated that you never pulled your hand away, even when you were in high school and even when all the parish boys tried to get your attention. You've always been a great daughter. So, how's school?"

"What school?"

"School. You know, college. University of Pennsylvania."

Thoughts flitter through his mind. She's always teasing me about school. Telling me she's taking the courses she knows I would like because I didn't have a chance to go. She took me to her classes one day. I paid attention, but I didn't take any notes. I understood everything they talked about, except a little bit in psychology. She understands everything, though. Smart girl. Maybe we'll go back there again before she graduates. I do wish I would've had a shot at it. It was a different world when I was young, though. At least she's getting her chance. Hope she makes the best of it. Seems to be.

"I graduated more than thirty years ago, Dad. But I understand the school is doing just fine. Would you like me to bring you something to read?"

He used to read everything, she thinks. Now he doesn't seem to want to read anything. Not even the newspaper. Luckily, he still listens to music, although it seems his hearing is fading as quickly as his vision is dimming. Unfortunately, his mind seems to be going even faster.

"Well, I hope Rosa comes back soon. She went to the drugstore to get some aspirin just before you came in from the grocery store. She said she wouldn't be long. Did you get the strawberries?"

She's always forgetting my strawberries. I like to put them in my cereal with peaches or bananas. If she's going to go out without telling me, she should at least get me some strawberries.

"It's me, Rita. Mom's not here. I didn't go to the drugstore. I asked you if you want something to read."

"Well, where were you then? I guess that means I don't get my strawberries today."

I can't blame Rita for not bringing me strawberries. She's in college now and doesn't have much money. Besides, she has other things on her mind. Soon she'll graduate and have to go out in the world.

"I can see if I can get you some strawberries. I'll be right back."

"If you run into Rita out there, remind her to pick up some aspirin. I want to try to get rid of this headache before we get ready to go to the wedding."

I know I have to get dressed for the wedding soon. Can't be late for the wedding.

"What wedding?"

"Come on, Louise. Stop kidding me. This is the biggest day of your life. You can't leave Angelo at the altar. He'd never forgive you. Plus, your mom and dad would be furious. They've already paid for the band and the food."

Sometimes Louise just doesn't think. She's been planning this wedding for months, and now she doesn't want to go through with it. I know she will, though. Angelo is a good man, and I know they'll be happy together. He has some skill for fixing appliances, so he'll also make some money.

"Dad, it's me, Rita. Aunt Louise's wedding was almost sixty years ago."

"Good thing. Wouldn't want all that good food to go to waste. Plus, the band is supposed to be very good. They play Glenn Miller and Tommy Dorsey, Benny Goodman and Jerome Kern. You know, all that good stuff."

I like that Jerome Kern. Very silky and smooth with lots of oomph to it. Not as pretty as Glenn Miller. I can listen to them all day. And this Sinatra kid. What a voice! Jersey kid. Of course, he'd be nothing without Dorsey's band behind him.

"Yes, I agree. Glenn Miller, Tommy Dorsey, Benny Goodman, and Jerome Kern are all very good. I'll go out and see if I can find some strawberries for you, Dad. Dad? It's me, Rita. Strawberries. Remember?"

"Okay, Rosa. I think we should dance now. After all, it's your sister's wedding, and we're all dressed up. Everybody expects us to put on a show like we always do. Are you ready? Back in the old days, we could go out dancing whenever we wanted. Now it seems we have to wait for a wedding. I liked the old days better. Everybody did what they were supposed to do. Too much freedom these days. Too many choices. Confuses everybody. At least we can still dance at weddings."

"Dad, it's me, Rita. It's not Aunt Louise's wedding."

"Of course, it isn't. How could it be? You weren't even born yet. How's Frank?"

Nobody will ever be good enough for my Rita. At least Frank is from the neighborhood, though, and he always shows respect. He comes from a good family.

"Who?"

It's getting harder and harder to follow him. I don't want to get frustrated with him, she thinks, but I can feel it happening.

"Frank. Your boyfriend. You two didn't break up, did you? I hope not."

Just when she finds somebody I think is okay for her, she walks away from him. I'll never understand women. At least she's not with that creep Mike anymore. Not a good kid. Lazy and dirty. Don't know what she saw in him in the first place.

"Dad, I've been married to Robert for a while now. I met him when I was horseback riding. Remember?"

"Yes, I remember Frank. You went to grade school with him, didn't you? What is he doing these days? Frank always said he wanted to work for the government. Mailman or fireman or cop. Something like that. Lost track of him. Never see him around the neighborhood anymore."

"I don't know, Dad. I haven't seen Frank for years. I think his family is still in the neighborhood."

"I'm worried about the neighborhood, Rosa. It seems like all the people we grew up with are dying off, and their kids have moved out. Sometimes, it doesn't feel like home anymore. I hope Rita and Nick Jr. will stay. Of course, we have lots of time with Little Nick. He's not even through high school. But Rita's in college. Maybe she and Frank will settle down in the neighborhood. That would be great, wouldn't it?"

Maybe Rosa and I will have to consider moving out at some point. When I was growing up, we didn't even think about leaving the neighborhood. Everything was always there for us—family, friends, and the guys on the corner. We have all the stores we need within walking distance. It's just a short trolley ride to center city, and it's only a little farther to Franklin Field. Of course, Shibe Park is farther up. It's in North Philly, and Municipal Stadium is the other way. It's only an hour down the shore. I love Atlantic City. The Million Dollar Pier and the Steel Pier. That horse is great. No need to leave this neighborhood. Hope it doesn't come to that.

"Dad, Nick has lived in the suburbs for years now. It's me, Rita."

"Hello, Rita. Mom asked me to see if you could pick up some strawberries for her. Do you think that's possible?"

If we don't get ready soon, we'll be late for Louise's wedding. We can't let that happen. Rosa and I are both in the bridal party. It wouldn't look good. I'm glad I could borrow Rocco's Lincoln. It looks like a limousine.

"Yes, I'll pick up some strawberries. I'll be right back."

That Rita. What a great kind. Straight As all the way though eleventh grade. If she keeps it up, she might get into the University of Pennsylvania. And Little Nick is just like her so far. What great kids! And Rosa, such a good mother. And wife, of course. I hope she remembers to pick up some strawberries. I'm sure she will. She never forgets anything. Everything's always just right with her. The house and the kids.

Everything. I wonder if Louise and Angelo will come over. Haven't seen them since the wedding. What a wedding! Great food and the best band. Everybody danced. Of course, Rosa and I were the best couple on the dance floor. Always are. We can really cut a rug. We need the whole dance floor, but that's the way it's supposed to be. I've been watching these kids dance nowadays. Stand in one place the whole time. No grace. No style. Kind of sexy, though, if you ask me. But it's not really dancing. More like a trip to lovers' lane. When there's music, you're supposed to be dancing. I hope Rosa comes back soon with those strawberries.

"I'm back. I have your strawberries."

"Thanks, Rosa. You just missed Rita. Didn't you see her out there? She was going to pick up some strawberries too. And some aspirin, I think. I don't know how you missed her."

Can't seem to get those two in the same place at the same time. I hope they're not avoiding one another. I don't think they had an argument or anything. I know Rosa likes that Frank boy for Rita. Maybe Rita thinks her mother is pushing her or something. They always seem to get along so well, though.

"Dad, it's me, Rita. Now that you have your strawberries, I want to talk to you. How are they treating you here?"

"Hello, Rita. I was just talking to your mother about you. I know she likes that Frank boys for you. Is she pushing you on that?"

The only way to find out is to ask. That should give me what I need to know.

"Dad, how are they treating you here? Is the food okay?"

"Food's great. Your mom has always been a good cook. She always knows exactly what I want and how I like it made. She seems to forget, though. Like how much I like strawberries. I think she just went out to get me some."

Dinnertime is the best time. The four of us sit around the table and talk about our days. We've had some funny conversations, though. I remember the time Little Nick asked why we couldn't have Indian children so he'd have somebody to play cowboys and Indians with. And when Rita was a little girl, she asked why they call the part of the church where they keep the Holy Communion a "tavern ankle." I think she might have picked that up from Rosa.

"I don't mean Mom's food. I mean the food you're having here at the home. Do you remember what you had for dinner last night?"

"Of course, I do, baby doll. Yesterday was Tuesday. Mom always makes spaghetti and meatballs on Tuesdays. So, we must have had spaghetti and meatballs. And a glass of red wine, of course. From the cellar. That we made last year. And salad. And fruit for dessert. You know, usual Tuesday."

I guess ever since she started college she's lost track of our normal routine. I guess that's to be expected. They grow up. Go out on their own. Find their own way. Break from the old ways. Just as long as she's happy. I hope Rosa comes back with that aspirin soon.

"Dad, today's Friday, and Mom is not making you dinner anymore."

"What? Is she mad at me or something? Just because I'd rather hang out with the guys on the corner and play pinochle than go to the movies? That's no reason to stop making dinner, is it?" I get so confused sometimes. What room is this? Where's Rosa? "Rosa, where are you?"

"Dad. What's wrong? It me, Rita. Are you okay?"

When he loses it like this, she thinks, I just don't know what to do.

"Rita, what are you doing here? Where's your mother? Go get your mother. Tell her we need to get ready to go now. I'm tired of waiting. She wanders off all the time. She never tells me where she's going. She never tells me where she's been. I'm tired of it. You understand me? Go find her. Understand? Tell her I'm tired of all this."

"Calm down, Nad. I'm right here. We have plenty of time to get reading for the wedding. We don't leave for a couple of hours. Why don't you take a little nap before we get ready? I'll wake you up when it's time to get ready to go. Rita just left. She had to go back to school. She left some strawberries for you, though, and she says good-bye. She'll be back later in the week. How's that sound, Nad?"

"Sounds good, Rosa. I miss you when you go out without telling me. I'm glad you're back now. I'll just take a little nap. You can call me when it's time to get ready for the wedding. What are you going to do? Sew?"

"Good idea. I think I'll sew a little bit before we go."

Nad closed his eyes and fell asleep. Rita wiped her eyes and left.

Tony DeSabato began writing by creating a short story series, *The Adventures of Merry Moose,* so he could read original works to his then-young son. From there, he began writing short stories about growing up in South Philadelphia. These are some of those stores. He describes himself as a recovering attorney, having practiced labor law for more than thirty years prior to his retirement. His full-time residence is in Narberth, Pennsylvania, but he has done much of his writing in Martha's Vineyard, either in his home in Edgartown or on the beach at Aquinnah. His novel, *Brewster Flats,* is set in Cape Cod.

His next projects are to ready *The Adventures of Merry Moose* for publication and to work on his next anthology of short stories.

Made in the USA
Middletown, DE
28 July 2017